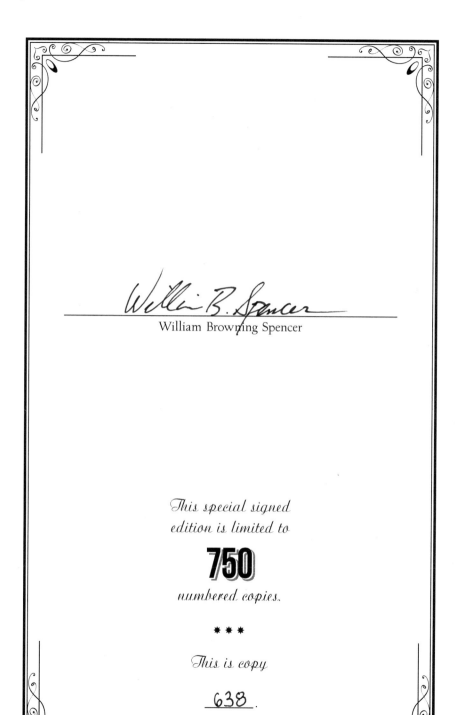

William Browning Spencer

*This special signed
edition is limited to*

750

numbered copies.

✱ ✱ ✱

This is copy

<u>638</u>.

The
UNORTHODOX
DR. DRAPER
and Other Stories

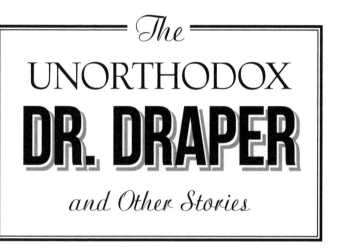

UNORTHODOX
DR. DRAPER

The

and Other Stories

WILLIAM BROWNING SPENCER

✻ ✻ ✻

Subterranean Press 2017

Subterranean Press
PO Box 190106
Burton, MI 48519

subterraneanpress.com

Dear Claire,
In high school, it seems you were
already drawing the light, warrior girl,
half-orphan girl, ablaze in a crowd.
And what were you thinking, leaving
Texas? I am so glad you are back.

Table of Contents

9 INTRODUCTION

15 HOW THE GODS BARGAIN

39 PENGUINS OF THE APOCALYPSE

77 COME LURK WITH ME AND BE MY LOVE

101 THE TENTH MUSE

133 STONE AND THE LIBRARIAN

159 THE INDELIBLE DARK

191 THE DAPPLED THING

215 USURPED

239 THE UNORTHODOX DR. DRAPER

277 THE LOVE SONG OF A. ALHAZRED AZATHOTH

How Irony Can Work for You

＊ ＊ ＊

HEN I AM asked what it takes to be a writer I always say, "You have to be willing to ruin the rest of your life."

Many successful writers clearly haven't ruined their lives. I'm an old guy who grew up at a time when ruining one's life for Art was a perfectly legitimate path. Now it's just an affectation. "If you want to ruin your life, go ahead and ruin it," someone will say, "you don't have to have a theme or anything, you can just be a *fuckup*."

＊ ＊ ＊

IN 1976, I was in a hospital psych ward in Rowan County, North Carolina, recuperating in a straitjacket after consuming an inordinately large volume of alcohol over the course of a week or two after attending the wedding of some friends in the wake of my first divorce.

Friends would come by to visit me in my hospital bed, but I found it hard to be a gracious host while restrained by various straps and buckles.

A doctor would occasionally materialize to recommend electro-shock treatments, and one of my fellow patients enthusiastically endorsed this cure. "It'll stop the shakes like *that!*" he said. "You might not be able to remember your name or what year it is, but that'll come back to you later. And if you never remember something, you won't know you forgot it, and you won't miss it." I thought he had a point there, but I declined the electro-shock. Sometimes I regret that. Maybe, out there in an alternate electro-shocked world, I am a better person.

✴ ✴ ✴

FASHIONABLE OR otherwise, I believe there are still plenty of troubled writers out there, writers who read Arthur Rimbaud as a child and practiced being dead in different places (dead in a tree, dead in the bathtub, dead at the top of the playground slide, dead and nothing but an inconvenience to all those normal kids shouting for their turn).

What I hope to do here is offer some practical advice in regards to interacting with that demanding exterior world that intrudes on our inner lives. We need to re-imagine the mundane world.

I could make a fortune if, instead of freely imparting this wisdom here, in this intro, I were to expand this concept to fill an entire self-help book. But I don't care about money. I write funny Lovecraft books. Does that sound like a guy who cares about money?

I'll start with a simple example. You come out of the grocery store, push your shopping cart, a wobbly, loose-limbed contrivance, across the hot asphalt, the air filled with the reek of dead dinosaurs and the feedback-like screams of grackles, and you arrive at your car. The rear fender on the driver's side has crumpled since you last saw it.

You immediately imagine the source of this damage: a group of teenagers, cretinous louts, their brains compressed to the size of golf balls by loud rap music, their conversations freighted with obscenities so tribal and social-network-new that you, a person fully grown before the death of civilization, cannot understand a word of the scatological nonsense they utter. You wish they were still around—they have driven away—because you would open your trunk, take out the assault weapon that the State of Texas gives anyone registering a car, and you would blast them into bloody bits.

They are gone, but they have ruined your day.

* * *

BUT WAIT! Maybe these teenagers don't exist. Maybe the damage was done by some sweet but addled little old lady, *exactly like the grandmother you loved so much*, who doesn't even realize she hit your car. She did hear something, and maybe her car jumped a little, and she said, "Goodness!" or maybe even "Land!" and she was so shaken she drove away rather than enter the store. She would be mortified if she knew she had hit your car.

You forgive your grandmother, don't you?

* * *

THAT'S A simple example of re-imagining, but the problem is often subtler. We are dealing with infuriating people and the infuriating things they do abound. Just yesterday I was reading a novel I checked out from my local library. Someone with a pen containing green ink had chosen to copy-edit the book. He had circled "Toyota Maxima" and written, "There is no such car, Mr. Editor! Do your job!" Some might say, "Well, he's right," but he has also changed "between you and me" to "between you and I," so his editorial skills aren't state-of-the-art, and anyway that's not the real problem. The problem is his *intrusiveness*, his belief that he is part of some larger world that would welcome his input.

Or what about the woman who was my co-worker at a large insurance company? She kept after me to give her one of my novels. "I'll read anything," she would say (ominously) and eventually I gave her a copy of *Zod Wallop*. I worked in the mold department of this giant company, and she worked in vermin or acts of God or something, so I didn't see her every day. When I did see her she would grow quite animated and shout, "I'm still reading your book. I'm not going to let it get the best of me. When I get ahold of a book, I don't let go until I have read every word of it! I'm no quitter!"

I would run across her once or twice a month, and she would utter something similar to indicate we were comrades in this arduous task. I would dread encountering her in the halls or cafeteria, but dread doesn't stop the inevitable, does it? When I left the company a couple of years later, she was still working on the novel, undaunted and optimistic that she would one day conquer it.

And then there are those people so dull, so transcendently boring, that their voices should be registered as weapons. There are depressed boring people and hearty boring people. Which, you might ask, is worse? Whichever one is presently stealing your time.

I could go on enumerating the varieties of people that can ruin your day, but instead—and this would be a workbook to accompany my self-help book—I suggest you reflect on your own encounters with annoying folks. What do they have in common, these psychic vampires? I think you will find that they are irony-free and cheerfully (or solemnly) self-important. How can you keep them at bay?

✳ ✳ ✳

FOR YEARS now, everyone has been saying that irony is dead. But what if it isn't? What if it has simply gone underground? Are you familiar with the work of Andy Kaufman? He was a comedian, but he wasn't interested in telling jokes. He was, more accurately, a performance artist. In one of his skits, he would maintain a sweaty earnestness while lip-syncing *only the chorus* of the *Mighty Mouse* song, waiting for the chorus to come around again on the record. That was clearly a joke, but his later career wrestling women blurred the line for many viewers who weren't amused. People began to think: *This guy is a jerk!* When he died at thirty-five, many people believed it was another one of his hoaxes. It wasn't; it was cancer, which is about as un-ironic as it gets.

So here's the secret. With the power of your private thoughts, you can transform those dimwitted people you will encounter into ultra-ironists, people who share their ironic selves with no one (*secret* ironists). The man who takes his library book and crosses out "between you and me" to write "between you and I" *knows* that "between" is a preposition, *knows* he is crossing out the correct form to replace it with an incorrect form, and he chortles in his living room when he imagines the next reader's righteous indignation.

My co-worker, with her loud assurances that she will get through my novel someday, hated the book and stopped reading after the first page. She is a failed novelist (whose overwrought romance, *Love is for Kisses*, resides in her attic after having been rejected by every reputable publisher and even declined by vanity e-book publishers who felt you had to draw the line somewhere). She is perfectly aware of how her feigned pluckiness will set my teeth on edge.

And boring people? They are dedicated undercover artists, always stretching the limits, seeking a personal best. *How long can I get him to stand there writhing while I describe my trip to Wal-Mart?* they wonder. That guy telling you about his miserable job until you feel that you are trapped in the sweatshop with him? He inherited money. He doesn't work for a living. He just gets a kick out of watching your eyes glaze over as he describes all of his tedious cohorts or tells you how his boss is always trying to screw him.

This sort of re-imagining doesn't imagine people who are nicer—they are sort of mean-spirited, I guess—but isn't it reassuring to pretend that the world isn't filled with literal-minded idiots? Isn't it good to think that irony is alive and well, ready to resurface when it is needed for some larger purpose, like undermining a totalitarian regime?

And don't worry about me. I stopped drinking in 1977. And I've gotten over that divorce. I've been married a couple more times and divorced a couple more times, and, to paraphrase Winston Churchill, I no longer have to avoid temptation; temptation avoids me.

And I wrote these stories because they were there, and nobody else wanted to write them. My publisher will agree that I gave other writers ample opportunity to adopt them. Anyway, I hope you enjoy them.

* * *

ONE LAST thing. Looking over these stories, I see that they are pretty dark. I just want to assure everyone that I am fine. Oh, I occasionally surf the Internet for suicide tips, but who doesn't? A couple of years ago, a friend of mine tried to kill himself by swallowing the contents of a bottle of aspirin. He spent a weekend in the hospital; I told him that aspirin was a ridiculously inappropriate means for shuffling off this mortal coil. I thought of telling him that he could get everything he needed to kill himself at Party Pig, but then, admirably I think, I refrained from speaking.

How the
Gods Bargain

W HEN MARISSA AND I were fourteen and in the freshmen class at Filmore High School, we fell under the spell of Harley James. The proximity of a genius can make one feel smarter, more alive, more aware of forces that abound beyond the shadows that most minds cast.

Harley was a junior at Filmore, and it seemed our extremely good fortune that he chose to mentor us, despite our youth and ignorance. At the end...well, it wasn't the end, was it? That's why I'm writing this.

Until recently, I hadn't spent all that much time thinking about Harley. When he did come to mind it was his voice that I heard, disembodied and querulous, usually in the form of a rebuttal. An example: last winter I was watching a famous television evangelist expound on intelligent design, defending it with the usual arguments, including evolution's inability to account for radical changes or the elaborate nature of such changes, and I could hear Harley's nasal voice in all its lofty disdain: "Two- or three-hundred million years is way smarter than you! Time is bigger than your pitiful little bully of a god."

After the show, I found myself remembering Harley-anecdotes, all of which were second- or third-hand reports, hall rumors. And the more outrageous these tales, the more apt they were to be true. Like the rumor that Harley had jumped up in class during a discussion of capitalism and shouted, "That's not a symbiotic relationship, that's a fucking parasite!" which got him suspended for three days, during which time everyone in school learned what "symbiotic" meant and someone slipped into the gym and painted THAT'S NOT A SYMBIOTIC RELATIONSHIP, THAT'S MY FUCKING GIRL-FRIEND! on the wall.

Harley was Marissa's friend before he was mine. Her parents lived right next to him, and for whatever reason—perhaps he spotted her beauty, her enthusiasm, her guileless nature—they hit it off. Harley lived in the only big house on Welch Street, and he lived there alone, virtually alone. There was a father, although I had never seen the father, and Marissa had only seen him a couple of times. Marissa said the father was a handsome guy—"really good-looking, like he could have been a movie star"—with a thin mustache, and he wore baggy pants with lots of pockets and sleeveless white t-shirts. Harley said his name was Felix, and he worked for the CIA, which might have been true, because Harley never seemed to lie about anything.

He taught Marissa how to play chess. They would sit at the kitchen table in his house and play on a faded black-and-white chess board with wood-carved pieces whose ravaged condition, Harley explained, was the work of a beagle named Monkey who, as a puppy, teethed on the chessmen. So Harley taught Marissa chess, and Marissa taught me chess. Later Harley said that chess was for kids, and he taught Marissa the game of Go. Marissa never taught me Go, and if I hadn't been clueless I might have given that more thought.

* * *

I'M GETTING away from where I need to begin. I need to begin
with my thirty-sixth birthday.

On the day of my birthday, Dan and Ethel Miller and
Swan showed up as I was closing the lab, and they insisted
on taking me out on the town. I found the prospect daunting; I'd had a long day that ended with my firing two student
interns for hopelessly fouling several promising trials, and I'd
put myself in a bad mood in which it seemed to me that the
entire world had turned its back on integrity and humility,
required virtues if one wanted to do good work.

I told my colleagues that I was too weary for anything
celebratory, birthday or no birthday, but they were persistent
and rowdy, Dan Miller shouting, "*Carpe beer!*" as though he
were already drunk.

Swan was his usual sketchy self, unshaven, wild-eyed,
mumbling inaudibly (perhaps a mantra like *kill-them-all kill-
them-all kill-them-all*). Swan was undoubtedly brilliant, and
he always arrived for work in a suit and tie, but if you were
asked to write his name under one of two columns derived
from a Robert Louis Stevenson story, you'd write it under
Mr. Hyde, not Dr. Jekyll.

Dan and Ethel, on the other hand, glow with rationality
and a heartiness that you occasionally see in long-married
progeny-free couples—they have already been married
twenty years and neither of them can be much over forty—
and they are well-liked by everyone. They are liked, I think,
because they don't inspire envy. No one would wish to be
them. They have smooth, smiling faces and, in the asexual
lab coats we all don in the morning, they are intelligent
androgynous twins with the sex appeal of Silly Putty. They
work and publish as a team and are often referred to as
"The Millers." I have also heard them referred to as "The

Coneheads," those happy aliens featured in old Saturday Night Live skits.

I see I have presented portraits of my colleagues that are not entirely flattering. I have a hard time describing anything in a thoroughly positive manner (salient details are, so often, unpleasant), so I should note that I am fond of all three of these people and fortunate to have them for friends.

And their insistence won me over. Even Swan, a man of few outwardly-directed words, entreated me to come out. "The Millers said we were celebrating your birthday. If you don't come, it will be just me and The Millers, who are always an embarrassment when they drink."

"It's true," said Ethel. And she and her spouse laughed like happy Pekingese.

* * *

SO I went—on the condition that we *didn't* go to Woozy's, which is a college bar catering to the young women of Legrasse University (Miskatonic University's sister college). Legrasse was born out of: 1) the recognition that women made excellent scholars and research scientists and 2) the fear of losing some of Miskatonic's finest scholars if women were introduced into its monastic walls.

Woozy's was also a big favorite with the male researchers at Enderson. The Lab has a reputation for recruiting the brightest and paying them well, and aspiring young scientists from Legrasse are a little in awe of us. I have seen Lumpy Caldwell, slovenly and troll-like, surrounded by a rapt group of lovely young women, regaling them, no doubt, with exaggerated tales of his bioscience prowess while guzzling beer like Falstaff: a scene that speaks to the power of Enderson's reputation and not to any charm, physical or intellectual, exuded by poor Lumpy, whose employment is a textbook example of nepotism, his father being *the* Dr. Elmer Caldwell.

It occurred to me that it would be easy enough to steal Enderson's most coveted secrets. Drunkenness and the promise of sex would loosen the tongue of any male employee at Enderson. You'd have to be a dedicated spy, though, since you'd have to piece together a lot of disparate bits (i.e., you'd have to kiss a lot of toads).

But I'm digressing...

I wanted something less youthful, less desperately ambitious, than Woozy's, so we settled on a bar just off Main. I wasn't familiar with the place, but The Millers said it was "fun for all ages." It turned out to be big and gaudy, featuring neon cowboy hats and boots and blinking stars. It did have a sizeable middle-aged crowd, which I found reassuring.

I intended to drink no more than three beers and then, having fulfilled my conviviality obligation, slip away, calling a taxi if need be. But I got a second wind after that third beer. There was a warm golden light suffusing the room we were in, and boisterous laughter mingled with jukebox-generated country music. I was thinking that life was good, and it seemed reasonable to try to sustain that ridiculous notion as long as possible.

Later in the evening, I was drunk. I haven't been drunk many times in my life. I do not, generally, enjoy the absence of control that comes with inebriation, but this time I felt omnipotent. I solved several vexing problems in my head and realized that all the botched trials I'd been lamenting could simply be re-purposed around data that had not been corrupted.

My bladder began to ache. "I need to urinate," I told my comrades. The Millers were clearly drunk, oddly entangled, their arms linked at the elbows, and drinking from each other's mugs while bellowing something that was not the song on the jukebox, singing against the tide, as it were. Swan was talking to a woman who had sat down next to him. She wore a cowboy hat and a red-and-white shirt with white fringe. Her makeup was heavy enough to suggest a disguise.

I got up to pursue my quest, and I got lost. This place was bigger than I thought. There were lots of rooms and plenty of people to fill them up. I was trapped in one room where a couple of fat guys with ponytails were good-naturedly wrestling while a crowd stood around them. My bladder chose this moment to become hysterical, and I ran behind a silver counter and into what proved to be the kitchen. Several people with hairnets and white aprons screamed at me, but I raced on, banging through gray swinging doors and into a brick-lined corridor where I instantly spied a door labeled Gentlemen.

My bladder vented violently as I leaned over the urinal, which was an older model, not like the ones at Enderson's which flushed discreetly when you backed away from them. When my bladder was satisfied, I flushed and zipped up. My peace of mind restored, I looked around me. This restroom was, I realized, for the employees. It wasn't bright and shiny; there were old crates shoved up against one cinder-block wall, two urinals, a floor of cracked linoleum, two stalls—

Something was making lots of scratching sounds behind the door to one of the stalls. Claws whisked on a hard surface: *scritch skitter, skitter scritch*. There was another noise, something dragged, swishing along. My heart caught the panicky rhythm. I thought I recognized it. *Jeez!*

The linoleum was a mottled gray and darker gray embellished with dried brown mud and black tar from the last time the parking lot had seen a new coat of asphalt. I bent down for a closer look and saw the bright red marks: blood in the shape of small, clawed feet. The tracks swirled about before disappearing under the stall door. I guessed four, maybe five of the creatures.

I've seen a few rats. I work with them every day. I lift them up and hold them in my cupped hands, and I look them in their vacant little eyes, so why would I let the sight of this rat-spoor rob my legs of strength and knock me back against the urinal where, blindly fumbling for support, I released a new downpour of water and the harsh effluvia of disinfectant? I was scared sick. *Recon rats!* I thought.

I tore my gaze away from the stall door, and I fled. In the corridor I stumbled toward an exit and found myself outside in a small enclosed area. Through the chain-link fence, I could see the parking lot. Since I'd last been outside, a wind had arisen, aggressive and chill, winter on its way.

I sat down on the top concrete step and thrust my hands in my pockets. I needed to talk myself out of this...what... misapprehension? But in my mind I could see the flourish of all those tiny paw prints, documentation of some frenzied dance—and I could see the thicker, sinuous lines that suggested fat-bodied snakes, washed in more bright blood, writhing in ecstasy.

I stood up and leaned back to look at the sky, seeking some comfortable alignment of stars, but the lamps that blazed in this gated enclosure rendered the heavens in glaring gray and white, a mist that something malign might hide within.

The thought of returning to the corridor behind me didn't appeal to me. I'd have to move past the restroom, and I didn't know...I didn't know if it knew me, if it was, perhaps, seeking me. Was I being paranoid? I didn't think I could overestimate the danger, knowing what I knew.

It occurred to me that I could depart via the gate on my left, run to the front of the nightclub, and beseech a bouncer to go get my friends. But then I saw the padlock and chain. Of course: this fence guarded the dumpster from the depredations of the homeless—

The dumpster! More rats were on the dumpster, not overly large rats but deathly *aware* creatures, and they were connected by what Harley called umbilical cords, although, always precise, Harley admitted that the term was for convenience only and awaited some understanding of their function before a more accurate nomenclature could be applied.

I counted nine rats, sticking to the side of the dumpster like spiders, each of them connected to its fellows by long cables that no one would mistake for cables, segmented tubes that rippled with life. The rats sniffed the air and regarded me with fierce sentience, an intelligence too acute to be their own. Something eager and immense watched me through them, and the scientist within me sought—and not for the first time—some way of defining what manner of creature that might be, but, in fear and its consequent confusion, I retreated to some limbic memory that shouted, *"Something evil!"*

I stood up with care, never letting the creatures out of my sight. I slowly moved my right hand back, seeking the door's handle. It didn't move. I exerted more pressure. It still didn't move, and my heart revved up as I imagined—or remembered—a slight click as the door had closed behind me.

I turned away from the altered rats and shook the handle, which served only to shake my body. I looked back over my shoulder. One of the rats...it was hideously cold now, an ancient cold that was disorienting...one of the rats moved down the dumpster's side, its comrades closing around it, the cables that connected them shrinking to accommodate this new condition. More of them had crept over the edge of the dumpster, and there were a dozen, maybe more, teeth and glittering eyes sparkling in this V-shaped rat-platoon.

I did not think to scream, and, in retrospect, had I been in possession of all my faculties, I still would have refrained from screaming. Who would come? Who would come with sufficient speed?

Something boomed on my left, a rattle of metal, a rush of hot air. I jerked my head to the left and saw that the door to the kitchen had banged open and a stout man in an apron was silhouetted in light and steam. He wrestled a heavy trash can down the steps, nodded, scowled at me, and dragged the trash can toward the dumpster.

"Don't—" I shouted. I turned again to point at the rats. They were gone.

The man emptied the trash can's contents into the dumpster, turned, and said, "You cannot be here."

"I got locked out," I said.

"You cannot be locked out here!" he shouted, flapping his arms like some flightless bird's ritual of aggression. I nodded, turned and ran into the kitchen as he shouted after me.

* * *

WHEN I woke up the next morning, I didn't have a hangover, but I was not at the top of my game. I was halfway to the lab when I realized it was Saturday. I drove home, stared at the phone, went upstairs and lay in bed but couldn't sleep. Finally, I called Marissa.

The phone rang a couple of times before it switched to the answering machine. It occurred to me that I didn't know what to say, and when the machine beeped, I still didn't know what to say.

Marissa picked up then. "Jerry?"

I hadn't talked to her in nine years. "How'd you know it was me?" I asked.

"Caller ID."

"Oh."

"What do you want?" she asked. The chill was still there; I hadn't been forgiven. Fair enough.

"I saw some of those rats. You know, Harley called them *recon* rats. He felt they were engineered to scope out the territory before…before the Big Event. Whatever he meant by that."

"It figures. I knew something was happening. It's back."

"What's back?"

"The General Store."

"Elders?"

"Well, let's see. How many general stores do we know that go away and come back?"

"I thought it was gone for good."

Marissa was silent for so long I thought the connection had failed. "Hello?" I said.

She spoke then: "I guess I thought it *would* come back."

* * *

ON THE drive out there, I had half an hour to think about the past. Marissa lives less than thirty miles from me, and we haven't met, we haven't *spoken* to each other for the last nine years. We avoid each other because we share an obsession.

* * *

HARLEY JAMES liked to go hiking, and he brought us along, his two acolytes. He was tireless, dragging us up and down mountains, through forests, into tick-infested fields and snarls of thorny vegetation. I remember how he lectured us while he waded in a muddy creek: "I'd be a naturalist if it wasn't such a discouraging career, checking a box each time another species goes belly-up, watching habitats disappear, watching humanity *infest* this world, yes an *infestation* of busy, greedy, arrogant apes so completely out of touch with their natures that 'animal,' that vibrant word that describes a joyous bounty of extraordinary creatures, means, on humankind's sour tongue, *brutish!*" His hand then plunged into the water and retrieved a crayfish which he displayed as though this squirming crustacean were the tangible proof of his words.

He had become more orotund in his rants, some part of which was self-parody, I'm sure. I told Marissa I suspected him of taking amphetamines. I suspected no such thing, but I hoped to dampen her hero worship with whatever reservations I could engender. And, of course, I didn't make a dent in her adulation. She was falling in love (by which I mean she had already fallen in love, and I was slowly assimilating this new state with shock and dismay).

Symbiosis was one of Harley's favorite subjects during the time we knew him. For him, the word meant something very specific. Generally, the biological definition defines symbiosis as an association existing between two very different organisms which may or may not benefit both individuals. Harley was only interested in relationships that were, in fact, mutually rewarding, "a bargain for both," as he put it.

He had no use for the notion that lichen, because it consisted of a fungus and one of several green algae, was a symbiotic organism. "That's like saying a man's heart and his liver are engaged in symbiosis." Indeed, when in the course of one of our walks, he came upon pale blue lichen decorating a rock and very much resembling one of my grandmother's doilies, he reviled it at length, as though he considered its existence some personal affront. When we moved on, Harley returned to his paean to the yucca moth, an insect that he regarded as the "true embodiment of symbiosis."

The yucca moth and its yucca plant were Harley's heroes. The female yucca moth very deliberately pollinates the yucca, first gathering pollen from the flower's anther, then pausing to lay her eggs, and then—O busy insect!—carrying her pollen to the flower's stigma where she carefully inserts it. No bumbling honeybee, this moth seems to know more about the yucca's reproductive process than most college students.

Harley acted like he'd discovered symbiosis and had the right to rail against those who applied it wantonly. He would shout: "And a burrowing owl that lives in a tunnel made by a gopher turtle. That's symbiosis? Come on, that's simple opportunism."

I could go on, but why? I was no longer Harley's doting disciple. And when I thought of that wretched moth and its obsessive botanical foreplay, I realized that there was a downside to this symbiotic bargain: *If one of them dies, be it moth or plant, so does the other.* When he graduated from Filmore, I assumed that the fall would find him in some elite university where he could surround himself with a new lot of admirers. I wished him well, and I wished him away from Marissa and me.

* * *

I MISSED the turn onto Griffith Lane and had to pull into the rest stop where a couple of forlorn picnic tables had sunk to their knees waiting for happy families, frolicking children, and frisbee-chasing dogs. *Let's take our smart phones on a picnic!* Maybe not. Forget picnics, Mom and Dad. Your kids have moved into the virtual. Wave goodbye. No, wait, *text* goodbye; they'll never see you wave.

I rolled down the window and took some deep breaths. It was still cold, but bright, the sunlight meticulous in its illumination, every blade of grass, every leaf getting its goddam due, while I was morose, sullen, afraid, and hopeful, a motley bunch of emotions that you'd think would shun each other's company, but I know they were all there because I took the time to sort them out. Marissa tells me men aren't very self-aware, and I think maybe we are, but not in a good way. I know I haven't had much luck with self-awareness.

I turned around and found Griffith Lane and followed the winding road to Marissa's little faux farmhouse on the edge of the forest and thought—I swear, for the first time—that she had moved into this house to *wait* for Harley. I hated not being able to tell her that Harley was gone for good. But I couldn't tell her without telling her how I came by that knowledge, and there's no way she would have been happy with the truth.

Marissa came out on the porch. She was wearing a backpack, and she held another by one of its straps. *That would be mine.* I got out of the car and walked up to her, and we both were uncomfortable in a dozen ways, and I said, "You're looking well," and she frowned. She was looking better than well. She had been a cute teenager in an all-American way: dark curls stirred by the breeze, brown eyes catching the light of any sun or candle or stadium light. Now—I hadn't seen her in years—she looked amazing.

We hugged—or rather I hugged her and she endured it. Neither of us knew how to act; we were chaperoned by our miserable pasts.

"Are we going to trek into the forest—" I began, but then I realized there was a more pressing question. "How do you know the store is back?"

"I saw it last night," she said. She paused, not wishing, I suppose, to diminish the truth of this statement, then added, "In a dream."

"Okay."

I didn't doubt that it was out there. If the recon rats were back, so were their masters. Their spaceship, or whatever the hell it was, would be resting in the middle of the forest, looking like...well, not a house made out of candy...an old-fashioned General Store. That's right: Elders General Store, a sort of run-down, silvery structure that would have been unremarkable in an earlier America, say 1930. On closer inspection, Harley had noted that the wood had been replaced by quartz and other more exotic materials. "It's petrified wood...sort of," he said. "That would require an absence of oxygen and maybe fifty million years, much longer I think." And when we had entered the store, which was so much bigger on the inside, limitless, perhaps, Harley had said, "Hundreds of millions of years."

❋ ❋ ❋

WHEN HARLEY graduated from Filmore, he didn't go on to college. Marissa, who I hadn't seen much that summer, told me he was still in town.

"I thought he was going to college," I said. We were sitting in the cafeteria, three days into a new school year, and I was already sick of the months of boredom that lay before me. The hopeless smell of overcooked food, as unforgettable as torture, did battle with the hormonal noise of my fellow scholars.

"Harley said there was no way he was going to spend the next six or seven years defending his mind from the depredations of tired dogma and academic senescence," Marissa said. She had acquired the irritating habit of tossing Harley-phrases into her conversation, even reproducing the snooty inflections that indicated disdain for the vast, benighted bourgeoisie. "Harley says that if you look at the progress of science in nineteenth century Britain, it's the people who *didn't* go to school who did all the heavy lifting, all the innovative thinking."

I didn't think that was true, but I didn't say anything. I wanted to get away from Harley-pronouncements, from all things Harley, actually.

But Marissa kept on about Harley. Apparently she and Harley had done lots of hiking and exploring that summer, and no one had thought to ask me along. I pointed that out, and Marissa said, "Harley says you don't like him."

I didn't like him, so what was I going to say? I just sulked some, which is every young male's strategy in the face of unrequited love.

❋ ❋ ❋

THAT, AND I stalked her, although not in a creepy way. I had a used car (a 1985 Dodge Aries purchased from an aunt who no longer drove). My parents bought it for me when I made all A's, and I happened to be driving by Marissa's house when I saw her come out of Harley's house. *Where are your parents, Marissa?* I thought, with the righteousness of the unloved.

Harley followed her out, and they tossed backpacks and other stuff into the back of his car (a new Jeep because, I guess, the CIA paid better than my Dad's job, which was selling stuff to restaurants). Without much ado they drove away.

I followed them. I stayed way back, and Marissa didn't even know I had a car, much less what kind of car, and when they turned off on this little winding road called Barker, I slowed down, pulled over at a farm gate and sat there for a while. I knew where they were going. They would park beside the old barbed wire fence, carefully insinuate themselves through its rusty strands, pay no attention to the No Trespassing signs, run across the meadow and enter the forest. This was Old Man Turnip's land, and he was still alive then, and sometimes he would chase kids off his land with unintelligible shouts, firing his shotgun in the air and generally filling a folktale niche in the history of any country-born boy.

I waited for about twenty minutes, and then I continued on up Barker and passed Harley's Jeep about where I expected to find it. And that was all the tailing I did that day. Overzealousness is, I suspect, often a stalker's undoing.

The next day was a school day, so I cut class. I wasn't worried about my folks getting a call from school. I was a model student, never missed a day, so everyone would assume I had a good reason for not showing up.

I figured Marissa would be at school, and I wanted to see what I could find in the forest without accidentally running into her or Harley James.

I guess.

I didn't have a plan. I desperately needed a plan, but I didn't have one. I just wanted to be doing something. I wanted to save Marissa from the malign influence of Harley James whose interest in her was not—I was sure of this— remotely intellectual.

I followed their trail, which was marked according to Harley's ingenious system that utilized nature's variety to encode a series of instructions far more precise and less destructive than anything achieved by stripping tree trunks of their bark. I was one of the three people who knew these codes, and as their language came back to me, I felt sadly abandoned.

I had brought a sleeping bag and other supplies in case I would have to spend the night. Harley was an intrepid explorer, and, to my credit I think, I was willing to endure some hardship myself. I might not have had a plan, but I was prepared to suffer for the sake of love. Youth is in thrall (and often betrayed) by a thousand romantic notions, never seeing the brute hand of Nature, whose sole obsession is the next generation.

It was getting dark, and I told myself I needed to stop and establish camp, but I pushed on, ignoring my good advice. I spied an arrangement of rocks that was not random, and I approached it, reaching for the flashlight on my belt. Before I could decipher the rocks' message, my feet leapt out from under me and I found myself upside down, a human pendulum describing ever shorter arcs.

We learn in school that the eye, that marvelous machine, presents an upside down image that our brain is required to flip upright and does, reflexively and effortlessly. This is always presented as a marvelous accomplishment, but I would be more impressed if this same brain could refrain from that flipping when we find ourselves upside down, since, at such a time, the upside down image would be just the ticket.

In any event, I recognized the sneakers right away, and then there was a light blinding me, and a voice: "Jerry!"

Harley leaned his face in, illuminating his features by holding the flashlight under his chin. "It's just me," he said. "Sorry."

He got me out of the trap quickly. I waited while he reset the trap, and then we headed back to his campsite.

"No offense, but that was a disappointment," he said. "Like stringing a line for catfish and getting a snapping turtle."

I didn't much like being compared to a snapping turtle (an ugly and belligerent species), but I was feeling too sheepish for a rebuttal, and that's when Marissa popped her head out of Harley's tent and smiled shamelessly.

"Excuse me," Harley said, and he went into the tent with Marissa. I assumed they were discussing me, so I just sat there steaming. In truth, there had been no betrayal. I had never kissed Marissa, never said I loved her.

They took me to see the store that night. "It's not far...if you're up for it," Harley said.

"Sure."

I didn't really want to see whatever it was that had them so enraptured. I should have turned and walked away. That was my first impulse, and I should have obeyed it.

* * *

NOW MARISSA and I stood on her front porch. It's hard to contemplate millions of years and imagine anything that feels like the truth, but contemplating twenty years isn't that easy either. It wasn't that anything much had happened. I'd gone to college, grad school, had a couple of really bad jobs. The jobs frightened me, and I went back to the university, acquired more credits and contemplated the academic life, and then I wound up back at my parents after an unfortunate affair with a lap dancer named Dawn—anyone can make a mistake, especially the sexually sheltered—and while I was home my parents said I should apply at Enderson Labs, and, to appease them, I did and was shocked when they hired me.

Marissa had moved away for a few years, but when her mother died of cancer she moved back to look after her father who had always been a sad man in an ill-fitting suit. He called me "Harry," and seemed to get most of life's details wrong, maybe lacking the stamina for recalling names and faces and facts. He had inherited a good deal of money, and, too apathetic to spend it, he was still rich on the day he died. He killed himself with an automatic pistol he'd bought at a gun show. He shot himself in the stomach, in the leg (probably an accident, the coroner noted), and finally through the heart. I wasn't in town for the funeral, but I was surprised when I moved back in with my folks to find that Marissa had bought a small farmhouse out on Griffith Lane.

* * *

HERE WE were.

"Maybe we should leave it alone," I said.

"Why?" she asked.

I thought that was obvious. "To avoid being killed," I said. "That's what comes to mind first."

Marissa glared at me, and I thought I saw Harley's disdain in her eyes. "I thought you were a scientist. Isn't curiosity sacred? Don't you want to know what happened?"

"We'll never know what happened." I think I raised my voice; I was exasperated, but that's no excuse. Marissa seemed to think that the world was a tidy place. She'd missed quantum physics or something. Hell, she'd missed television and the Internet. "Even your boy genius Harley was stumped."

"He would never have stopped seeking the truth!" Marissa said.

"Oh!" I was getting really worked up—I supposed guilt had something to do with that—and I knew I would say something hurtful. "What good is the truth if you're dead? If you fling yourself into the abyss you won't come back whole. Would you seek the truth if you knew your mind couldn't contain it; if you knew it would shatter all the convenient objects of your reality as though they were china; if you knew knowing would bring madness?!"

I realized in that instant that Harley understood this. That I *was* one of his disciples. It was another one of his symbiosis-inspired rants. Like all his rants, it came out of nowhere, a long *non sequitur* (because Harley's conversation was almost entirely internal—and divisive). He'd been speaking of ants he called amazon ants (I can't remember the genus, but they weren't uncommon; there were species in Europe, in America).

Harley said, "So these ants enslave other ants, in this case ants of the genus *Formica*. The amazon ants go into the nests of the *Formica*, kill any ant that opposes them, and steal the cocoon-encased pupae. The amazon ants are great warriors with large mandibles. But these warrior ants have no other castes. The amazon ant is essentially helpless without its slaves; it can hardly feed itself much less attend to the complex needs of the colony. All it can do is enslave other ants, but what does that anthropomorphic verb 'enslave' mean to the ants it captures? Nothing. Business as usual. You now have a *Formica* colony that nurtures some ants with long, killing mandibles. That's it. And the *Formica* will seek out other colonies of *Formica* and lead the amazon ants to that nest. So are these *Formica* evil collaborators? Of course not. This is all just ant-life in the ant-world. Where did these amazon ants come from in the first place, these helpless warrior ants? You've got me."

Harley hesitated. It was a rare thing to see him confused, but there it was. "It's as though nature, whatever you want to call it, cannot avoid going down these paths, it doesn't, in fact, resolve into simplicity. Nature perseverates. It's neurotic, insane really..."

He didn't finish the sentence. It was the first time I can remember Harley being at a loss for words, and (I confess) I was pleased.

∗ ∗ ∗

I HAD no idea how or what I felt as we drove up Barker. I was worn out and resigned to whatever bad thing happened. This was the closest I ever got to a Zen state. Small talk was in order: "Does this property still belong to the Turnips?"

"It never belonged to the Turnips," Marissa said. "That was kid-speak. It belonged to the Turners, and as far as I know it still belongs to them. They are probably sitting on it until the rich real estate developers come along, which is a ways off."

"Way beyond the horizon," I agreed.

We chatted as we had always chatted, and I enjoyed this strange displacement in time. The mood changed when Marissa parked the car—not, it seemed to me, where we used to park it. We got our gear, crossed over the dying meadow and into a forest guarded by evergreens that opened into the first scatterings of fall color: yellows and browns and reds, curled leaves that crackled under our feet.

By the time we got to the store, it was dark, and I sensed it before I saw it, and I was afraid and assaulted by images from twenty years ago and time hadn't improved the vibe.

"We'll go in," Marissa whispered in my ear, and the words hummed as though read in a ritual.

"Yes," I said.

Although it looked like wood, it was cold and hard as stone, silver-blue and luminous. The door was halfway open (as always; it could not be opened or closed, it couldn't be budged) and we slipped inside to where the blue light was brighter and the weirdness weirder. I could hear Harley's whispered voice: "Everything has been replaced: some exotic substances, although common quartz seems to predominate."

I stood in the center and turned slowly in a circle, as I had the first time I came here, as anyone would. Everything had leapt up and pressed itself into the walls: an old oil stove, counter-tops, signs advertising soap and elixirs for health, cans of beans and carrots, a bag of potatoes that had burst open and set its contents free so they now resembled the backs of great bloated beetles burrowing into the plaster, a tall, ornate cash register from which coins tumbled, each stuck to another. Whatever had pasted everything to the walls had also robbed everything of color—the jelly beans were either white, black or gray—and it was this absence of color that had made the man stuck to the wall seem—surely—a manikin. But where the flesh flared raggedly on the left side of his jaw, the teeth and dusty-black tongue were difficult to explain, as was the single skeletal foot (the other encased in an elaborately-decorated boot). "He was," Harley had whispered, "no doubt the proprietor until... well, perhaps he still is. Maybe he's Elders like it says on the sign outside. But he's definitely *not* the sole proprietor."

"Same as ever," I said, wishing to sound at ease but discovering a voice that was thin and lacking in conviction.

Marissa must have heard it. "Let's get on with it," she said.

I hastened to follow her as she crossed the room and slipped through another half-opened door. We walked down a flight of wooden steps (*real* wooden steps) and entered what was an underground storeroom that had succumbed to the usual laws of entropy. This room existed in a sort of eternal twilight, and I could never ascertain where this light came from, but, surrounded by bigger mysteries, I was content to let that one lie. This is where I first encountered what Harley called recon rats. "I think their masters send these out to look around. But these masters don't have much love for their servants. They are ill-used. When they come under any light, you'll notice they are red. Their little metabolisms have been pushed to the max, and they are sweating blood."

Across the room, Marissa opened another door. I raced after her, descended stone steps and encountered, as though for the first time, the Hall of the Warlords.

That is what Harley called the place; he found it, he gets to name it.

But naming it doesn't describe it. I don't know how these giant, grisly murals and carvings were created, although I think they might have been created in some malleable material and later subjected to the process that turned the store to stone.

* * *

I HAVE never traveled the miles of this underground labyrinth, and I don't intend to, and not because the undertaking would be too physically arduous. No, what I fear is eventually *understanding* this catalogue of what must be eons of war. There isn't any single artist, or any single species. It's nondiscriminatory interspecies carnage.

As a teenager, seeing all the images, feeling the outrage that younger generations bestow upon the previous generation, I despised the very impulse that generated life. What I saw—and what I was still seeing twenty years later—was one generation of monsters recounting its triumphs only to be overwritten—no, defiantly written *beside*—the next race of extraterrestrial barbarians. This was the universe's graffiti wall where the boasts and venom of cosmic gangs could share a moment of art.

Every kind of monster, every atrocity, every dark, festering need is depicted on these walls. To see it is to despair.

❊ ❊ ❊

MARISSA CALLED my name, and I saw her farther down the hall. I started walking toward her and hesitated when I thought I saw a shadow behind her.

"Jerry," she said. "He came back."

It was, in fact, Harley, or the image of him. He seemed immediately at her side.

"My old friend, Jerry," he said.

"What are you?" I asked.

"And why would you ask that? Don't you believe your own eyes?"

"You aren't Harley."

Harley turned toward Marissa, lifted a hand to her cheek and said, "Jerry thinks I'm dead. He thinks that because he remembers killing me. But he didn't kill me; he only wanted to." Harley looked at me. "How did you kill me, Jerry?"

I couldn't speak.

"With a rock hammer, *my* Estwing Supreme rock hammer, in fact. Couldn't even bring your own murder weapon. And why? Because Marissa loved me, not you."

"No."

"The Elder Gods still live here, although this *here* isn't in a forest on old man Turnip's land. They are not gods, of course, but they might as well be. They are, however, more complicated than earth-made gods. They are in alliance with us because—and this is true symbiosis as I never understood it—they want our defiance, our hatred, and then they *make us love them!*"

Harley threw his arms around Marissa who returned the embrace silently and looked past him to me with an expression beyond my dark-hearted understanding. And there was a noise, like the unfurling of a huge sail in violent weather, and something like vast black wings rose up behind them and they disappeared in a rush of darkness that rolled out and toward me too fast for me to flee.

And it was gone. I was in a clearing in the forest, and I pushed myself to my knees and rose up and thought, *It's gone for good.*

And I have thought about it and thought about it and haven't grown any wiser. I still go to my job, and it is no better or worse than it ever was.

And at night when I am trying to sleep, it is not a cosmic question that troubles me. It is what I saw in Marissa's eyes. Sometimes I think it was simple fear. More often I think it was pride. But most of the time I think it was pity.

Penguins of the Apocalypse

I WAS WATCHING A nature documentary on the small television I'd taken into exile with me. Several thousand hapless Emperor penguins huddled together on a vast plain of snow while blasts of ice-laden air furrowed their feathers. Tough little birds, sleek little stoics that made my flimsy misfortunes (unemployed, divorced, alcoholic) seem like the hothouse complaints of a pampered child. But wait…perhaps these birds weren't even roughing it. If I could zero in on a single bird amid this huddled mass, if I could read its mind, I might find it thinking: "This is great, the lot of us here, comrades, all for one and one for all. Would you look at the way the sun blazes on the ice! Beautiful! What a magnificent day to huddle together. And there's a nice breeze, too!"

I live over a bar, and when my own thoughts get too much for me, I go down to the bar and Evil Ed, the bartender, draws me a free beer from the tap. This should not be mistaken for generosity. Later, he runs my tab up extravagantly, claiming I've bought beers for people I don't remember and who, I suspect, are the imaginary spawn of Evil Ed's accounting practices.

Evil Ed and I both have apartments above the bar. I rented my apartment through Evil Ed, who was representing our landlord, Quality Rentals, Inc. QR resides, as do we, in Newark, New Jersey, or, at least, that's where QR's post office box is located.

Evil Ed is an ex-con, his muscled arms covered with primitive tattoos, the strangest of which is a heart among many knives with the initials A.B. in the heart's center and a little banner over that with the single word WHITE printed on it. Why a black man would wish to have an Aryan Brotherhood tattoo is beyond me, but I don't know him well enough to ask. Evil Ed keeps to himself, and he doesn't feel compelled to engage in the sort of small talk that passes for social interaction between strangers. I appreciate his self-containment. Surely the virtue of silence, of allowing others their space, should be taught in kindergarten. Such schooling shouldn't have to wait until prison.

Anyway. It was a Saturday, which might suggest a crowd, but this wasn't a Saturday-night kind of bar. This was more the sort of bar you went to because you had gone to it the day before.

The place could get a little rowdy sometimes, and Evil Ed had nailed a holster up under the counter near the cash register. Lodged inside that holster was a Walther P38 that looked old enough to have been pried from a Nazi's cold dead fingers. As far as I knew, no one had ever tried to rob the place. Evil Ed's demeanor did not suggest a man willing to hand over cash without a fight.

This Saturday night, the bar (which, by the way, has no name, being identified only by the vertical neon letters B-A-R) was sparsely populated with regulars (Rat Lady, Freddie Famous-Long-Ago, Bullshit George, and The Nameless Perv). There were a couple of Goth kids, happy to be miserable,

and three bulky guys wearing dresses, transvestite empower-
ment night, I guess, and, somewhere in the shadows, Derrick
Thorn, waiting to meet me, waiting to befriend me.

The television over the bar had the same penguin show
on, and now a seal was chasing a penguin through the water.
The seal, its mouth wide and bristling with pointy teeth,
shot through the ocean, shedding iridescent bubbles, its eyes
black, demonic, the eyes of some angry ghost-child from a
Japanese horror flick. I had never seen seals from this perspective. Scary stuff!

A voice that was not mine seemed to pluck the thought
from my head: "It does not seem right, a seal animal to eat
a penguins, the both of them slippery, swimmy things that
should be happy brothers together in the oceans."

I turned to behold a large pear-shaped man, smooth-
faced, hairless as a cave salamander. His face was oddly
blurred, and he may have tried to remedy this lack of definition by the application of eyeliner to his forehead, but the
eyebrows created in this manner only seemed to emphasize
the absence of any assertive facial features. He wore a black
sweatshirt with the hood thrown back and pleated black
pants. The contours of his sweatshirt suggested lumpy pud-
ding flesh beneath; pale hands, small as a child's, sprouted
from black sleeves. I assumed that this much strangeness had
to be calculated, that he was some sort of artist.

"Let us make of each other the acquaintance," he said.
I'm not the least bit fastidious when it comes to drinking
companions, so we moved to a corner booth, and we drank a
lot of beer, which he must have paid for, because my bar tab
didn't grow at all that night.

It's not clear what Derrick Thorn revealed of himself.
I came away with the knowledge that English was not—
surprise!—his native language ("It fall down on my tongue,

these English"), but if he told me the country he called home, my brain failed to log it. He was in some sort of business requiring a lot of travel, and he lived alone. He must have volunteered this info; I know I didn't ask. A maudlin, drunken state had overtaken me, and at such times a drinking companion is merely an opportunity for a monologue. I told him I was divorced, unemployed, and paying child support to a woman so mean that her death would cause a thousand of Hell's toughest demons to opt for early retirement. I was exaggerating, out of bitterness and an alcohol-induced love of hyperbole.

Derrick nodded as I spoke. At some point during the evening, he took out a handkerchief and mopped the sweat from his brow, eradicating one eyebrow and smearing the other.

I was flickering in and out of a blackout, that alcoholic state in which the mind visits the moment, departs, and returns sporadically, illuminating scenes as might the world's slowest strobe. A moment that my mind chose to save consisted of Derrick, solemn and slick-faced, leaning toward me and saying, "At end times, the penguins will remember those who friended them." I recall this (now) because, in the context of whatever I was saying (and I can't remember what that was), it seemed profound.

It was very late when I found myself back in my room. I turned the television on while waiting for the floor to settle. Another nature documentary was in progress. Monkeys were eating mud.

When I woke in the morning, the television was taking it easy, some people slumped in sofas, talking about social ills with the calm resignation of people who only expect things to get worse.

* * *

I CAN'T always tell when I'm ill, because I drink a lot, and the aftermath of drinking has many flu-like symptoms. But I was sneezing in the morning, and my forehead felt as hot as heated asphalt. My thoughts were trying to devour each other, a sign, I've found, of fever.

I thought of calling Victoria and telling her I couldn't make it, but she'd accuse me of being a selfish drunken bastard who cared nothing for anyone other than himself. I hate defending myself against accusations that are fundamentally true, so I made some coffee and drank it and rallied as best I could.

At night, I empty the contents of my pants pockets on the floor, and I was reassigning these items (car keys, lighter, artfully wadded-up bills, sundry coins, pens, et cetera) to the pockets of a clean pair of jeans when I found a business card of the inexpensive thermal-printed sort you might purchase from an Internet site for a pittance. It read:

Derrick Thorn
businesses • helping persons • solving problems
good deals by mutual bargain
friendship and opportunity guaranteed
please be calling at ➜

A telephone number was hand-printed on the other side of the card. Well, I thought, not a misspelled word in the lot. Not that it made any sense. I tossed the card in the nightstand's drawer, where it would lie with other business cards, many of unknown provenance.

I got dressed, regarded myself in the bathroom mirror, said, "If no one has told you they love you today, there's a good reason for that," and left my apartment. Evil Ed was in the hall, a garbage bag on his shoulder, heading to the stairs that led to the dumpster out back. He nodded to me and I nodded back, neither of us compelled to smile or speak.

* * *

IT WAS snowing, slow dizzy wet flakes that turned black in the gutters. Aside from a couple of homeless people hunkered in doorways and a skeletal dog that was tearing apart a black plastic trash bag, spilling empty beer cans into the street, it was quiet the way Sunday mornings are in my neighborhood. The God of Church has either got you, swept you up and dragged you into some storefront salvation shop, or you are lying low, hardly breathing, feeling the oppressive holiness of the day coming for you like a hearse.

We were in the holiday season, almost Thanksgiving, and I could already feel Christmas bearing down on me, a black cloud of obligations and money-draining events. My bank account was no longer being fed by a salary—BC Graphics had fired me three weeks ago for excellent reasons that have no part in this narrative—and I hadn't informed Victoria of this reversal in my fortunes. I couldn't imagine her saying anything helpful.

Victoria, my ex, has never entirely approved of me. She married me, I suspect, because her father despised me. In marrying me against his wishes, she was getting back at him for being a distant, aloof parent during her formative years. As time went by, the old man warmed to me. I turned out to be his ally in a sea of women—five daughters, no sons, a harridan of a wife!—and Victoria felt betrayed.

I married Victoria because I loved her, and, in the fullness of time, that love disappeared as though a magician had snapped his fingers. Behold this shiny love. Keep your eyes on it, ladies and gentlemen. Are you watching? Voila! Gone in a flash of smoke, vanished in a whoop, and before I could catch my breath, there it was again, transformed, love sauntering in from offstage, grinning, the magician's misdirection flawless, as good as a miracle, there: Danny Boy Silvers, our son.

He was five now, and I was on my way into the heart of the suburbs to pick him up and take him to the zoo in West Orange.

* * *

"CAN WE stop at McDonald's?" he asked, looking out the car's passenger window at the falling snow.

"If you don't tell your mother," I said. This was a Sunday tradition, covert McDonald's, a small father-son conspiracy against a powerful regime that could crush us without raising a sweat.

"I won't tell," Danny said. He waited. Waited and grew impatient. "Why shouldn't I tell?"

"Because she'd slap us so hard our spines would fly out our butts!" I said.

Danny giggled.

"She'd stomp us so hard we'd pop like bugs on a griddle."

My son laughed, leaning forward.

"She'd knock us all the way into next year. She'd whack us till our tongues jumped out of our heads. And once a tongue gets away, it burrows down into the earth, quick as a snake, and you have to get a spade and dig like crazy, and by the time you catch it and put it back in your mouth...well, it doesn't taste very good, I can tell you that."

A stand-up comic is only as good as his audience. My audience was small but enthusiastic, giggling and hooting, his knees bouncing, his nose running, spittle flying.

"She'd shake us until we were so dizzy we couldn't tell up from down, and we would fall right into the sky and keep on falling until our asses hit the moon!"

In the McDonald's we both ordered Egg McMuffins, hash browns, and chocolate shakes, the major food groups.

"When we go to the zoo, can we see the snakes?" Danny asked.

"This isn't a really big zoo or anything. I don't know if they have snakes."

"They do! Mom went on the Internet and showed me a picture. They have a Reptile House."

"Okay," I said. "Sure." Secretly, I was a little miffed. What was Victoria doing, prematurely unwrapping my gift to Danny, my zoo? Oh, how petty are the skirmishes of the heart.

* * *

FROM THE parking lot, the zoo didn't look very imposing. There were two round towers from which flags fluttered, suggesting one of those Renaissance fair events in which one is harried by costumed jugglers, street musicians, and mimes. Once we got our tickets and got through the gate, jostled by a group of elderly women wearing identical bowling league jackets ("Queen of the Lanes" emblazoned on the backs), we consulted the signs and settled on a plan: monkeys to big cats to otters to hippos and rhinos to giraffes to birds and, saving the most anticipated for last, to reptiles. The Reptile House was near the gate and a logical last stop before leaving the zoo.

These things never go as planned.

* * *

"DAD! WHAT are those monkeys doing?" Danny was wide-eyed, open-mouthed.

"Fornicating," I said.

"What's that?"

"It's like fighting," I said.

A tall guy next to me, obviously another divorced, weekend-dad with two small, identical girls, each clinging to a hand, nodded his head. "You can say that again."

There were lots of small, fidgety monkeys that seemed completely baffled by their cages, as though they had been caught earlier that day and were still thinking, "What the hell? I'm trapped! I'm getting the hell out of...what's this? I can't get out this way either! What's going on here?"

In a large cage with black bars, a reddish-brown orangutan slumped in the crook of a tree. His boredom was palpable and made me ashamed of my scrutiny. Forget spying on people having sex or practicing some special perversion. What is sadder, more dismal, than witnessing another person's boredom, the slow, dim-witted crotch-scratching lethargy that is often the existential lot of a person alone? You might note that orangutans are apes, not people, but that didn't keep me from hurrying Danny on to the Lion House, which, if possible, smelled worse than the Monkey House.

✳ ✳ ✳

AND ON we went: to the zany otters, the bloated hippos, the absent rhinos (on vacation? escaped? indisposed? deceased?), the really tall giraffes, and into the raucous bird house. As a father and font-of-all-knowledge, I read out-loud the various plaques that described the animals, their habits, their character, their troubles, and Danny listened politely. Other weekend fathers were also reading these plaques to their kids, and I felt a certain disdain for their efforts. As if they knew anything beyond what they were reciting! Pathetic.

We came to a great, curving arc of glass, a vista which promised a view of—yes!—penguins. I had much to say about these amazing birds, the saga of their days fresh in my mind, and was dismayed to find myself gazing at brown concrete curves, blackened and desolate, an emptiness as unwelcoming as some demolished urban block. A sign announced that the penguin habitat was closed for renovation, and my mood worsened, which, I confess, caused a bit of bad behavior. A guard caught me trying to teach an intellectually-overrated gray parrot (said to have a vocabulary of over two hundred words) to say, "Kiss my ass"—and Danny and I were escorted out of the building.

That left the Reptile House, and Danny loved it, loved the brightly colored poisonous frogs (not reptiles at all, but always welcome in reptile houses), the lethal, arrow-headed vipers, the boas and the immense anaconda. And the penguins! I couldn't believe it when we came upon them. But it made sense. They had to stay somewhere, and here's where they were, slumming with the reptiles. Since birds evolved from dinosaurs, it even made some taxonomic sense, I guess.

I was glad to see them, shuffling around in a glass-fronted cage that might, at one time, have housed alligators or crocodiles.

They weren't Emperor penguins. According to the plaque, these were Fiordland crested penguins, an endangered species, with long, pale-yellow slashes over their eyes, like an old man's eyebrows.

"Danny, did you know—"

"They have captured these penguins! What crime the penguins perform to make them prisoners, I do not know. The snakes! Hah, that is easy, they bite the peoples, and they are, anyway, Satan's spawn, as is said long ago in your Bibles."

I jumped, I think. I turned, and there he was.

He was dressed exactly as he had been last night. The lights in the Reptile House were muted, and his pale flesh seemed to glow with a faint blue sheen. He had restored his eyebrows since I'd last seen him, and he appeared to have added purple lipstick to his cosmetic effects.

"It is good to meet you again, Mr. Sam Silvers. I hope you remember me. I am Derrick Thorn."

"What are you doing here?"

He nodded vigorously, as though I were a good student who had asked a clever question.

"I am enjoying the seeing of the animals that are here for their offenses." He spread his arms and turned slowly to the left and right to demonstrate how his enthusiasm included all the creatures in the room.

Odd didn't begin to describe this guy.

"Did you follow me here?" I asked.

"I am coming after you did. Would that be to follow? You told me you were to come to this zoos with the child person of your support."

"I did?"

"Yes, and I am pleased to be here and to witness the progeny of your troubles."

"Well, fine. Look, I've got to be going. Derrick, you have a nice day."

I grabbed Danny's hand and headed for the entrance. Derrick shouted after me, but I didn't turn around.

"I will be pleased to be having the nice day, Sam Silvers," he shouted. "I will make for you the nice day also. I have not forgotten our bargains."

The temperature had dropped, and the snow was falling with new purpose, frosting the parking lot, glazing car roofs and fenders. I dug through the glove compartment's summer detritus (day trip maps, sunglasses, suntan lotion, an amusement park brochure) until I found the ice scraper.

I got out of the car and went around to the front windshield where I began scraping a gritty mix of snow and ice from the glass. From within, Danny waved at me, grinning.

Back in the car, I had to sit for a minute, catching my breath, as though I'd been engaged in heavy labor.

"Dad, who were you talking to?"

"Just some guy I met recently," I said. I looked at my son. Danny was frowning, puzzled.

I leaned over and ruffled his hair. "Your mom says you've got a girlfriend."

Danny grinned. "Her name's June. She's got a snake for a pet."

"All right!" I turned the key in the ignition. "My kind of woman," I said, as the car moved slowly forward.

* * *

I RETURNED Danny to his mother, the usual sense of loss already rising in my chest like black water.

"I tried to call you on your cell," she said. She knelt down in the doorway and brushed snow from her son's hair and shoulders. She looked up at me. "It's out-of-service. Why's that?"

I shrugged. "I decided I didn't need a cell phone."

She stood up for a better, unimpeded glare. "If this arrangement is going to work, I need to be able to get ahold of you. The roads are bad. I was worried."

"Nothing to worry about," I said, squeezing Danny's shoulder. "We had fun at the zoo, didn't we?"

"It was great!" Danny said, and began to catalog its many wonders. Feeling hollow in a superfluous-dad sort of way, I waved a goodbye and headed for the car.

* * *

I STOPPED at the bar on the way to my apartment. If I was going to quit drinking, it might make sense to move to other lodgings, but I wasn't going to, was I? I dispatched two beers and went on up to my apartment, pleased with my restraint.

There were two six-packs in the fridge, and I drank them, unintentionally. As I remember it, I drank a single beer and didn't wish to leave an odd number of beers, so I drank another one. After that, my reasoning grew convoluted until it occurred to me that drinking all the beer in the fridge, thus leaving none to tempt me in the morning, would be a good start on a new, beer-free life.

My phone rang in the chill of the morning, and I burrowed under the covers, a rabbit fleeing the hounds, and I heard my answering machine click on—"This is Sam Silvers. I'm not here"—and Victoria's voice: "Sam."

I leapt from the bed and snatched up the receiver, hearing the fear in her voice, and knowing, instantly, the precise sound of this fear, its only possible subject, our only shared and immutable bond. "Danny's gone," she said.

✻ ✻ ✻

WE SAT on the sofa while the detectives interviewed us. "On a school day," Victoria said, "Danny gets up at seven. He sets his alarm at bedtime, and sometimes, when it wakes him in the morning, he turns it off and goes back to sleep—not very often, but sometimes—and I have to go in and get him up. This morning the alarm just kept ringing, and when I went in, the bed was empty, and I thought he might be in the bathroom, but he wasn't. He wasn't anywhere in the house."

To someone who didn't know her, my ex-wife might have appeared calm, purposeful, in control, the slight tremor in her folded hands understandable enough. But I could see the care with which she answered every question, as though each word, the order of each word and its cautious articulation, might restore the world to sanity, might, by its intense rationality, restore our son. She would not break down; she would not show emotion. To do such a thing would be to collaborate in Danny's disappearance. She would not, by hysteria, acknowledge its reality.

This I knew of Victoria, and my heart ached for her, as it ached for myself. And Danny? Does a five-year-old get up in the middle of the night and walk out into a snow storm, leaving his winter coat in the closet? Or does someone come for him, silently, in the middle of a ghostly storm, enter the locked house without any signs of forced entry, and walk away with the boy without awakening his mother, just down the hall and a light sleeper, always restless. How often, in our marriage, in the years we lay beside each other, had Victoria come awake at the sound of midnight rain, tree branches shaken by a wind, a car passing on the street at three in the morning? I'd wake, oblivious to the noises that had roused her but attuned to Victoria and called awake by her wakefulness. That seemed a long time ago, in a distant, implausible past.

* * *

WHEN I left Victoria, it was to accompany the detectives back to my apartment. I was aware that I was a suspect—or at least an obligatory part of the investigation—and I wasn't surprised or offended by this. How often had an ex-husband, frustrated by circumstances that kept him from seeing his child, simply grabbed the kid and run? They weren't going to find Danny in my apartment, but I guess, if I had spirited him away in the dead of night, I could have stashed him with a friend.

I answered all their questions. Most of the questions were asked by the shorter cop, a black man with high cheekbones and a formal way of speaking, the word "sir" punctuating his sentences with sibilant force. The other officer was taller, older, white and balding, and I noticed he would occasionally interrupt to ask a question his partner had already asked. I guess he was interested in what my answers would sound like the second time I gave them.

After they had been gone a couple of hours, I glanced out the window and saw three uniformed cops out back. A female officer, dark, Hispanic, held the taut leash of a German Shepard as it nosed around the back of the dumpster and then moved out across the vacant lot that separated the bar from the rest of the strip mall. Only then did I realize that I might be suspected of something worse than kidnapping my own son. They might be looking for his body.

And why not? You read the papers; these things happen. Some enraged psycho wants to make his ex-wife regret leaving him, and he knows the way to her heart, he knows how to do real damage.

I made it to the bathroom in time to vomit in the toilet, retching up Victoria's coffee, something in my skull rumbling. Something big, monstrous, had broken free and was lurching around on the deck of a world so fucked-up that the worst stuff, the unthinkable, had a hundred, a thousand, precedents.

I lay on the bed for awhile, and then I got up and went down to the bar. Evil Ed saw me and brought me a beer.

"You need to lawyer up," he said. I was impressed: advice from Evil Ed!

"Thanks," I said. "But I didn't do anything. I don't have anything to hide. And Danny—" I stopped. Water rushed into my eyes, violently, as though I'd been shoved under a river and was being held there, breathless. I marshaled my paltry resources, gulped the beer.

Evil Ed shrugged and mopped the counter with a gray cloth. "You notice I don't ever take a drink? Might be you are bringing yourself bad luck, swallowing it right down your throat."

"What are you talking about?"

"They got this old Chinese saying goes like this: 'First the man takes a drink. Then the drink takes a drink. Then the drink takes the man.'"

"I still don't know what you're talking about."

"I guess you don't." Evil Ed slapped his palm down on the counter. Beneath it was a white envelope. He took his hand away, revealing my name on the front of the envelope, printed crudely with what looked like black crayon. "This was here on the counter when I opened this morning. I don't know what's inside it, and I don't want to know, and I should have handed it on to the cops when they were talking to me earlier today, but I didn't. It's yours. You do what you like with it."

I took the envelope and turned it over. It was sealed, and too light to contain anything more than a sheet or two of paper. I looked at the front again. All caps: SAM SILVERS.

I turned away from my unfinished beer and went back up to my room. I lay on the bed, my heart beating fiercely. I was afraid to open the envelope. Should I call the police? Perhaps it was a ransom note, and in opening it I'd destroy evidence. Forensics could do wonders, right?

Should I call Victoria? But that would be the same as calling the police; Victoria trusted authority. And I did not. I was raised on media tales of law enforcement agencies that bungled kidnappings, hostage situations, terrorist confrontations. Too often the innocent died with the guilty.

Hands trembling, I tore open the envelope and pulled the single sheet of paper free. A ball-point pen with blue ink had printed words whose letters jumped above and below the baseline, investing the sentences with a childish energy.

This is what I read:

I have solved your child support! If there is no child there can be no support of a child and no need

*for these moneys of which your wife makes you pay
and pay! Ha! I am very clever you must agree. This is
bragging, but it is so. All your worries are overboard!
I hope to talk to you sooner. —D.T.*

I walked around the room, sneezing. My body ached, an
aggressive pain, as though I'd been injected with poison. My
throat was on fire. I was not feeling well. But that wasn't
the problem, except to the extent that this flu-thing might
keep me from thinking clearly. Why, for instance, hadn't I
said anything to the police about Derrick Thorn? Did I really
think it was a coincidence that he had shown up at the zoo?
Did I think he was harmless? Did his crooked diction make
him somehow childlike, did an innocence of English syntax
indicate moral innocence? Hardly.

I sat down on the edge of the bed and tried to recall what
I'd thought and said to the detectives. I shook my head to clear
it, which made the room waver like an undulating funhouse
mirror. At Victoria's…the thought of Derrick Thorn had
not once entered my mind. It was as though I'd completely
forgotten the man's existence. Surely he was too strange to
forget. I tried to picture him now, to bring him into focus by
an act of will, but all I could see was his stout, pear-shaped
body, a silhouette in the Reptile House, his face in shadow,
his words…something about Danny…about child support.

How would I describe him to the police? A fat man in
black who might, or might not, be sporting purple lipstick
and false eyebrows? Wait, Evil Ed must have seen him. Sure.
He brought us drinks. He came to the booth with the drinks.

* * *

I RAN downstairs, too fast, slipping, saving myself from a
sudden dive forward by snagging the wooden railing just in

time. I stumbled into the bar. Evil Ed was at the opposite end of the bar listening to Rat Lady, who appeared to be wearing a bathrobe.

"Hey!" I shouted, and Evil Ed looked my way, saw me, and nodded, no doubt pleased to be moving out of the range of one of Rat Lady's monologues.

He drew a beer from the keg as he made his way toward me, but I shook my head.

"I don't want a beer. I've got a question."

Evil Ed raised his eyebrows, set the beer down, folded his arms, and leaned back some.

"You saw him. Could you describe him?"

"Describe who?"

"The guy I was talking to the night before last. Fat guy, really pale skin?"

He shook his head. "Wasn't but you. Sitting in that booth, drinking yourself into a coma, talking to yourself, coming out with a laugh every now and then, nothing happy about it, that laugh."

I kept on: "His name was Derrick Thorn. He was some kind of foreigner, spoke funny." But no accent, I thought, for the first time. "He paid for the beers."

Ed frowned. "You paid for your beers your ownself."

I had him there. "Then how come I didn't have a tab run up?"

"You did. You paid it at the end of the evening."

"I never do that," I said.

Evil Ed laughed. "That's right. Took me by surprise. You was drunker than usual, which is saying something."

Reflexively, I reached for the beer. This was to be a medicinal beer, a beer for clarity. If I could slow my thoughts down, I could sort them out.

✳ ✳ ✳

IT TOOK more than one beer. A lot more. When Evil Ed came by, he would glower at me, maybe thinking I had more important things to do then sit and drink beer. But I was working, thinking, and finally it came to me: I remembered what I needed, staggered to my feet, and headed back toward the stairs.

Back in my room, I headed straight for the nightstand, grabbed the drawer, yanked it—too hard—and it flew out, and all the cards and pens and antacid tablets jumped up in the air and scattered over the floor. Shit.

There were a lot of business cards. And, of course, amid this ridiculous surfeit of self-advertising, there wasn't, of course, of course, any card bearing the name Derrick Thorn and promising "good deals by mutual bargain" a phrase goofy enough to lodge in my mind even if the creator of that inanity was as elusive as truth at the White House, even if—

I let out a whoop of triumph and pounced on the card. I turned it over, saw the number, and without consulting my fever-riddled and almost worthless mind, I ran to the phone, snatched up the receiver, and made the call.

The phone rang and rang. Having no alternate plan, I was willing to sit there with it ringing. Maybe it rang for thirty seconds, maybe thirty minutes, I don't know. Then the ringing stopped and static rushed in, like an ocean wave over the sand.

I thought I heard a voice. I shouted, "Hello! Hello, Derrick Thorn!"

The tide of static ebbed. "Yes," the voice said.

I couldn't speak. Who was this? But then: "Hello Mr. Sam Silvers. You are calling with the congratulations! Yes. Ha, Ha! No more the child support, no more the, how did you say, blood from the turnip!"

"You son of a bitch!" I screamed. "Where's Danny? Where's my son?"

"Do not be worried. I will take the care of it. Trust me, like money in the bank!"

I was squeezing the receiver as though it were Thorn's throat. "I need to see you," I said. That was better, much better than saying I intended to kill him. Oh, I am clever in a clinch. There was a long silence, in which I thought the phone might go dead. But some urgent certainty told me I couldn't speak again; I had to wait.

"Yes. Sure. We make the bargains," he said. "Now you help me, one hand scratching the other. I will meet you tonight. Look at your watch and I will look at mine. Just us to meet, no body elses. At ten of the watch tonight. At the zoo."

"What?"

"At the zoo. To bring justice to the penguins."

"What?"

"The penguins, they do nothing wrong. They are good birds. But they have the enemies just the same, the seals and others. I think they are political. I am sure they are prisoners of the government."

I wasn't following this. "I will be there at ten tonight. Is Danny there? Let me talk to him," I said.

He hung up.

* * *

THE ZOO'S parking lot hadn't been cleared. The unseasonably nasty weather had closed the zoo for the day; temperatures were supposed to rise tomorrow, and, despite the desultory falling snow, I could see stars sprinkled between the clouds.

The parking lot was a white expanse, blue in the shadow of a bare-branched tree, gold under the single street lamp. I looked at my watch. It was ten minutes to ten. The tracks of my boots were all that marred the lot's smooth surface, which meant that Derrick Thorn hadn't arrived yet.

I waited, shivering with fever and the chill air, my breath coming out in white clouds. Ten came, and 10:05, and 10:10. I could feel the gun in my coat pocket, its weight both threat and reassurance. When Evil Ed's back had been turned, I'd leaned across the counter and retrieved it. I had to hope that Evil Ed wouldn't notice its absence. And if he did? He wouldn't report a missing gun to the cops. But he might figure out who took it, and Evil Ed could be scarier than any cop I'd ever met.

In my room, I'd confirmed that the clip was full, and on my way to this rendezvous, I'd stopped the car along the highway and walked off into a patch of evergreens and indulged in some target practice, sending a bullet into the trunk of a dead pine tree. It worked, and the seven remaining bullets were seven more than I'd need, unless he'd harmed Danny, in which case all seven slugs would be residing in Derrick Thorn's flesh.

I am not a fan of guns, but I know something about them. My father had been a collector, and, when I was young and under his spell, we would bond at the shooting range. I lost interest when he left my mother to run off with his secretary, an ancient, dishonorable tradition (my father's dad had, incredibly, done the same thing). I was fifteen when Dad left.

So here was my legacy: I knew how to shoot a handgun.

* * *

AT 10:15, I was getting restless, panicky. I walked up to the gate, gripped the bars and peered in at the animal statues and kiosks. The gate swung open, taking me by surprise, and I slipped, falling forward, banging my head against the gate. My knees skidded on the snow-covered ground, but I managed to get my hands in front of me in time to prevent my face from colliding with the icy bricks. I knelt there on all fours, dazed, and then I saw the small blue-shadowed footprints that marched between my hands: the bare footprints of a child. The snow was wet and preserved the imprint of each toe. Were these my son's footprints?

I followed the footprints, moving as fast as I could but not running for fear I'd fall and break something. I looked up, and the Reptile House loomed in front of me, more imposing than I remembered it, its crenellated towers given authority by the night. The footprints were farther apart as they neared the steps leading to the door; Danny had been running—and, yes, I was certain it was Danny now, for no reason except that I knew it to be so.

The footprints climbed the steps and ended at the door. I gripped the door's handle and pushed. Locked. No, it moved, but there was resistance. I leaned into the door with my shoulder, and it moved reluctantly. There was light from within, gleaming on the blue marble floor, and black, no red... There was a great smear of blood—another thing I knew with a certainty beyond logic: *blood*—curving away, under the door, behind the door. I entered the room and closed the door, and the body lay revealed, up against the wall, where I had shoved it with my shoulder against the door.

The security guard had been a small man, but bigger than my son, much bigger than Danny, and he lay curled on his side, oddly crumpled as though thrown there by some vast malevolent force, and in my horror and fear I felt a rush of relief because that's the way our hearts are made and this was not my son.

I turned away from the body and saw Derrick Thorn across the room in front of the glass cage where the penguins resided. Danny stood on his right, and Thorn had his right hand resting on my son's shoulder, a companionable pose. Danny was wearing his *Harry Potter and the Order of the Phoenix* t-shirt and bunny pajama bottoms. His feet were bare.

"Hello Mr. Sam Silvers!" Derrick shouted, raising his left hand as though hailing a taxi, his voice reverberating in the high-ceilinged room. "I have been worrying of your coming, thinking you did not keep your bargains."

"Move away from my son," I said, walking toward him. I had my hand in my pocket, my fingers already around the pistol grip, my forefinger on the trigger. Waves of dark power rushed up my arm, filling my heart with rage.

Thorn lifted his hand from Danny's shoulder and waved an admonitory finger at me. "You are angry because the child of your support is still here and you think, 'We had a bargains but it is broken because, before my eyes, the boy is still here.' Do not be full of the worry, Mr. Silvers. I, Derrick Thorn, have always the keeping of my word through time longer than you know."

"What do you want?" I asked.

"I have been thinking of the penguins and our agreeable conversations," he said. "We like the penguins. But they must do something wrong these penguins to be in jail, I think." He lifted his right hand this time and waved it toward the penguin cage.

"Danny," I said. "Come here."

Danny looked up, but his eyes failed to focus. There was no glint of recognition within them. Was he drugged?

"I think," Derrick continued, "that the government does not like the penguins, and I ask myself why this is so, because the penguins are good birds who have only, for enemies, the seals who are hungry to eat them, which is sad but is Nature's Law. 'Why,' I say to myself, 'is the government hating of the penguins?'"

"Danny," I said. "Come to me."

And Danny's eyes widened, and he took a faltering step forward, then stopped again, as Derrick continued, "And then I think of the canaries, the little yellow birdies, and how, in a coal mine, the canary dies and everyone says, 'Oh, the canary has died and we must run away,' and so they all run away and the bosses say, 'The canary is bad. She dies and no one will work. Stop looking at the canary,' but peoples look at the canary and say, 'I quit!' and run away and business is bad."

Danny began to walk again. He raised his arms and walked toward me, arms out, and I walked to meet him. I took my hand out of my pocket, and I lifted him in my arms and hugged him. He pushed his face against my neck and made a small, muffled noise, a child's displeasure at being jostled in his sleep. "It's okay," I said.

"The penguins," Derrick said, engrossed in his rant, "they are birdies like the canaries. They die and people say, 'This is of the global warmings! Stop the global warmings of the factories and the cars and the coal that is burning! The penguins are dying!' And the government says, 'Pay not the attention to these stupid penguins! Don't look at them! They are trouble makers!' And so the governments are putting the penguins in the prisons, you see?"

"Derrick," I said. "I don't know who you are or what you are"—I could admit this, to myself, at least—"but I am taking my son and leaving. If you attempt to follow me, I will kill you."

"But we have the bargains," Derrick said. "We must set the penguins free, and I will save you the child support."

"No," I said. "We have no bargain."

I expected some reaction, but my words seemed to deflate him somehow. His hands dropped to his sides and he stared at the floor.

I turned away and walked back toward the door of the Reptile House. When I reached the door, I looked back. He was gone.

The security guard's ravaged body no longer lay in the shadow of the door.

I carried my son out of the building and past the statue of a smiling hippopotamus and out the gate. I unlocked the car door and put him in the passenger seat. I pulled the seatbelt across his chest and snapped it into its latch. I got the scraper out of the glove compartment and scraped ice from the windshield. I noticed that the sky was full of cold light, but finding myself in what appeared to be the afternoon of a different day did not strike me as remarkable.

Danny was waking up when I climbed into the driver's seat. One of his shoelaces was untied, and so I tied it. Something seemed wrong with those shoes—and his winter coat, which, I noticed, was buttoned wrong. I re-buttoned the coat. For whatever reason, the image of Harry Potter, famous boy wizard, flashed through my mind.

"Dad, who were you talking to?" Danny asked, still woozy.

* * *

VICTORIA WAS angry. She'd tried to call me on my cell, and when I told her I'd discontinued the service, she said, "If this arrangement is going to work, I need to get ahold of you. The roads are bad. I was worried."

* * *

AND FOR a time, I remembered none of this. And why should I remember a thing that never happened? Had it happened, had my son actually disappeared, Victoria and Evil Ed would certainly have refreshed my memory.

* * *

I DRANK more, every day, sometimes passing out in the afternoon, and then getting drunk all over again in the evening.

Evil Ed told me about a drink taking a drink, and it sounded familiar. One time, I woke to find the television on, not unusual in itself, but this time cartoon penguins were tap dancing, and I was filled with improbable terror, caught in the sheets, falling out of bed. Unable to find the remote, I crawled to the television and slapped the power button, saving myself from...from what? Not for the first time, I thought, "Maybe I need to stop drinking."

In the newspaper, a photo of someone named Calvin Oster surprised me with another frisson of déjà vu. He had been a security guard at the Hillary Memorial Zoo in West Orange and, it appeared, a victim of gang violence. That explained it: I had, no doubt, seen him at the zoo and—what an amazing magpie, the mind—recorded his image without knowing it. That did not, however, account for my certainty that no inner-city gang had killed him.

Then, one day, somewhere between Thanksgiving and Christmas, somewhere in a stew of bad weather and strangers and a mugging (my own) that I tried to prevent, being too drunk for discretion's better part, I woke in a hospital ward with a bandaged arm and an I.V.

"How am I doing?" I asked a large, truculent nurse wearing green scrubs.

"Depends," she said. "That cut on your arm ain't nothing. But you got bad alcoholism. You been thrashing around considerable, plain out of your mind, and there's an orderly here name of Joshua, real big boy, six feet ten inches. He don't want to come round you. He says you got a demon, need to be exercised."

"What do you think?" I asked.

"I think I should have learned computers, stayed clear of all the misery and blood of this here nursing profession. An alcoholic ain't nothing but a sorry tale unfolding, lessen he gets sober. There's a fellow came in asking about you. I see him sometimes at the meetings they bring here on Tuesdays and Thursdays. He says he'll be back. Hope you don't owe him money."

"Why's that?"

"I wouldn't want to be crosswise of him is all. He got an evil eye on him."

* * *

SURE ENOUGH, Evil Ed visited me. We went down in an elevator to the second floor and listened to some guy tell his story, how drink had ruined him but then he had embraced the twelve steps of Alcoholics Anonymous, sobered up, and was now the president of a bank.

"What did you think about that?" Evil Ed asked.

"I don't know," I said.

"You could do a lot worse than that answer," he said. He said he'd come around some more.

When the hospital discharged me, I started going around to AA meetings with Evil Ed. I drove. Evil Ed said he didn't want to take his car; it might get stolen, whereas no one would covet my ratty Escort, which was true I guess but hurt my feelings.

* * *

WE WENT to a lot of AA meetings, traveling around to church basements and storefront clubs. Some of the neighborhoods were rough, and the AA meetings reflected that, with drunks sleeping it off on ratty sofas and old winos trying to steal a couple of bucks from the coffee-money can. One time a furious fight erupted between two members over which of the AA founders was wiser, Dr. Bob or Bill W. Sometimes I was the only white guy in the room, which didn't bother me particularly since I often thought I was the only guy on the planet. There are levels of alienation, and mine was way beyond racial.

I wanted to drink, but I didn't. Evil Ed couldn't always make it to a meeting, and I started going to meetings by myself. I went to a meeting every day, sometimes two, sometimes three. There was a club called "The Into Action Group" that was within walking distance of my apartment, so I went there a lot.

And if I got restless, I could always go down to the bar and talk to Evil Ed. He was almost chatty on the subject of alcoholism.

"Drinking has got consequences," he said. "You get a tattoo when you're drunk, it's still there in the damned morning. I been sober nine years, and people say, 'You should get that tattoo removed or inked up so it's different,' but I say it's a reminder of the consequences of drinking, and anything that reminds me why I don't want to go drinking again is a good thing."

One day I saw a help-wanted sign on the door of a print shop, and I walked in, talked to the manager, and got a job on the graphics side, not quite the art director position I'd left at BC Graphics, but it paid the rent and required me to get up in the morning.

A couple of days before Christmas, Evil Ed's sponsor was celebrating at a big speaker's meeting, and we went and listened to him tell how he'd wound up in AA and how come he hadn't had a drink in thirty-two years. He was a small, India-ink-colored old man with white hair, and he wore a three-piece suit. After the meeting, Evil Ed and I went to a party someone was throwing for him.

I was feeling my usual alienated, awkward self, so I found a place on the sofa, out of the way of all the hilarity. The television was on, and the station was showing an old Jimmy Stewart movie called Harvey. It was about this sweet-tempered alcoholic who is befriended by a giant rabbit that only he can see. I watched the movie with more interest and trepidation than it warranted. It was a harmless, mildly-amusing piece, but I was so caught in its spell that I jumped when Evil Ed's sponsor sat down next to me.

"Still a little jumpy!" he said. He squeezed the back of my neck and laughed.

He leaned forward and peered at the television set. "Well no wonder you're jumpy. You're watching a movie about a pooka! That's what they call that invisible bunny in the movie, say it's a mischievous spirit. They got that right! But mischief isn't a strong enough word. A pooka can do a world of harm. They are entities that attach themselves to alcoholics, and they can do more harm than a rabid dog. I've seen them destroy a man. They have great power to shift time and space. They can bend reality like a pretzel. It's not uncommon for a drunk to have acquired a pooka or two. Used to be, when I'd go see an alcoholic in detox, I'd get old Sally LaBon to come along with me, and she'd pray and work her potions, and once—you don't have to credit this—I saw a dog-like creature come howling out of a poor fellow's mouth and fly right through the ceiling. No one holds with praying out demons anymore. And I guess the program itself can rid a man of his demons, but I've seen times when some of Sally's righteous magic would do a world of good."

A pretty young woman came up and hugged the old man; such women have the power to dominate an elder's mind, and he forgot I was there. They got up and went off, to dance, I think, and I finished watching the movie. Despite its happy ending, I felt a sense of deep disquiet.

* * *

CHRISTMAS DAY didn't go well. I'd bought Danny some stuff that I knew he'd wanted, and he'd been really excited and happy with his presents, but I thought Victoria was acting odd, and when her friend Julie arrived with her husband, I figured it out. Julie and her man had brought another of Victoria's office mates with them, a big-smiling, handsome-and-he-knew-it guy with carefully tousled, jet-black hair.

His name was Gunther, and when he walked in the door, Danny looked up and grinned and said, "Hey, Gun!" and my mood deteriorated. I decided not to stay for the meal, and Victoria accompanied me out the door to tell me that I needed to reflect on my selfishness and think of my son for a change, and Gunther came out, asking if he could be of any help. By throwing the first punch, I may have managed to break his nose, but I didn't win the fight. When I came to, I was lying in the snow on the front yard, a couple of yards away from my car in the driveway. The car's driver-side door was open, suggestively, and I got up, collected myself—no large bones broken—and drove away.

* * *

"WHAT HAPPENED to you?" Evil Ed wanted to know.

"Christmas dinner with the ex," I said.

"Looks like the turkey got the stuffings knocked out of him," he said.

* * *

IT TOOK a week of stewing, of feeling ill-used and done-wrong, of wallowing in self-pity, but, finally, I picked up a drink.

There was this little well-lit delicatessen with a liquor license, right next door to the print shop. It wasn't some dive filled with comatose barflies. It was clean and bright, you might even say wholesome. I drank a couple of beers there before going home one evening. It didn't seem like such a big deal.

But it's the first drink that gets you drunk, even if that first drink takes a few days to really kick in.

* * *

SO I was drunk in my room in my underwear. I hadn't gone to the print shop for a week or so. After the second day, my boss had stopped leaving messages on the answering machine. My guess was I didn't have that job anymore.

The television was on, as it often was, babbling away in its news voice, a serious Iraq-Darfur voice over a blighted grayscape, muddy video-people moving around, digital zombies. I wasn't watching closely, but the voice droned on, the non-stop monologue of a demented relative. Then the voice turned hearty, and I looked up for the good-news segment, some cheery thing about toddlers helping the homeless or octogenarians climbing a mountain, human interest as opposed to the tedium of human death.

A reporter was standing in front of the zoo in West Orange (I recognized the crenellated towers and little flags). I tapped the remote's volume control, raising the volume in time to hear her say, "...going home. That's right, these penguins, extremely rare, are on their way back to New Zealand where they will be re-introduced to their native habitat. The Fiordland crested penguin's numbers have been reduced by..."

I stared at the full-screen close-up of this endangered penguin as it tilted its head back and forth, flashing those familiar eyebrows. I reached for the remote and punched the power button.

Where did this penguin dread come from? Penguins were not, generally, considered creatures capable of inspiring much in the way of horror and loathing. Was I losing my mind?

That was a question I rarely asked myself. I knew where my mind was. All right, in the years I'd had this mind, I hadn't always used it carefully, hadn't checked off every single 5,000-mile oil change, hadn't even done a crossword puzzle or read a challenging novel in the last ten years, but was there anything fundamentally wrong with my mind?

There was this penguin glitch. But I could work around that. How hard was it to avoid penguins? And the zoo was sending those penguins back to New Zealand, in any event, so I could even go to the zoo with Danny...go again, that is.

I was starting to panic. My heart shivered, like some small bird in an ice storm. I heard a sudden loud, thumping sound, and I looked to the door, but the sound was behind me, coming from the kitchen. I got up from the bed; my legs felt boneless but, by an effort of will, I was able to walk.

I reached the doorway to the kitchen and leaned against the frame. The sound was coming from within the refrigerator, a muffled, booming sound. The fridge rocked from side to side, and half a dozen cockroaches skittered out from under it and shot across the dirty linoleum.

The refrigerator's door banged open releasing billowing clouds of gray mist that blew over me, soaking me, plastering my hair to my forehead. I closed my eyes, and when I opened them, he was there. He was wearing a tuxedo, and his eyebrows were now complete circles around his eyes. He'd drawn a small purple patch of mustache above his purple lips. These embellishments still failed to define him. He was a sort of manic blur, a creature my mind refused to bring into focus.

"Derrick Thorn," I said.

He clapped his white-gloved hands. "Yes. I think some-times you forget me, but then I come back because you remember me, you remember me and you keep your bargains!"

I did remember him. It wasn't like remembering, though. It was like entering a room that held stuff you'd lost, stuff you'd completely forgotten about, and now, here it was. You recognized it immediately, and that was the word, really, recognized.

I recognized the bloodstains on his white dress shirt and on his gloves.

"What did you do?" I asked.

"We have the bargains, you remember? You say, 'Forget the bargains. I take my son of the child support and I leave, and no more bargains.'"

He shook his head ruefully, studying the floor. "That is the rule. Is up to you. No bargains? Very well, no bargains, and I go away."

"And now? Why are you here now?"

"Ha, ha! I am always around, but you cannot see me, and so you must drink the alcohol and then—ha! ha!—I am clear as sunshine."

"You came because I started drinking?" I was talking to a supernatural creature, a pooka. Or maybe I was talking to my hallucinatory self. Did it matter?

Derrick shook his head. "No, I come because you of the slyness are. You say, 'No bargains!' but then you be the clever one and go through the channels! Yes, the channels! The penguins at the apocalypse they will be of rejoicing and singing your name 'Silvers! Silvers! Silvers!' They will say, 'We be always holding for you gratitude and love!'"

"I don't understand," I said.

"You be joking all the way through, I see. Okay! But the penguins, you give them the freedom! You get them out of the prison and to going home! Hooray!"

I remembered. "No bargain," I had said, and this creature, this pooka, had let Danny go. And now this creature thought that I had set the penguins free and—

"So I keep the bargains!" Derrick shouted. "We make the deals! Is done! Done deal! I see you at the Christmases with the ex-wives of your anger. I confess, I be the spy on the wall. I see your true wishes, and I obey them. And no troubles for you, be so assured of this."

"What have you done to Danny!" I screamed, and I lunged forward. Maybe I expected my hands to slide through him; I don't know what I expected, but my hands found his neck, and his flesh was cold and boneless, and I squeezed, and his neck, like some balloon thing, no, like paste in a tube, his neck collapsed beneath my fingers, and his head swelled, seemed to leap at me like a child's toy, his head round and smooth and big as a basketball and growing bigger, tongue out—bright blue!—and teeth every which way like a ragged shark's mouth and, from this mouth, a high, keening sound that was, I'm sure, laughter.

Derrick's head exploded with a bang, so loud that my eardrums seemed to have burst in sympathy. I fell back and watched as Derrick, headless, ran in circles, making a *huh, huh, huh*, sound, flapping his arms like some big water bird slowly building for take-off, before he came to rest with his back to the wall, and slid down the wall, legs straight out in front of him, convulsing briefly, and finally growing utterly still, above him a great swatch of bright red like a thick exclamation point ending in his body.

I went back into the bedroom. I didn't have any plan, exactly, but I didn't need one because the phone rang. I answered it. It was Danny asking if I still planned on taking him to the ice-skating rink next Sunday, and I said sure. He wanted to know if I could pick up June too; she lived close by, and it was okay with her parents. "Sure," I said.

Danny said goodbye, and I put the phone down, got up and went back into the kitchen. Derrick Thorn was gone, it seemed, leaving nothing but a lot of blood. On closer inspection, I found a tiny, balloon-like skin. I was able to make out the bowtie, even the tiny, polished shoes. I carried this deflated cast-off to the sink, turned the garbage disposal on, and dropped it down. The disposal made a stuttering, chugging noise, as though gagging.

I walked to the refrigerator and opened the door. The fridge was empty except for a six-pack of beer and Gunther's head. I poured the six-pack out in the sink, and went back and regarded Gunther's head again.

* * *

I DON'T feel good about this. I mean, I'm not a complete asshole, and I realize that my problems with Gunther weren't Gunther's fault. I could have explained that to that stupid pooka if he'd taken the time to ask.

I do have to say that even in death Gunther had managed to hold on to his deeply-refined, disapproving air. He wasn't wearing a horrified grimace; he seemed sort of serene. I guess I'm saying that he didn't appear to have suffered. I double-bagged him in black plastic trash bags and took him down to my car.

They never did find Gunther's body. They won't find his head, either.

* * *

I KNOW I had a part in Gunther's demise, but it would be hard to explain the nature of my involvement to the police, and I'm not going to try. You're my sponsor, and I trust you. This is fifth step stuff, and I know it won't go any further.

I know one thing: I'm done with drinking. I'm back to a meeting a day, two-a-day on weekends. I know I'm powerless over alcohol. And I know I don't want to ever see Derrick Thorn again, and I'm pretty sure I won't. Oh, I don't think he is dead. In fact, I'm certain his departure was just another one of his jokes.

Remember that hospital meeting you took me to last week? There was this guy sitting across the room in a hospital gown. He stared at me throughout the meeting, and he headed straight for me when it ended. He looked bad, the left side of his face scraped raw and something seriously wrong with one of his legs so that he moved up and down and left and right like some busted wind-up toy. The worst thing, when he got up close—and he got close, his face six inches from mine—was the death in his eyes, the cold-water craziness at the bottom of those muddy, red-rimmed pupils. Or maybe the phlegmy sound of his voice was worse, I don't know. Maybe it was the sum of his infirmities, the weight of ruined days, the dank reek of his breath. No, probably the worst was what he said: "I know you. We got a friend in common. He says, 'Don't be a stranger.' He says maybe he'll see you around, and you can share a few beers and have good times." He shambled off, just another wretched, booze-ruined derelict. But I had to sit back down in a chair and ride out the vertigo, because I didn't think it was a case of mistaken identity.

If I take a drink, he'll be waiting. I'll walk into a bar somewhere. I'll sit down on one of the bar stools. I'll look up at the television, and I'll see a lot of penguins tobogganing on their bellies down an ice slope, and behind me, I'll hear his voice. "Oh, the happy penguins!" he will shout.

Pookas are called up by alcohol, by the darkness that blooms in an alcoholic's soul after that first drink, and with AA and these steps I think I can avoid that drink.

Maybe I'm arrogant, but I'm honestly not that worried about my sobriety. I am, I guess, still a little worried about global warming, and I still wonder what we'll say to the penguins when the end times are upon us.

Come Lurk With Me
and Be My Love

W HEN WALLY BENNETT was a kid, his parents taught him to say this prayer:

Now I lay me down to sleep. I pray the Lord my soul to keep. If I should die before I wake, I pray the Lord my soul to take.

❋ ❋ ❋

HE HAD stopped saying the prayer at nine or ten, and he had always found it disturbing, for two reasons. One: Dying in his sleep was not a pleasant thought, not something Wally wished to entertain; the idea that the Lord was poised above his sleeping form like some immense holy vulture waiting to grab his soul—and do exactly *what* with it?—was unsettling, to say the least. And two: There was always the implicit suggestion that, should he *forget* to say this prayer, something awful would occur. One of Satan's minions might drag him into the abyss.

Wally hadn't thought about God much in years. Now here he was, reading a book entitled, *Of Pandas and People,* and thinking about...well, actually, Flower. Her name was Flower, oddly imprecise for one so much *herself*, as though her parents had wrestled with names like Daisy, Violet, and Rose, lost their way amid so many choices, and settled for this generic solution.

Wally was in love with Flower, love like a rat in his vitals, love that gnawed at his sleep, love that made his time away from her feel like bad television, like exile.

He had met Flower at a craft fair in Warrenton. Like all males, Wally hated craft fairs, but he had accompanied his married friends, Ben and Sarah, because they had insisted—well, Sarah had—that he needed to get out more. Wally and Sarah both worked for a small, desperate ad agency (Blitz Media) in Arlington, Virginia, and, more often than not, Wally worked on Saturdays, preparing for some Monday presentation while the rest of the office, people with lives, celebrated the weekend.

"You've got to get out of this office," Sarah had said. "You're like one of the undead, like a blind cave salamander."

So Wally had said sure he'd go, why not?

* * *

AT FIRST, the fair seemed to answer that question. Unruly children screamed and chased each other through the crowd. Coils of smoke unfurled from the slow-cooking carcasses of pigs and chickens and rose into the cloud-heavy sky. The beer in cardboard cups was tepid but, alas, not undrinkable, and Wally drank way too much, and a bluegrass band wailed, miserably authentic, thin, clenched voices harried by a banjo and a mandolin. The day, unseasonably chilly for late April, threatened rain, and Wally wished he'd worn something warmer than a t-shirt.

He stared at the crafts and the people who had crafted them and was appalled at how the creative impulse could so easily lose its way. The beer got him and, for a moment, a rush of idiot compassion urged him to hug a pinch-faced man in brown overalls who sat on a stool surrounded by primitive paintings of Jesus engaged in various farm chores (milking a cow, driving a tractor, killing a hog) but the desire to comfort the untalented, the misguided, left Wally before he could act.

He had lost sight of his friends amid the milling throng, but Ben had anticipated that possibility and suggested that they meet back at the SUV at 4:00 should they become separated.

Wally looked at his watch. It was only 2:15, and he felt exhausted, which manifested itself in a flare of self-pity: *I am thirty-two years old, and the best I can do on a Saturday is accompany my married friends to a craft fair.* The thought inspired an instant twitch of self-loathing, because it was such a lame lament. You put something like that in your suicide note, and the cops would have a good laugh. "My wife burned dinner," someone would say. "I think I'll hang myself." Another wit would say, "Hell, nothing but reruns on. I'm gonna get the shotgun out of the attic and blow my damned head off."

Wally found himself resenting these imagined cops. What did they know about his life? A shy person, Wally had grown up in a family of extroverts, shouters, backslappers, people who could tell a dirty joke, heartily curse the referee at a football game, watch sitcoms and laugh like crows. He was the youngest, with three brothers and two sisters. He could never shake the feeling that he had arrived at the party too late. Everyone assumed he knew what the celebration was about, but he didn't have a clue.

"So, do you want to buy that?"

Wally looked up and saw the most exotic, most beautiful creature he had ever seen. Her eyes were a breathtaking blue, her lips full and dark purple, almost black, and she stood, bare feet planted on a small stool, swaying slightly as though to music, perhaps practicing some feminine martial art. Clouds had obscured the sun, but a single shaft of light escaped to bathe this child woman in gold, as though God were throwing a spotlight on His glorious creation.

She had a Goth look to her, spiky black hair, a black t-shirt, and black cargo pants, but Wally knew—the way you know a thing when love pierces you like a sword—that she heeded no one's fashion, was, indeed, incapable of being, of looking, like anyone other than who she was. And Wally knew, having beheld her, that an after-image would burn in his mind for the rest of his life.

* * *

NOW, THREE weeks later, sitting on the sofa in his apartment with *Of Pandas and People* on his lap, Wally thought again about that first meeting. Had he been immediately smitten, or was this a lover's revisionist history? It was, he thought, every bit as real as a car crash he had been in when he was twenty-four and a car filled with teenagers had run a stop sign and broadsided him. His car had seemed to spin slowly, leisurely, and images of the surrounding buildings, the clouds, and the stark winter trees had been shuffled like cards and slapped down one-at-a-time in the middle of his mind, too surreal to comprehend and yet leaving him with the reality of a twice-broken arm. In just this way had his heart been altered, irrevocably, by Flower. Why else would he be reading *Of Pandas and People?* He read:

> *Of Pandas and People* is not intended to be a balanced treatment by itself. We have given a favorable case for intelligent design and raised reasonable doubt about natural descent.

* * *

THIS WAS the book that the people in Flower's commune were using to homeschool their children, and Flower had urged it on him with a mixture of diffidence and desperation. Clearly, his opinion of the book was important to her, so important (Wally suspected) that his negative opinion could scuttle their fledgling romance. All right: Wally knew that this intelligent design thing used to be called "creationism," which maintained that mankind did not evolve through the random action of physical forces. Intelligent design (aka God—and a Christian one at that) had to get Life going. And once Life got going, something as complicated as a giraffe was never going to evolve without divine meddling.

How would one know when something was created by the application of intelligence? How could one *recognize* intelligence? According to the authors of *Pandas*, seeing and knowing this intelligence was largely common sense. "Most of us do it without even thinking," they wrote. Consider those ripples in the sand that you observed when walking on the beach. Anyone could see that this pattern was a natural phenomenon created by the rhythmic action of the ocean's waves. But, suppose you walked down that same beach and came upon the words JOHN LOVES MARY written in the sand. You'd know the waves hadn't created that pattern. These words were created by intelligence! Probably, the authors added, by an intelligence named John or Mary. To illustrate this principle, the authors included a photo of sand in which the words JOHN LOVES MARY were written. *Proof!* (Wally was inclined to think that the *photographer* was the intelligence behind this pattern and that neither John nor Mary had anything to do with the words; he realized, however, that this thought was completely irrelevant.)

Wally read on, but his question wasn't "Can I honestly say I believe this crap?" No, his question was a simpler one,

"Can I lie to Flower to win her love?" And the answer to that was a resounding, "Yes!" Love that can't trump intellectual integrity isn't worth the name.

* * *

ON THAT day when they met, her first words were: "So, do you want to buy that?"

He could not say whether she repeated this sentence or whether the words simply hung in the air until he was able to process them. He saw that he was holding in his hands a small, smooth object, a carving of some sort.

He studied it. It was a primitive wood carving of a man, standing, his legs disappearing into the blocky base of the carving. Cradled in his arms was a child—no, a tiny woman; her breasts were fully developed—and this woman was also holding something in her arms, a dog-like creature whose mouth opened to display ragged teeth. Man, woman, and dog-thing all faced forward, eyeless, mouths open. *Howling*, Wally thought.

"What is it?" Wally said, or heard himself saying. Was that a rude question? He couldn't think.

"You don't have to buy it," the girl said, jumping down from the stool. She was smiling, dimples in her cheeks.

"How much is it?"

"Twenty dollars, I guess." She looked at him, as though trying to puzzle out the effect such a sum would have.

"Okay," Wally said, and he fished in his pocket, pulled out some crumpled bills, and found a twenty among them. He handed this to the girl, who beamed, a smile worth all the twenties he had. She laughed, a musical trill that made Wally dizzy.

She took the carving from him and placed it in a small brown paper bag. She creased and folded the bag's top carefully, as though there was a formula for this folding, and, as she bent over, engrossed, the thick spikes of her hair leaned forward, suggesting the fronds of some jungle plant. Wally watched his hand move toward her hair, a hand in thrall. She looked up, and he dropped his hand and looked away, saw the card table covered with carvings, and examined another one. This one was a sort of frog creature with its mouth open. Within its mouth, he could see another frog peering out.

"You want that one, too?" she asked.

"Did you carve all these?"

"Yes," she said.

"That must have taken a long time." *Jeez*. Was this his best shot at conversation?

"I got a lot of time, that's for sure. Dah always says, 'More you wait, the sooner you're late!'" She giggled. "You can have that one, too, if you want it." And she looked down when she said that, at once demure, shy.

"How much?" Wally didn't know how much money he'd brought with him. Whatever, it was hers.

She shook her head, not looking up. "Free, is all," she said.

"That wouldn't be right. I really like it!"

She looked up, rocked him with her smile again, and said, "That's the price then. Liking. I give it to you for the liking of it. And because..." She was coy now; her head canted to the side and away, eyes looking back.

"Because?"

"I like you, too."

✻ ✻ ✻

THEN IT was after four o'clock and Ben was standing by his side, miffed. "We said we'd meet at the car at four," he said. "I've been looking all over for you. Sarah's got a headache. We need to get going."

Wally had lost track of time, sitting there with the girl.

"This is Flower," he told Ben. "She lives on a commune, and she carves these amazing figures."

"Nice meeting you," said Ben, but he was in a hurry, almost rude, a quick dismissive glance at her art, and Wally reluctantly stood up and followed him back to the SUV.

* * *

THE NEXT morning, Wally was in the parking lot before the craft fair opened. He'd come alone this time, and he spent the morning sitting with Flower, talking to her, passing the time, watching the people go by, ambivalent when people stopped and purchased one of her carvings. He liked seeing the smile a sale induced, but he didn't want anyone to own something Flower had touched and laboriously carved and sanded and graced with the sweet weight of her concentration.

At noon, Flower stood up and announced that she was closed for lunch. She walked around the table and out into the aisle, where a new batch of craft fair attendees jostled each other, picked through jewelry and junk, and purchased hot dogs and giant pretzels from a vendor wearing, for reasons of his own, a Spiderman costume. Wally and Flower purchased fried chicken and fries and soft drinks from another food vendor and climbed to the top of a hill where they could look down on the fair. Flower pointed to the blue mountains to the west. "I live there," she said.

"Can I visit you sometime?" Wally asked.

"Oh, sure. I'd like that. I'll have to draw you a map, though. It's not easy to find, kind of a lurk, you know?"

"Lurk?"

"You know, like a hideaway. We don't want people to come mucking around in our business, so we lie low."

Flower reached forward and squeezed his arm. "If you really want to know about us, there's a book you should read. I mean, it's important. I can't even tell you how important." She let go of his arm and hugged herself, as though constraining something wild and sensuous within— or perhaps she was just responding to the chill, for the day had grown overcast, blustery, and was full of the stubborn remnants of winter.

＊ ＊ ＊

THREE EXTREMELY long weeks had passed since he had last seen Flower. He had watched her climb into her van, a wobbly, ancient vehicle, dirty-white with patches of gray primer, and he had waved goodbye—*idiot that he was!*—and, dazed by the kiss she had bestowed on his cheek, he had failed to follow her. Yes, he had the map she had drawn for him, and he had her promise that she would call him—she had carefully tucked away the business card he gave her (a card he'd made when he planned to escape the drudgery of Blitz Media by going freelance)—but he should have followed her. Because he knew just how forgettable he was.

Back in the days when he went to bars, when he made some effort to pick up women, he saw in their eyes this phenomenon of effacement. He would evaporate, even as he spoke. At first these women he approached would seem slightly annoyed, aware that their attention was being demanded by someone unremarkable, but then they'd look dazed, bemused, and turn to the girlfriend who'd accompanied them or shout to the bartender for a refill. Wally would know that, as far as they were concerned, he was gone, not even snubbed, which would have left some mental residue, some knowledge that he had *been* there.

Perhaps, driving down the highway, Flower had glanced in the rearview mirror, seen him waving, and wondered who he was. *Oh yes: a customer.*

He had asked her for a phone number, and she had told him there was no phone because "Dah don't hold with them. Not the lines nor the cells." She said she would drive to where there was a phone and call as soon as she could. And she had warned Wally that she'd have to "acclimate" her father (the formidable "Dah") to the notion of a visitor from the outside.

Naturally, Wally had grown impatient and tried to find her with her map. The map led him west on Lee Highway and north on 688, traveling through rainy, smudged-watercolor fields, black cattle and barns as red as blood. He stopped at gas stations and antique shops and asked about the Hewlitt farm or Skunk Cabbage Creek, but no one had heard of Flower's landmarks. Both weekends he'd hunted her, quitting at dark and driving home to study the map, which he had memorized and could see with his eyes closed—and which now looked so spare and unforthcoming that he wondered why, when she gave it to him, he hadn't laughed bitterly, shook his head, and said, "If you don't want me to visit, just say so."

Once he thought he was close. He'd driven past what looked like an abandoned gas station, but he'd seen the screen door swing open, emitting a cat before banging shut, so he'd turned around and gone back. He'd gotten out of his car and gone up to the screen door and peered in. He couldn't see into the gloom, but someone shouted "Hey!" and he turned around and saw an old man who must have come around the side of the building. He wore brown gloves and gripped a hoe in his right hand. His chin was pocked with white stubble, and the gray of his eyes was the color of rain water in a tin cup.

"You don't want to peep into a man's house like that. You give an honest knock is what you do."

"I was just—"

"We ain't got any gas. Does this look like a flourishing establishment?"

"I just wanted to ask directions. I'm looking for some people." Wally walked back to his car. He opened the door and prepared to get in. It didn't look like he was going to get anything but aggravation from this old buzzard.

"What kind of people?"

"I believe they live in a commune."

"Like hippies?"

"Well no, I think this is a Christian-based commune, actually."

"Something like those Mormoners, with their sacred underwear and their child brides?"

"No." Wally climbed in the car and turned the ignition on.

Just then the screen door opened, and a woman came out. She was wearing a green bathrobe over a blue nightgown, and pink slippers. She was as ancient as the man, but fleshier. Her eyes seemed very large behind her gold-framed glasses.

"What does he want?" she shouted to the old man.

"Wants to know where some people are, but he's mighty vague about them, mostly knows who they aren't."

That's when Wally saw Flower's carvings on the seat next to him. He couldn't say why he'd brought them with him. "For luck," he would have said if anyone had asked. Now he realized that there was an absolutely rational reason for bringing them along. They were evidence of Flower's existence.

Wally reached out and picked up the man-woman-dog carving and swung back out of the car, leaving the engine running.

"Maybe you've seen someone selling these carvings?" he said, holding up the carving. "At a fair or—"

"Damn you!" the man shouted, and he ran at Wally, swinging the hoe, and Wally ducked, which wouldn't have saved him, but the hoe's blade overshot, banging against the car's roof, and Wally slipped on the cracked asphalt, and thought he heard the old man grunt with frustration. He heard shouts, the old woman hollering, he couldn't make out what. The rusty blade winged by again, quick as a bat, inches from his left eye, and he heard a sharp bang, something cracking, and then he was standing, lurching forward, and the hoe's shaft slammed down on his left shoulder, knocked him to his knees, and he hollered, "Ow!" which seemed, even in the moment, a pathetic expression for the considerable pain.

"Okay, okay! That's enough, Paw! What the hell you doing, anyway!"

Squinting, hands in front of his face to fend off the next blow, Wally looked up to see the old man struggling with a thin, hard-muscled man in a flannel shirt and jeans. The family resemblance was obvious, the same muscle in the jaw, the same taut frame, same eyes.

"I ain't gonna let you go till you calm!" the younger man said, clutching the older man's arms from behind. The older man said nothing, glaring, the hoe on the ground by his feet.

Wally sat on the asphalt, his legs stretched out in front of him, his back against his car door, and rubbed his shoulder. He became aware that someone was casting a shadow over him, and he looked up and saw the old woman. She leaned over and offered him a can of beer.

"Thanks," Wally said. He popped the top of the can and took a long swallow.

"It ain't your fault," the woman said. "You just poked a sore."

After the old man and his son had gone back in the house, she explained about the sore. There had been a grandson, their daughter Laurel's boy. The boy, Dean, wasn't right in the head, and he was too much for Laurel, so she'd run off.

The old woman and her husband had had the raising of the boy. "And no trouble at all. He was the sweetest little fellow, addled, but angel sweet."

One day they found him dead in a creek bed, his neck broken, and likely it was an accident, but Horace, her husband, had had a run-in with some gypsies who'd stopped at the station—that was back when the place was a going concern—and these raggedy folk had been selling carvings that must have looked like the one Wally had (although she couldn't say for certain they were the same; she hadn't seen them).

She hadn't been home when Horace had the encounter, but he told her about it. Apparently, a big old whiskered fellow, the leader, had seen Dean and it set the old patriarch off. He said that Dean was nature gone awry, was an abomination to the great plan (something like that) and had no business living.

"You ever heard such a thing?" she asked. And it was no more than a week later that Dean was dead, and Horace went crazy, sure it was those gypsies, and he kept after the sheriff, who, to his credit, did what he could, but those travelers were gone, and no one else had set eyes on them.

"Not a bit of that is your fault," she told Wally, "but here you come, ignorant as a newborn, and stick your hand right in the hornet's nest."

Wally had thanked her for the beer, found Flower's carving where it had rolled up against the back tire, and climbed back into his car. His shoulder throbbed like a bad tooth, and he just wanted to get out of there. He was worried that Horace might give his son the slip and return with a shotgun. He was clearly a volatile man.

As he backed up, the woman shouted after him, "You seem like a nice man. You remind me a little of our Dean, though. He was always one to rush in without thinking. You might not want to find those people, is all I'm saying."

* * *

WALLY WAS convinced that he wasn't going to find Flower. So why, then, did he continue to read *Of Pandas and People?* He supposed he read it because Flower said it was important. The book was a connection to her—and a stupid waste of a Sunday, no doubt. He was drinking beer on top of the pain killers his doctor had prescribed for his shoulder, and that was, no doubt, interfering with his concentration, but, really, what was so damned important about reconciling Genesis with evolution anyway? He read on, and in a chapter entitled "Genetics and Macroevolution," he read that the intelligent design blueprints were actually *protected* by natural selection. An evolutionist improbably named Bumpus had made a study of English sparrows and discovered that those sparrows killed by a severe winter were "more extreme in their physical characteristics." The normal sparrows survived. What the book called "stabilizing selection" kept the optimal (intelligence-designed, God-wrought) sparrows alive and eliminated the mutants.

Wally put the book down and walked to the window of his apartment. The view consisted of other apartment buildings and a parking lot. Heavy rain swept over the parked cars, pummeling them, generating a silvery nimbus that enclosed them. As he watched, a figure emerged from between two parked cars, surrounded in the same shimmer of atomized raindrops. This lithe, elegant apparition strode purposefully across the lot, oblivious to the downpour. *Flower!* Wally knew her instantly, by her grace, the way she moved as though partnered with some elemental force. She looked up and stared directly at him. He thought she might have heard the hitch in his breath and felt the rush of joy that flooded his heart. Wally turned, ran to the door of his apartment, flung it open, raced down the hall, down two flights of stairs, and ran out and into the rain, ran to her, and she smiled, hands at her sides, waiting, and he threw his arms around her and felt the lovely curve of her spine, the sweet animal truth of its history. What could be more wonderful, more mysterious than two creatures, shaped by huge forces, by fire, wind, and rain, by boundless, implacable time, finding each other in the terrible random turnings of the world?

The rain was a roaring in their ears and she had to shout: "I ran away!"

* * *

SHE WAS shivering, from the chill of the rain, from fatigue, and from, Wally understood, her own recklessness, the wild thing inside her that had torn her world asunder. Wally had read of children raised in strange cults, immersed in inflexible systems of belief, defined by rituals; children warned, more often than not, of the horror and death that awaited them if they turned away from the one true path. How hard it must be to forsake one's kin and country.

While she was showering, Wally undressed, toweled dry, and put on clean clothes. Then he fumbled through his closets for something that Flower could wear. Everything was too big, of course, but she could roll the cuffs of the pants... they'd have to buy stuff...he could wash and dry what she'd worn...had she hitchhiked? How could anyone be so brave?

Wally emptied the pockets of her sodden pants. There were some coins, a few bills, an ink pen, the business card he'd given her—which, incredibly, must have led her here—and a curious medallion about the size of a quarter. The medallion was warm to the touch and etched with a holographic image of something that looked a little like a trilobite, that ancient arthropod that suggested a many-segmented cockroach and turned up in fossils that were two or three hundred million years old. When Wally turned the medallion over, he saw the same hologram on the other side, although the effect was more one of the image *rolling* over to the other side than of a second image being revealed. He closed his fist on the medallion, and the sensation was quite pleasant, like holding a warm stone that sent waves of warmth pulsing up his arm, filling him with cozy omniscience.

✳ ✳ ✳

HE WAS sitting on the couch when Flower came out of the bathroom. She was wearing the clothes he had found for her, and she looked like a child playing dress-up. *Good God! What if she isn't even eighteen!* Without makeup, without the spiky hair and the deep purple lipstick, she seemed newborn, no more than fourteen.

"How old are you?" he asked.

Flower frowned. "Dah says likely 411 years, but the birthing logs were lost in a fire in 1810, and he says he might not have the count-back right."

Wally nodded. No problem, then. He was feeling pretty good, the thrum filling up his body with a soft, cottony certainty.

Flower said. "Did you take my little pocket piece?"

Wally nodded. "Yep." He uncurled the fingers of his fist to show her, but the medallion was gone. *Poof!* Like a magic trick. He giggled. "Gone," he said. He felt a little drunk. He remembered Flower's bravery, and he wanted to comfort and reassure her. "I read the panda people book you lent me. I don't have any problem with your being a Christian. I mean, if you think God created the world in six days, if you think dinosaurs shared the earth with men, that's okay with me."

"But I don't," Flower said, eyes wide. She seemed shocked, possibly offended. She frowned, then a knowing light came into her eyes, and she nodded as though in agreement with some internal voice. "You mean because of the book, how it's Christian and all. I just wanted you to read the book because then I wouldn't have to explain so much. I mean, it tells how we made the world and all, but the god of that book, he's not real. He's just a story. Dah says there are more story gods than you can hit with a stick."

Wally nodded, although he didn't think he was understanding her perfectly.

Flower's next words didn't seem to make complete sense either: "You're being sorted right now. I think it is a good sign that you found the kinstone before I gave it to you. Dah teases me, calls me superstitious, but I believe in omens. You finding it yourself, that's a good omen."

"Okay," Wally said. He was tired, maybe a little queasy, and he needed to rest before he examined all this new, confusing info. He closed his eyes.

✳ ✳ ✳

HE WAS jostled awake. He was lying on a thin air mattress in...it took a minute to get his bearings...a van. He had no memory of walking to the van. He saw the back of Flower's head and shoulders, and he pushed himself into a sitting position.

Flower must have seen the movement in the rearview mirror. She turned around, her smile more radiant than ever.

"Dah wasn't going to let you visit. So I ran off to fetch you. He won't fuss so much now, because you been sorted and you are definitely kin. You aren't some stranger he can smite with his wrath."

"Good," Wally said, but he was nervous all the same.

"If you are feeling better, why don't you come on up front and sit with me," Flower said.

Wally nodded. "Okay." He stood up, felt momentarily dizzy, and braced himself with a hand on the van's wall. They were still bouncing over rough road, but Wally wobbled and lurched his way to the passenger seat, clambered over it, and slid down. Rain splattered the windshield, but it was nothing like the earlier deluge.

"Where—" he began, but Flower yanked the wheel to the left and pointed them straight toward a cluster of massive granite boulders protruding from a sheer wall of red clay in which some gnarled, stunted pine trees had found grim purchase. Wally screamed. Darkness enveloped them, stole the light, stole the thoughts in his head, stole the sound of his scream. He had no idea who or what he was. And then they were back, or at least they were somewhere.

"Here we are," Flower said. She turned the engine off, turned in her seat, threw her arms around Wally and squeezed him. "This is a pretty good lurk, huh?"

Wally climbed out of the van and turned slowly in a circle. There were thousands of tiny lights overhead, and, at first, he thought they were stars, but he realized that they blinked on and off, creating patterns that shifted and repeated.

"Come on," Flower said, taking his hand. She led him down a flight of metal stairs. Yellow lamps on the tunnel's walls illuminated other doors. Wally heard what sounded like the rush of water, the creak and clang of ancient machinery. "Where are we?" Wally asked, his words echoing around him like startled birds.

"We're inside a mountain," Flower said.

Wally didn't think there were any caves in these mountains. The caves were all farther west where underground streams carved elaborate limestone caverns.

Flower might have read his thoughts, for she said, "Dah says these caves were created by the Ur Gods and here is where they birthed the world. This is where they created the Gatherers, who were the first sons of mankind."

It seemed to Wally that he marched down countless steps and navigated a vast labyrinth before Flower opened a door that revealed the living room of what could have been a somewhat rundown Victorian home. It was a chilly room, ill-lit by several dim gas-fueled globes. Logs were burning in the fireplace, and shadows licked the faded wallpaper, an intricate ivy print. Flower called out, "Dah, I want you to meet someone."

Several overstuffed armchairs faced the fire, and from one of them a figure emerged, expanding as it turned toward Wally and Flower.

"What have you done, daughter?" The voice was deep and bullhorn loud, and the man stepped into the light. He looked like Walt Whitman, Wally thought, if that great poet had weighed an additional 300 pounds, had a thick slab of a brow that kept his eyes in constant shadow and a voluminous beard, mottled with gray-green moss or lichen.

"I've found a man to love," Flower said. "For the line and for love."

Her father seemed to have some difficulty breathing. Each expansion of his lungs—a visible effort—was accompanied by a rusty wheeze. He wore a ragged, ancient suit that appeared to be fashioned out of burlap or hair. "I told you, daughter, we cannot deal with the daylighters. We lurk in the shadows for a reason."

Flower walked up to her father and stood on her toes and said, "He's kin, Dah."

"Kin?"

Flower nodded her head.

"He's been sorted? You've had a stone look him over?" he asked.

"I have."

"Well." The monstrous man approached Wally and leaned forward. "Are you looking to marry my daughter or merely mount her?"

"Ah—" Wally began.

The old man's face loomed close. Where the flesh surfaced amid whiskers, it was infinitely creased, and Wally could see the man's eyes, as blue and quick as Flower's. "I'll know a lie," the man cautioned.

"Marry," Wally said.

"Good answer," the old man said, and he extended his hand. Wally shook it. Flower came up and hugged him.

Flower turned to her father, bowed, and left the room.

The old man gestured to another armchair, indicating that Wally be seated.

"My name is Garth, and you may call me that," he said, sinking into his own armchair. "I am glad you are one of the true, glad you are kin. My daughter has been disappointed before."

"Disappointed?"

Garth nodded. "She has loved unwisely, found outsiders who proved impure." He paused, slapped his massive hands down on his knees, and leaned forward. "You read the book?"

Wally didn't have to ask what book. "Most of it," he said.

"Well, the book is true, and then again, it's all cockeyed. Does it say why all this fuss was made? Does it say why some vast intelligence would fashion us?"

"I don't know," Wally said.

"Of course you don't. I do. I will tell you. The Ur Gods live in the vast reaches of time and span universes but their eyes are finite. They cannot monitor every future. And so they came upon this planet and thought, 'In time it will have its uses,' and they planted a seed. They drew man to their specifications and made him breathe. And what are we designed for?"

This time Wally was pretty sure the question was rhetorical, so he waited.

"We are designed to gather information. Yes! We assimilate the universe. We study, we experiment, we compile. And when the Ur Gods return, they will find us and our knowledge will be theirs."

"Well," Wally said. "That's something." This was fairly confusing stuff. "How exactly will they acquire this knowledge that we have gained over thousands of years?"

Garth smiled, as though a bright student had asked a particularly astute question. "They will devour us."

"Devour? What—"

Garth nodded. "Eat. Chew up and swallow. Devour. You make a sandwich and you devour it. Fry some eggs, bake a cake. What for? To eat!" Garth put his hands together. "What a fine thing. To be swallowed by a God!"

Wally was stumped. He couldn't think of a thing to say. Wait, there was something else he wanted to ask: "I understand that I am one of your line, an intelligently designed ancestor, not some strayed mutant, right?"

"Yes."

"How exactly do you know this?"

"My daughter gave you a kinstone. This is a technology from the stars, bequeathed to us by the Ur Gods. It glides beneath your flesh. It looks within you. And if it finds you wanting, it kills you."

"I could have been killed?" Wally said. Flower had been playing with his life? *Jeez.*

Garth shrugged. "You are alive. The Gods have blessed you. Among those my daughter has taken a fancy to, you are the first one who has survived. Be grateful." He sighed.

"I only wish her mother had lived to see Flower's joy. But Rachel was burned for a witch. That is the nature of our calling: Mostly we weed, but sometimes we are weeded."

* * *

GARTH SHOWED Wally to his room. They climbed a narrow staircase and came out, again, into the vast light-speckled cavern. Far below, Wally saw several shadowy figures moving, illuminated by the light from a ghostly projection, a flickering holographic statue, a fifty-foot homage to some ancient alien voyager, perhaps, that resembled nothing so much as a giant trilobite.

They re-entered a world of shabby Victorian furnishings, and Garth ushered Wally into a dingy bedroom.

"We will talk tomorrow about your wedding," Garth said, and he extended his hand again. "I am pleased to welcome you back to your family."

* * *

WALLY SAT on the bed. He was too tired to make a careful assessment of his surroundings. He untied his shoes. He was tugging his shoes off when something fell onto the rug. It glittered there, like a malevolent insect, silver wings twitching. Wally recognized it. He guessed it had been lying in the cuff of his pants where it had fallen. This was the medallion, the *kinstone*, that was supposed to have slid beneath his flesh and vouched for his pedigree. Only it hadn't. It had fallen out of his hand because he had been drunk *and* wrecked on oxycodone.

Just great. He could pick it up. He could close his fingers over it and let it do its job. He suspected he was genetically fraudulent, an off-shoot, and so it would kill him. So what? If he just went ahead and married Flower, she'd find out soon enough, wouldn't she? *If you were a human being, could you marry into a clan of vampires without them noticing you weren't one of them?*

Wally took his shoe and pushed the holographic medallion under the bed and out of sight. *I am so screwed!* he thought. And then, because he was already on his knees, he put his elbows on the bedspread, folded his hands together, and began: "Now I lay me down to sleep—"

The Tenth Muse

1.

I LISTENED TO MY agent's voice on the phone, not wishing to pick up the receiver immediately for fear Max was seeking another loan. Traditionally, it tends to be the other way around: writers borrow, or attempt to borrow, money from their agents. My agent, however, was Max Felwin, who was, by turns, impecunious and rich, his fortunes falling and rising as a result of drugs, frequent marriages, and manic states. When he was down on his luck, he would hit up some of his clients for a loan.

If he was calling me for a loan, then he was in big trouble, indeed, and his mind had slipped back a decade or so to a time when my financial health and prospects were happier. My last novel had sold three thousand copies. I carried photocopies of the reviews (excellent) in my pocket as a talisman against complete ego collapse, but money would have been more eloquent praise.

"Marsh," he said to the answering machine, "I've been talking to Priest over at *American Promise*, and he's committed to a piece, a three- or four-parter, first North American serial rights, and I'm thinking there's a book in it too. This is for a Morton Sky piece with an interview. I—"

That's when I picked up the receiver. "Morton Sky doesn't give interviews," I said.

"Marsh," Max said, "I knew you were there." I could tell by the sound of his voice that he was in his hearty, triumphant mode. "And I knew you'd say that! Sure, he doesn't give interviews! If he gave interviews, we'd be in trouble, because the world would no doubt have grown sick of his pompous proclamations long ago. But he has remained blessedly silent, and—"

I made an interrupting sound which he brushed aside with a laugh.

"I've got you an interview, Marsh. I did that before talking to Priest. Give me some credit."

"Why would—"

"Maybe because you were his next door neighbor."

"I was a kid. He never noticed me at all."

"Your father was his friend. You have memories in common. Besides, you're a huge fan."

"We tried that before."

"That's right, we did. But he's older, and I got lucky, got the old fart on the phone, and he sounded sort of weakened, not the same old thundering windbag, and he said, 'Marshall Harrison?' and I said, 'Yes, Harrison,' and I was going to explain what that meant, but he said, 'All right,' so we settled on a time. I was stunned. I had this whole sales pitch ready to go, and it was good, but I didn't need it. And get this, you're invited to stay at the house while you conduct the interview. He said there isn't a decent motel in town, so you might as well stay with him."

* * *

I **NEEDED** the money, but that wasn't my sole motivation for flying the next morning from my home in Austin, via a disorienting stopover in Dallas, to Kansas City, renting a car, and aiming that car east on 152. I was curious about what Morton Sky had to say, and, in truth, I couldn't resist this opportunity to contemplate my past through the patina of accrued wisdom and regret. I'd always intended to return to Empire to see if it made any more sense now than it had when I was ten. This was my chance. The aging, almost irrelevant Morton Sky and his overly-venerated relic of a novel would serve as the catalyst for deeper philosophical concerns.

And I'd write about my father and mother, remarkable people, volatile people. My father was, for a while, famous himself, having written a collection of poetry, *Imploding*, that captured the spirit of the late sixties with such passion and anarchic wit that it sold several hundred thousand copies, an extraordinary feat for a book of poetry, an unheard of feat for a book of poetry that was rigorously metrical and assumed an educated, literary background on the part of its readers.

My father wrote *Imploding* when we were living in Durham, where he taught literature courses at Duke University.

I remember the students, ragged and exotic to my child's eyes, who sat at his feet while he declaimed, waving his arms, standing on a coffee table. My father knew everything and could grab, from the air, any secret a book had ever held, any dead author's words, any thought the mind of man had formulated in the face of the terror and beauty of the world. My father was the spokesman for all that was important. I couldn't have articulated that when I was a kid, but I know it is what I thought, because I still think it, reflexively, and it requires an effort of willed objectivity to think otherwise.

My mother is a more elusive shape in my mind, because she is still alive, and I am older.

When we moved to Empire and rented the house next to Morton Sky, Marshall Harrison was the celebrity author, and Morton Sky was an odd, morose man tending to his dying grandmother who had been ill for years and who expired a month after our arrival.

If I could portray my father in juxtaposition to Sky, I might have something quite powerful, something worthy of a book.

* * *

ON THE plane, I'd tried to read *The Resolution of My Dread*, the only novel Morton Sky had ever written, but I couldn't get beyond Jenny's description of Main Street. I don't know why, on first reading, I (and the rest of America) hadn't paused to wonder at narrator Jenny's eleven-year-old voice, slangy, naive, and yet peppered with words like "elucidate" and "lambent" and "benign." This female Huck Finn with a thesaurus stuck in her throat should have created a convulsion of disbelief, but she didn't. Instead, America fell in love with her.

On publication in the spring of 1976, the novel leapt onto the *New York Times* bestseller list, where it resided for 82 weeks. It has, even more impressively, achieved classic status, never going out of print, required reading in many high schools and progenitor of an equally famous movie. It still sells a quarter of a million copies a year.

Critically, the novel has followed the inevitable arc of such popular phenomena, first lavished with praise by reviewers who marveled at its authenticity, then applauded for its success, later venerated in critical studies, and finally disdained by younger critics who, having been bludgeoned by its thousand imitators, see nothing original in it and wonder how an earlier generation could have been so smitten by such a formulaic account of coming-of-age angst.

What can I say? I had loved the book; I was a little embarrassed by it now. There are certain novels that you only get if you come upon them at the right time, when your life is poised over a chasm of change. I was seventeen when I read the book. There are a lot of us who came upon *Resolution* at just that age.

On highway 291, I stopped at a gas station, filled the rented Buick up, and bought a soda inside, where coffee cups and bumper stickers certifying that I had visited Harry Truman's home in Independence were to be had for a pittance.

I passed on the souvenirs, got back in the Buick, and drove on into the Heartland. I turned the radio on and REO Speedwagon jumped out, freed from someone's attic. The Midwest liked to hang back a little, politically, theologically, musically, maybe twenty years behind the parade in case something went wrong up ahead. If the present went belly-up, they'd have a shorter run back to the fifties.

2.

I ARRIVED in Empire in the late afternoon, the last stretch of road flanked by tall rows of corn. Farms and crops gave way to houses with manicured lawns, and the speed limit shifted from 55 to 35 to 25 quickly enough to guarantee a steady stream of speeding-ticket revenue from incoming motorists lulled by the monotony of corn and soybean vistas. I passed the old Moose Lodge, saw it was sporting the same ancient sign, much the worse for wear, and then I entered the downtown area, where slow time continued to have its way. There was a McDonald's that hadn't been there before, and a big Bank of America building that had replaced Art's American Five & Dime, but the Empire Barbershop remained, and I knew it would look the same inside. The courthouse, although shrunken and diminished by time, retained its dignity and managed to convey a certain admirable stoicism.

Driving slowly, I peered into several empty store fronts and tried to locate the movie theater I had frequented but could find no trace of it. A yellow dog took its time getting across the street as the July sun sucked the finish from the dozen or so cars and trucks parked along Main; no parking meters existed to count the hours. Empire wasn't close enough to K.C. to be adopted by well-heeled commuters, and it was wearing away, drifting into stuporous old age.

In other words, it was much the same as it had been when my family arrived here.

Downtown consisted of two parallel streets and eight or nine blocks, so I made the tour in about five minutes and then drove around some until I located Emory Street. Halfway down the second block, on the left, was Morton Sky's house, a large faux Victorian edifice with a black, wrought-iron fence surrounding it and a lawn that hadn't seen a lawnmower in months.

I had been surprised to learn that Sky had never moved. I had known he was still in Empire, that fact being something the press always noted, as proof of the author's abiding love for his town, or proof of his humility, or proof of his fear of the larger world. Well, no one agreed on just what it was proof of, but it was one of the few solid facts the press had, so they can be forgiven for hoping it was a fact that carried some truth or revelation within.

What I hadn't realized until Max gave me the address was that Sky had not only remained in Empire, he had remained in the family home, and, if he had made any repairs to it in the years since I'd been gone, time had unraveled them again.

To the left of Sky's house was a newer house, a small, tidy white house of two stories with purple shutters and a porch full of bright, multi-colored flowers in pots. And to the right of Sky's house was a vacant lot. I imagined I saw the faint outlines of the house that my father had rented in the spring of 1974 and in which we had lived until February of '75 when it burned down.

It had been a big house, although not as big as the house next door. In Durham, we'd lived in a modest ranch house, and my older brother Andrew and I were fascinated by the new dimension of a second floor. We would race each other up the stairs, banging into the wall at the landing and pushing off it for the last flight of steps that brought us to the second floor hallway. Looking up, I'd see the soles of my brother's tennis shoes—he always won—and beyond his shoulders I'd see the attic's trapdoor, and I'd stop running. I was naturally wary of that door.

Three weeks after we were settled in our house, I ran up the stairs alone; I'd almost reached the top when that trapdoor flew open, and my father hung suspended in front of me like some ghastly magic trick, his face twisted, hands clawing at his throat, and before I could scream, something exploded, a loud reverberating *crack!* that shook the ceiling, and my father fell to his knees, the rope descending beside him to lie in coils by his side. My mother rushed out of their bedroom at the end of the hall and ran to him, screaming, "You sonofabitch! You stupid sonofabitch!" She fell on him, fists flying, screaming. Then she was lifting the rope from around his neck—I saw the red burn mark and blood on his pale throat—hugging him, sobbing deeply, while my father said nothing at all. I can't remember if we went to the emergency room that night or not. Sometimes we did, and sometimes we didn't. Not all the trips were prompted by my father's destructive proclivities. My mother was overly fond of sleeping pills.

"Christ, Louise! Sleeping pills!" my father would shout at her slumped form, there on the passenger seat. Andrew and I always sat in the backseat, saying nothing, dragged out of sleep, groggy. I suppose it would have been bad parenting to leave us alone at three in the morning. My father would lean over the steering wheel, concentrating, speeding to the hospital, which, conveniently, was only two miles away. "Fucking sleeping pills," he'd mutter, as though he were offended more by her method than her intention.

* * *

I DIDN'T get out of the car. I didn't knock on Morton Sky's door and avail myself of his hospitality. I'd arrived a day early, and I had a reserved room waiting for me in a bed-and-breakfast in the neighboring town of Cale. I thought I'd revisit some places; see what memories I might revive, and take notes for the philosophical and thematic underpinnings that would transform my article into something more than a sighting of the great man breaking the surface of his silence.

3.

"MUCH OF my past," I wrote, "is a matter of hearsay. This is true, to a lesser or greater degree, of every human being." I admired this opening while finishing off the last of a glazed donut and a cup of coffee. I hadn't slept well in the small bedroom of my Victorian B&B in Cale. With its glut of ancient chairs and trunks and dowdy lamps, the room could have been serving as storage space for the effects of some long-dead relative, space that had been hastily adapted to accommodate an unexpected guest. I am sensitive to dust and mold, and I spent the night coughing and sneezing and exhausting an entire box of Kleenex.

I'd risen early, dressed and gone driving around Cale until I came upon Dale's Donuts and Coffee where a couple of parked cars suggested it might already be open in the first gray glimmer of dawn. It was.

I sat at a small table next to the front window. This was Main Street again, but a slightly more prosperous one than that of Empire. All the customers seemed to know the waitress, and good-natured banter reached my ears until I lost myself in my writing.

* * *

BEFORE LEAVING for Empire, I'd called my mother to inform her of the proposed interview with Morton Sky. My mother had remarried in 1988. That husband, a man of great decency and no discernible personality, passed on six years ago, and my mother now resided in an assisted-living apartment in Greensboro, North Carolina.

I was hoping she'd talk about our time in Empire, although I knew it was unlikely. In the past, whenever I'd tried to get her to talk about Empire, she'd refused.

She surprised me this time. On learning that I'd be interviewing Morton Sky, she said, "There were always some who said your father wrote that book. After all, what did Morton Sky know about writing? He didn't know anything about life or literature. But, of course, the people who suggested your father wrote the book didn't know anything about your father. Really, why would he do such a thing? Why would he waste his time writing another man's book?"

I'd never given any thought to the ridiculous notion that my father had written *The Resolution of My Dread*. It was not a book he would have liked at all, the sentiment too easy, the narrator's cynicism nothing more than adolescent attitude.

"I just read the book recently," my mother continued. This came as a surprise to me. I'd always assumed she'd read it when it came out, and that we had never talked about it for obvious reasons.

"They have a little library here," she said, "and I saw Morton Sky's book. I'd never cared to read it, didn't care for the title, but I took it and I read it right through."

The line was silent. I waited. Finally, I spoke, "Mom?"

"Well." She hesitated. "It wasn't a good book. But, I swear, some of the sentences, some of the language, it brought Marshall back, like he was in the room with me. There were tears in my eyes when I finished that book. Your father and I fought all the time, but we were close—we loved each other—and I know the sound of him, and it's in that book, not all the time, but sometimes. I think he must have helped with it. I can't really see it. Your father was a selfish man. If you were a pretty coed, he might give you some extra attention, but a man like Morton Sky? It seems unlikely. Well...they did a lot of drinking together; he was over there drinking a lot, sometimes all night. I guess he must have helped with Sky's novel. You might ask Mr. Sky about that, although when I saw him on television—that was decades ago—he didn't seem the sort of man who would give credit to another."

* * *

I DROVE back to the bed-and-breakfast, collected my stuff, paid my bill, and drove to Empire.

I visited the Empire *Gazette*, the Empire Library, the police station, Ronnie's American Restaurant (where I ate lunch), the Empire Barbershop (where I got a haircut), Thompson's Auto Repair & Tires (nothing; the car was a rental). I called

Jill Withers from Greta's Bar & Grill. Since I'd called her from Austin, she'd had time to think about meeting me. There was new reluctance in her voice. She thought maybe we shouldn't meet. "I don't know anything about him. I was just a kid when we lived next door."

I explained to her that I intended to write about my own boyhood in Empire, something to surround and give thematic substance to the interview, and that all I would ask of her is shared memories of that time. Our houses had flanked Sky's three-story ruin. The house Jill's parents had rented had been replaced by the new, purple-shuttered dwelling that I'd seen on Emory Street. If she had some thoughts on how she had perceived the man in the house next door that would be terrific, but I wasn't asking for anything that would compromise Mr. Sky's privacy, and if she didn't want to say anything at all about him, I'd respect that. "It will be good just seeing you," I said. "It's been a long time. I didn't expect you to still be in town. Calling your mother was a long shot."

"I'm just back," she said. And, letting me know she wasn't a fool, added, "I guess I could see you, but we ain't long lost pals, you know." I laughed and told her the drinks would be on me.

✳ ✳ ✳

I WOULDN'T have recognized her. Nor she, me, I'm sure. Which was what you'd expect. I'd been ten years old then; Jill had been eleven. In 1974, her hair was red, as red as a firecracker on the Fourth, with freckles splashed across the bridge of her nose and her eyes blue and fierce with life.

Her hair had turned blonde since then, the roots brown. Her eyes, outlined in black mascara, had faded from blue to gray, as though what she'd seen in the intervening years had leached the color from them.

She had described herself over the phone ("frizzy blonde hair, blue jeans, a Tigers t-shirt and the only woman in town who ain't fat") and that was the woman I waved at, and she came over, studied me, and sat down with a sigh.

"Marshal Harrison," she said. "Been a while, huh?"

"It has," I said. "You are looking well, Ms. Withers."

She waved the compliment away with a faint frown, rooted through her purse, and found a pack of cigarettes. "You can call me Jill. After all, we go back a long way. I'm gonna smoke," she said. "Want one?"

"I don't smoke," I said. It sounded priggish, a declaration of moral superiority. In Austin, no one smoked, not in a restaurant or bar; it was against the law, and I saw myself telling her that and the look she would send me.

The waitress came, and we both ordered beers. Jill didn't want anything to eat. A cheap date.

She took a long swallow of beer and slapped the mug down with a sigh of satisfaction. "I've only been back in town a week. When Mom told me there was a call for me, I figured it was my ex with some new line of bullshit. Instead it's you from a million years ago. I do remember. You and your brother...?"

"Andrew," I said.

"Yeah, Andrew. I remember we used to hang out a lot, kid's stuff, comic books, swimming... That was about a century ago."

A different century, I thought. It really was a different century.

She looked around the bar. "Maybe I could get work here. I need something, that's for sure. Living with Mom's the reason I ran off with an idiot like Lonnie in the first place. Now I'm back—and in a trailer park. There's a moral in there somewhere."

I can't take any credit for getting her to talk about Sky. In fact, most of the people I'd encountered that day had something to say about the man. The waitress at Ronnie's American Restaurant said Mr. Sky had never gotten over his grandmother's death ("She raised him, you know"), and that's why he didn't write another book. Bobby Thompson over at the auto repair said, "The man hit the ball out of the park on his first swing. He quit because he knew there was nowhere to go but down." Two customers over at the barbershop had nearly come to blows over my question. "He ain't writing," the one said, "because he's high on heroin, thinks Reagan is still the president, has a dope dealer drives out from St. Louis every other week with a briefcase full of heroin and a couple of hookers."

The other was outraged. "A man like that wouldn't go near heroin. If you could read, you might read his book, and then you'd know something of his character. He hasn't written another book because there aren't any people to write it for, just a bunch of assholes like you, TV-addicted, celebrity-gossiping assholes who wouldn't know a good book if it bit them on the ass."

They shoved each other some and knocked over a pile of magazines (*Sports Illustrated*, *People*, and *Missouri Fish & Game* among them), but the head barber, clearly the authority figure, said that the both of them were going to have to get used to bowl haircuts from their wives because they sure as hell weren't going to get any haircuts in his establishment if they couldn't act like civilized humans, and that quieted them immediately, with the one shaking his head in disgust and banging out the door.

When it came to Morton Sky, everyone had an opinion, but no one had anything much in the way of facts or even interesting anecdotes. Morton Sky had his groceries delivered to the house, and he didn't interact much with the town that he'd made famous. I was supposed to arrive at his doorstep at 7:00 that night, and the afternoon was rapidly fading away, so if Jill Withers didn't have anything substantive, I'd have to create the atmosphere for this interview out of the weak fumes of my own recollections.

* * *

JILL SAID, "I had a crush on your father. He was the handsomest man I'd ever seen.

"Maybe he knew about it. I mean, knew I had a crush, because he always took time to ask how I was doing, and he always talked to me like I was an adult. He used to call me his Muse, remember?"

I remembered it as soon as she said it.

"That reminds me," she said. "I haven't thought of it in years, but at the time I think it creeped me out some. I had come by to see you, I don't remember what for, and your dad and Morton Sky were sitting out back of your house, on that stone bench where there used to be a white gazebo, and your dad called me over. 'Here comes my Muse,' he said. He rattled off some Greek names, other Muses, I guess, and I knew that a Muse was a goddess that inspired artists, so even though he was kidding, I was flattered, and I blushed. I could feel my face, hot and red. Then I looked at Morton Sky, and he was staring at me like he'd never seen me before, and he said, 'That's what I need. I need a Muse,' but he wasn't joining in a joke. He had a serious, desperate look, and your dad said, still joking, 'Stop looking at my Muse that way! Get your own.' But even then, Morton Sky didn't laugh. He looked away from me, and I thought he might cry or something, and I went on off to find you."

She said she hadn't thought much of it at the time, but now...well, if Morton Sky had ever looked at her daughter that way she would have made a point of never letting her daughter near that man again.

I thought I'd leave that anecdote out. A creepy look did not a pedophile make, and it would be unfair to the man to portray him as exhibiting some vague, unhealthy interest in a child, when Jill, a child, could have easily misinterpreted the man's expression. Besides, Morton Sky may have radiated weirdness, but I'd never felt he was dangerous. You wanted dangerous? My parents were dangerous. My brother and I knew better than to get between them when they were fighting.

4.

EARLY THAT day, at the Empire *Gazette*, a newspaper that was still put together with hot wax, column-wide strips of typeset copy, and a plastic roller, I had been redirected to the library for its archives, and in the library, I'd found myself leaning over an eyepiece and staring at a halftone of my father who was smiling into the camera. Despite the halftone's rough resolution, my father's good looks shone through. I had heard people say he looked like Errol Flynn, meaningless back then because I didn't know who that actor was, but now the comparison seemed accurate. The headline read: "Poet Marshal Harrison Dies in Fire."

On a jump page there was a photo of me, my mother, and my brother Andrew, all of us standing in front of the fire-ravaged house (a scorched chimney and some black remnants of the frame) and squinting into the camera like tourists documenting a visit to some decaying shrine. Why would anyone take a photo like that? And why would we cooperate? My brother towered over me and seemed to be scowling. I was smiling with what looked like childish exuberance. I know I was intent on hiding, at any cost, the knowledge within me, and perhaps I thought that a smile was the best disguise.

* * *

JILL SAID, "I'm sorry about the fire and your dad. I cried and cried. I thought I'd go crazy, and it wasn't like I was family, like I had the right to go off like I did. My mom took me to Dr. McLachlan so that he could give me some pills to calm me down, and she wouldn't let me go the funeral, said it was unhealthy. It's a long time coming, but I want to say I'm sorry for your loss."

"Thank you."

"They never did learn what started the fire, did they?"

"My father drank; he smoked a lot in bed," I said, but I didn't really answer her question. The truth was, the investigators had thought it might be arson, because of the extreme heat, the way the metal bookcases were surreally twisted and an empty wine bottle had melted flat like something in a Salvador Dali painting. But they never discovered a source for all that heat, and the investigation went nowhere. The heat turned my father's body into a cinder beyond the reach of the limited forensics they had at the time. Pieces of his grandfather's ancient revolver were found in the debris, and he could have shot himself with that gun—as he had threatened to do on more than one occasion—but the fierce blaze destroyed any hope of ever learning what actually happened.

* * *

I HAD been awakened by ripping and snapping sounds and my brother's shouts. He was in the room, in his underwear, shaking me by the shoulders, telling me to get up. Groggily, I reached for my jeans, which lay on the floor.

"No time!" he shouted. "The house is on fire."

I was aware of smoke in the room, smoke tickling my throat. A tremendous crash came from below us, shaking the house, and I was wide awake, with panic in my lungs. I ran down the hall, and somehow I was in front of him, and I saw flames at the foot of the stairs, and I leaned over the banister and looked into the open door of my father's study. He was lying on the cot that he sometimes napped on when he was, as he put it, recharging his batteries. I couldn't see his face for the smoke. A circle of flames surrounded the cot—just like the students who used to sit at his feet—and I saw blood on one of the pillows, a splash of blood, and more blood on the sheet tangled at his feet.

I shouted for my father to get up, but his stillness was absolute. I would have tried to reach him, to shake him back to consciousness, back to life, but a roar from the flames at the foot of the stairs made me turn away from this horror, and I saw flames racing toward me, leaping and snapping as they ascended the stairs like hounds in a killing frenzy.

I turned, and my brother and I ran back down the hall to my parents' bedroom where we roused my mother, who awoke, listless and confused.

"A fire?" she said, as though the word itself were one she'd never heard.

My brother was in charge, and a good thing that. He made us go out in the hall again and run through the smoke to my bedroom, my mother screaming, "Where's your father? Where's your father?" Andrew shoved open the window, and we were able to lean out, grab the thick branch of the maple tree, and swing over to the trunk. My mother was an athletic woman, an avid tennis player and hiker, and the descent would normally have been no problem for her, but she was in one of her over-medicated periods, and, after successfully gaining the trunk of the tree, she slipped, fell through branches that slowed her fall, and broke her ankle when she hit the ground.

* * *

I LOOKED at my watch, saw that it was almost 7:00, and told Jill I would have to go.

"Thanks for coming," I said. "You can't think of anything else about Morton Sky?"

"No. I guess it's not so much loyalty that protects Sky from gossip. He just keeps out of the way, so there's nothing for gossip to feed on. It wasn't that way with his grandmother."

"What do you mean?"

Jill leaned forward. "Now that I think of it, that's something the town never did talk about. That's common knowledge that nobody cared to share."

"What's that?"

"Well, everyone agreed that Sky's grandmother was a witch. People would cross the street rather than walk by her door. My own grandmother was scared to death of her."

* * *

IT WAS time to go. She asked me to call her before I left town. I said I would. Maybe we could get together for another drink before I left.

5.

I PRESSED the doorbell, but I couldn't hear it ring within, so I took the big brass knocker in my hand and banged it three times. Some flakes of green paint fell from the door, and I waited a minute and knocked some more, and more of the door's dying paint job fluttered to the ground. Someone was coming. I heard the steady thump of shoes, and the door swung inward, and I was looking at Morton Sky, a really old Morton Sky sporting a brown tweed jacket over what looked like a striped pajama top. The fashion statement was completed with gray sweatpants and black dress shoes over white socks.

He regarded me from under hooded eyes. "No solicitors," he said. "Can't you read the sign?"

I looked around for a sign but didn't see one.

"There used to be a sign," he said.

"I'm Marshall Harrison," I said. "We had an appointment. I'm here to interview you."

Sky smiled. His teeth were long and yellow; his eyelids drooped, causing him to appear rueful, puzzled, and sly, all at the same time.

"Marshall!" He clapped his hands, the gesture mechanical, an imperfect attempt to show his real delight or a parody of that delight. He opened the door wider and backed up, ushering me into a gloomy corridor, the floor covered with an oriental rug so dirty and ill-used that various stains had triumphed over the original pattern, creating a more modern asymmetrical design.

He had already turned his back and was walking away, stooped at the shoulders, one finger held up in a gesture that, I assumed, indicated I should follow him.

He turned his head to look back at me. "Didn't recognize you. Guess New York changes a man from the inside out." He turned away and marched on.

I followed him. I had used the same book jacket photo for years now; maybe it was time for a new one.

"I live in Austin, Texas, not New York," I said.

He laughed and didn't look back. "As long as you're living, right?"

I didn't have a clue what that meant, but it did remind me of the early years when Morton Sky gave interviews. He had a pompous, overly fastidious way of saying things and a fondness for inscrutable epigrams. Humility, a virtue America loves to discover in its icons, was not Sky's long suit. His manner, in the recorded interviews that I had watched, showed a man who was dealing with fools and had just about reached the limits of his patience.

America had loved him in spite of the arrogance of his demeanor, but maybe—this just occurred to me—Max had been right in suggesting that the man's welcome would have worn thin had he chosen to stay in the limelight.

I entered a large room with several sofas, lots of overstuffed chairs, a host of bookcases, a massive antique wardrobe, a worn green carpet, and a hanging chandelier in which small, flame-shaped bulbs glowed wanly. No lamps were turned on, and the room was filling up with shadows and certain to grow darker as the light that glowed behind the window shades receded, following the sun over the horizon.

"Please have a seat," my host said, waving at a sofa. "I'll fetch us something to drink." And he disappeared down another hallway.

I waited, sitting on the sofa. I noticed that the bookcase closest to me held nothing but copies of *The Resolution of My Dread*, various foreign editions of the book and the numerous American editions and paperback reprints. I recognized the tan spines of the first edition, four rows, and it occurred to me that the contents of the bookcase would fetch a tidy sum. I counted the first editions and made a note to look up the going rate for a well-preserved, jacketed copy.

I was feeling a little woozy, not drunk, but tired. Drinking after a sleepless night and before an interview. What was I thinking? I closed my eyes, just the briefest respite...

"Hello, Marshall. Dropped off, did you? I do that all the time." Sky was holding a silver tray upon which resided two wine glasses and a bottle of wine. He put the tray down on an end table, turned the wine glasses right-side up, and filled both of them.

He offered one to me, and I took it.

Holding his own filled wine glass, he eased himself into a bulky brown arm chair. I expected dust to rise from the frayed and dirty fabric, and perhaps it did. It was too dark to tell.

The years hadn't treated Morton Sky well. He had been handsome once, but age had exaggerated the features that had made him so, causing me to doubt any youthful good looks that could morph into this dissolute, watery-eyed fat man. His size gave him the aspect of a hulking ruin that might succumb to gravity at any moment and crumble before my eyes.

I sipped the wine, neither of us saying anything. Not very good wine, I thought. Perhaps the bitterness was something that only connoisseurs could learn to love.

I decided to break the silence with a requisite bit of flattery, explaining how I was a big fan of his book, which I had read when I was seventeen, years after we'd moved from Empire. Only then, I told him, did I realize that I had lived next door to a genius. It is impossible to over-flatter a writer, so I poured it on.

He didn't answer. He might have been asleep, his chin resting on his chest, lips pursed and swollen, eyes lost in the shadows of his prominent brow. His big hands clutched the arms of the chair, and I could hear his breathing, a slow rasp.

"Mr. Sky—" I began.

He coughed. "Didn't recognize you," he said. "You look different without the mustache."

He seemed to recede. I was hideously tired. I shouldn't have indulged in those afternoon beers. I had never had a mustache. He was saying something else, muttering to himself.

"Don't want to kill you, but I'm no pharmacist. Ten pills for half a bottle. That seemed right." He held his own wine glass up, still filled to the brim. "I'll be right back," he said. "I just need to pour this out. Wouldn't do to drink it, and I might. I find I'm very absent-minded these days."

With some effort he got up, and he was slowly making his way toward the hall when I blacked out.

6.

I AWOKE with a jolt. I had been falling. My heart was racing, and I was sweating profusely.

Morton Sky was leaning forward, his face a foot from mine, the network of exploded capillaries that scrawled across his nose and cheeks like a map of bad living, his eyes blue and stupidly inquisitive.

"It worked," he said, and smiled.

I tried to stand but could not. I looked down. I wasn't on the sofa. My wrists were bound with duct tape to the wooden armrests of a straight-backed chair. My right arm was bare where my shirt sleeve had been rolled up. A drop of blood glistened darkly on my forearm.

I couldn't see my feet, but they too were bound. I looked at Sky again, and he was holding up a syringe, looking at the liquid that remained within.

His eyes moved back to my face.

"Epinephrine," he said. "Stuff you get in those little asthma inhalers. I know, you don't have to tell me, it's a little risky. But you don't look like a man with a weak heart, and I couldn't wait around all night, could I?"

My heart was beating as though it might sprout wings and fly. If I opened my mouth to scream, my heart would fly out. I was sick to my stomach, buzzing with nausea. I was going to die.

Morton Sky stood up, turned and walked back to the armchair he had been sitting in earlier. He sat down, slapped his hands on his knees, leaned forward, smiled, and said, "Okay, ask me anything."

"Why..." Too many words crowded my mind.

Morton Sky was oblivious to my confusion. "I never really thought you were dead, Marshall. I don't know why you came back, but I was glad to hear it. I've got something of yours."

He stood up abruptly and walked out of the room again.

He returned with another silver tray, this one holding a dozen tiny burning candles floating in the oil of oversized shot glasses.

He set this tray down, and returned to the armchair. "So ask me why I haven't written another book," he said, wiggling slightly before settling comfortably in the chair and giving me his full attention, as a parent might grant an audience with a child. "Go on, that's what everyone asks."

I said nothing.

He shouted: "Ask me!"

"Why didn't you write another book?" I said. My insides were dancing, but I thought, *No need to ask now. I know the answer: you lost your mind.*

"That's a good question," he said. "I did so well with that first book. I could have made quite a lot of money with another book. Even if the book was vilified by the reviewers, everyone would have to own a copy, wouldn't they? And here's what's really interesting, although it may come as no surprise to you..." He paused for dramatic effect, and then he leaned forward, shouting, "I did write another book!" He leaned back, composed himself, and spoke in a softer voice, "Quite a few more books, actually."

He got up and strode to the dark, looming shape of the wardrobe. He swung it open. I still couldn't see what was within, but Sky must have anticipated that. He reached out and flipped a wall switch which turned on a standing lamp to the right and in front of the wardrobe. I stared at stacked reams of paper, bound in bundles by thick brown rubber bands. The manuscripts rose to within two feet of the wardrobe's ceiling. Two feet and the wardrobe would be completely filled.

He let me stare at this manifestation of his industry for several minutes, and then he turned the lamp off again. He went back, got the tray of burning candles, and began arranging them around me. He placed one on the floor directly in front of me, and then, following some painstaking methodology known only to him, placed the others around me in a circle, with some of the candles in clumps, others spaced several feet apart. He arose from the last candle, surveyed his work, nodded, and walked to yet another bookcase, from which he withdrew an oversized book that looked to be bound in worn red leather. He opened it and looked up at me. "I am going to give you back something of yours. Can you guess what?"

I couldn't. I realized now that, in his eroded mental state, he thought I was my father.

"I'm not very good at this. Gran always said, 'You can teach a conjure, but those without the gift will be prenticed all their lives.'"

He began to read. What he read sounded like Latin, and it rose and fell in strange, unvarying cadences. I was unable to translate any of it, despite my two years of high school Latin, but I confess my mind was elsewhere. I was distracted by my racing heart, which had sped up even more when I saw the long, curved knife that hung from a chain around his neck. It dangled, naked and bright, over his pajama-striped belly, and I was pretty sure it was a new addition to his fashion accessories. Surely he wasn't wearing it when he opened the door.

All I knew was this: a sharp—it looked very sharp—knife doesn't bode well when the lunatic wearing it is chanting Latin and the audience (i.e., me) is tied to a chair.

He put the book down on the floor, slipped out of his jacket and let it drop to the floor. He unbuttoned his pajama top and tossed that away, too, revealing new proof of his madness, had any been required. Half circles of lurid red dots, wounds, some fresher than others, covered his chest and stomach. Scattered amid these red half-circles were dozens of livid scratch marks.

He clutched the knife, still dangling from the chain around his neck, turned his wrist outward and administered a quick, downward stroke. A five-inch vertical line of blood appeared, ending just above his navel. He held the knife against the wound, and blood flowed over the blade. Now he bowed his head to lift the chain from over his head.

Jesus, I thought. *Kill yourself! Please just kill yourself.*

He lifted the knife, and I saw his eyes, and I was out of luck, so far out of luck, but maybe, maybe, not tortured, okay, just not tortured. Please.

And this is where the chance of selling this piece to *American Promise,* a magazine that prides itself on its rationality, pretty much goes out the window.

Still muttering something, Sky shook the knife blade over the bound book, and I watched as small drops of blood spotted the moldering cover. Instantly, the creature was with us, within the circle. I don't know what Morton Sky was doing at that moment, because I couldn't take my eyes off the thing.

It was, I want to say, insectile, but that suggests a remote and alien creature, an unknowable intelligence, and much of this thing's horror lay in its familiarity. It emitted a stink of yearning, of sewn together desires, perverse and vile and yet shared. It moved toward me while my mind tried to comprehend what it was—and, somehow, what it meant.

* * *

IT WORE a kind of ghostly shroud, like a translucent, hooded raincoat, which obscured its actual form. It was no bigger than a child, but not a child, more like a dog standing on its hind legs, and it moved with ragged, illogical speed, a motion that filled me with vertiginous nausea. The creature glided to the book, prodded it with a clawed finger and turned toward me. Jill's face appeared, the red-haired, eleven-year-old Jill, and my gasp of recognition called the whole of her into being, and she was standing in front of me, but not Jill, never for a moment a plausible illusion. She was translucent, and the thing within her moved with its own logic. But she was gathering substance as though—and only later, on reflection, did I think this—some feedback from my emotions, my thoughts, fine-tuned the simulacrum.

The Jill thing came up to me, extended a finger, touched my bare arm just above the elbow, and I felt an excruciating pain. Slowly, while I writhed in agony, she drew her finger down, toward my thumb, and a line of blood followed the track of her nail. Then she drew back, blinked, and hissed. Abruptly she turned away and moved quickly toward Sky who had backed beyond the circle of candles.

He watched her approaching, and he cringed, a big man trying to squeeze himself into some other reality, anywhere not here, bent forward as though he'd been punched in the stomach, his arms out in front of him, the fingers of his hands splayed. This was an overwrought performance, exaggerated gestures from a silent film. You had to be there to appreciate its accuracy.

He pointed a trembling finger at me. "There's your master," he whispered. She did not turn to follow his finger, nor did she give any indication that she had heard him. She came on.

When she reached him, her arm shot out, and she clutched his naked forearm and pulled him close. Her head darted and turned, with inhuman speed, and her mouth opened, and she bit him on the pallid, trembling flesh of his upper arm. He shrieked. Immediately she released him, and I saw the mark of her teeth, a black semi-circle in the gloom. Blood ran down his arm, she spoke. "Right now!" she said. "Now!" Her voice was a whisper, but loud enough to fill my head, vicious, full of unholy need.

And Sky staggered toward her, whimpered, and she spun him toward the hallway, and into the hallway, and his whimpering came back to me, rapidly diminishing, as they climbed the stairs to the second floor.

I listened, still and attentive, and I heard nothing but my own heart for long minutes, and then, finally, I heard something, faint but unmistakable, a sound like no other, the precise, authoritative *thak, thak, thak* of an electric typewriter.

I looked at my own bloodied arm and saw that the clawed nail that had slid through my flesh had also cut the duct tape cleanly, as a razor might. I yanked my arm back; I writhed in agony as my heart beat faster, and my wrist came away, free, throwing me backwards with the chair. My head hit one of the candles as I came down, and I felt the flame bite my ear, and I smelled my burning hair. But my arm was free, and that was all that mattered. I quickly tore the tape from my other wrist and both ankles. I stood up, alive. I turned and started for the door.

I stopped. I was not going to climb those stairs. I was not going to risk my life for Morton Sky who had, I believed, hijacked my father's Muse by occult means and, possibly, murdered my father. But I was going to satisfy my curiosity regarding Sky's literary efforts. I walked to the wardrobe and, bending forward, I dragged one of the bound manuscripts from the middle of the pile, causing the others to spill around me, a literary avalanche. I fanned the pages with my thumb, satisfying myself that I held typewritten pages, just as Sky had said, and then I walked to the front door and let myself out, closing the door behind me.

* * *

I CALLED Jill Withers from my cell phone on the way out of town. Something had come up, I said, and I had to leave immediately. This news didn't devastate her.

"So did you learn why he never wrote another book?" she asked.

I gave her the generic answer: "Success was more than he could handle."

I suppose she sensed my reluctance to pursue the subject. She thanked me for calling, wished me luck, and said that she had a cousin in Austin and would look me up if she ever got down that way.

7.

SHE HASN'T called. Almost three years have gone by, so I don't expect she will. A little over eighteen months ago, Morton Sky lost his life when his house burned down. Who knows what exorcism he was attempting? Every newspaper, every magazine, every television news station dusted off his bio, and the resurrected hype and conjecture surrounding his famous book caused a new spike in its sales. No one noted that the house next to Sky's had burned down years before, carrying off another writer, famous once himself. Surely some of Empire's old-timers marked this coincidence, but the reporters, with access to famous writers and celebrities ready to testify to *Resolution*'s impact on their lives, didn't seek out Empire's anonymous residents.

✳ ✳ ✳

THE DAY I left Empire, I drove to Kansas City and checked into a Best Western to wait it out until my flight the next evening. I studied my wounded forearm in the shower; stitches might have been a good idea, but I saw no signs of infection. Supernatural creatures, I thought, are probably germ-free.

I lay down on the bed, and I woke on top of the bed-spread, shivering in my jockey shorts, at 3:15 in the morning. I turned up the thermostat, which had been set to sixty-five, and crawled under the sheets, but I couldn't fall asleep again, so I got the manuscript I'd taken from Sky's ward-robe stash, plumped up the pillows behind me, and turned on the nightstand lamp. The first page was a blank sheet of paper. "Chapter 1" was centered at the top of the next page. The text (double-spaced, courier) began: "My name is Lisa Anne Jenkins. If I had someone handy, I'd just talk to her or even him. I wouldn't write this down. If you are reading this, you are probably going to use it against me later. Don't take umbrage, that's just the way it will be."

Umbrage, indeed.

Word-for-word, except for the heroine's name, this was the opening of *The Resolution of My Dread*. I flipped through the manuscript and quickly confirmed what I'd guessed: except for name changes, this was the same book Morton Sky had written in 1975.

On some of the manuscript pages, I found rust-brown smears (blood, I assumed). One page near the end of the manuscript contained a bloody handprint.

A bad day, I thought.

I lay in bed and stared at the ceiling. I thought of all the typed pages, each page its own arduous, sacred task (no word-processing magic to call upon). I thought of the wardrobe, tall and wide and jammed with dozens of *Resolution* clones, all created on an electric typewriter. Perhaps, every day of his life, Morton Sky thought he was writing something new, something powerful, revolutionary, and imbued with fire and passion.

Until he read what he'd written.

Maybe the creature that drove him no longer graced him with any inward light. I had heard it command him, in that uncanny, imperious voice, and the urgency I heard was undeniable, but what she (it) had uttered, I realized, was: "Write now!"

The thing had turned on him, and he had tried to give it back to the man he'd stolen it from, but the one he could have returned it to was dead, and I was not a suitable substitute, even if the same blood flowed in my veins.

* * *

ALL THIS was long ago. My agent, Max Felwin, is gone. A woman he refused to marry shot him dead, the price he paid for trying to change his ways.

I had called him the day after my return from Empire. He had been gracious when I told him I couldn't write—or even talk about—the interview with Sky. He was used to projects that failed to materialize, having dealt with writers and editors for almost fifty years.

* * *

I AM compelled to add something to this narrative, which isn't to be published until after my death, at which time you are all free to question my sanity. I have no reputation to preserve, and I'm not interested in posterity's good opinion. I write to hear these words in my own mind, to stand back and read them later and judge their truth from a distance.

* * *

THIS MONTH, in the mail, I received the galleys for a book of my father's collected essays. These are essays my father wrote for various magazines and journals after the success of *Imploding*.

I was sure I had read all these pieces. They are not his best work, being the rants of a man who had let his celebrity status lull him into sloppy prose and self-importance. But there is an essay, the first in the book, that I had never read before.

"My Suicides," filled me with a growing sense of dread and revelation. I could hear Andrew's voice saying, "I wish he'd just do it right!" after another of my father's failed attempts.

In the essay, my father describes the various ways in which he tried to kill himself, with alcohol, drugs, and by his own hand. He even speaks, with humor, of his failed attempt to hang himself, although he fails to note that his youngest child was present for this performance. He writes frankly, without self-pity or melodrama, about his mental illness, its various diagnoses and the delusions it inspired.

He writes these lines:

> I had called Calliope my Muse, because *Imploding* aspired to epic poetry, but later I strove for something more personal and Polyhymnia, the Muse of sacred poetry, befriended me. In my drunkenness, my drug stupors, my derangements, I didn't understand that

I was summoning something more ancient, a banished sister whose atavistic heart burned with rage and terrible need, a tenth Muse that was nameless and moved without mercy through the darkest night. The Muse that offered the shotgun to Hemingway, the arsenic to Chatterton, the ocean to Hart Crane, the river to Virginia Woolf, the pills to Jack London, and the pistol to Robert E. Howard. This is the Muse of oblivion, of negation and obsession, and her voice is as sweet as any of her sisters.

* * *

FOR THE first time, I felt my father's absence, and I wept.

Stone and the Librarian

"Civilization is unnatural. It is a whim of circumstance.
And barbarism must always ultimately triumph."
— Robert E. Howard

I
IN AFRICA, AGAIN

HE **WAS A** child of seven years when the Librarian's men came for him and carried him from the small village where his father labored in the mines.

They came in the afternoon, with his father away, and his mother fought for him, and the Librarian's soldier slew her with a single stroke of his broad axe so that all the child took with him from that day was the image of his mother sprawled on the ground, her garments in disarray, one arm flung out, fingers grotesquely clutching the dirt as though attempting to retrieve her head, bare inches beyond her reach.

Bad luck for her, he thought, or later thought. He left the village forever, owning nothing but his name—and that given to him by a stranger.

* * *

HE HAD acquired his name on the day of his birth, when his father, old Seamus McGarn, reeled into the pub. Already well-oiled through the diligent application of strong home brew, McGarn called out for a beer.

"Me heir has arrived!" he shouted. "A wee stalling at the gate, but he's here!"

Someone in the crowd yelled out, "Likely he didn't care to come into the world, seeing his inheritance."

This might, at another time, have precipitated a brawl. McGarn was quick to anger and quick to use his fists, as were his fellows, for the poverty that clung to them did not teach brotherly love and tolerance but encouraged a constant Darwinian struggle.

McGarn was feeling uncommonly proud and pleased to be released from the long vigil of the birthing. "He'll be man enough to wrest a living from this blighted world, I tell you that. Fourteen pounds!"

"My God," someone blurted. "A full stone!"

Amid laughter, he was named.

* * *

STONE LOOKED up at the hills ahead. Hundreds of birds, brown carrion feeders, flew over the green canopy and commenced to spiral slowly into the trees like muddy water down a drain. He had seen a dozen of these creatures on the plain below, a hunchbacked rabble pushing and shoving each other, snatching at the entrails of a dead antelope with much shrieking and flapping of wings. In the air they had a wind-borne grace that vanished when they touched the earth.

Stone inhaled deeply. For all its dangers and grotesqueries, he loved the jungle. This primitive continent had surely saved his life and set his soul free. The wildness of these African gods, with blood on their teeth and tongues, with not an ounce of mercy to quench a prayer, had renewed him. Without Africa, the sentences might have bound him fast, might have fastened round his chest like iron bands and pressed the air from his lungs, the blood from his heart.

He owed his freedom to the one called Hemingway. Not directly, of course, for the old man had killed himself in another world, another time.

The Librarian had asked him who, of the writers he was forced to read, did he admire most, and Stone had said, "Hemingway," although, in truth, Stone hated the lot of them, hated the way the books bred inaction, turned everything into words, the sun and the moon and the wildness of the sea and the lust for battle or for women. But he had learned that the Librarian's questions were always to be answered. He was not suited for solitary confinement.

So when the Librarian asked why, Stone answered, "He stands up."

The Librarian had not understood this, was not, perhaps, familiar with the habits of this Hemingway, and so Stone explained. "I've read that most writers slouch in chairs as they write, and those that don't lie in bed scribbling away on pads of paper. Hemingway stood as he wrote." Hemingway's words showed this, showed a man who might walk, or run, from the words, forsaking them for the turbulent world of combat, of women, of storms upon the ocean.

"Ah," the Librarian said. "Yes." And yet it seemed the Librarian thought Stone's answer was a metaphor (an honest mistake, for many of the students deemed plain-speaking contemptible), and Stone did not disabuse him of this notion, did not say that Hemingway's attraction lay not in his writing but in his willingness to forsake it, that the man was rightly skeptical of a vocation that harbored so many effete and degenerate types.

Stone's supposed admiration for Hemingway had lodged in the Librarian's mind, and not six months later, the Librarian called Stone into his office and said, "What would you say to seeing that Africa your Hemingway so loved? Seeing Kilimanjaro *itself.* What would you say?"

Yes was what Stone would say and did, his only reservation being that he had not killed the Librarian yet and now, if he wished to secure his freedom, might never have the chance.

As soon as the opportunity to leave the tour group presented itself, Stone took it and was gone.

✻ ✻ ✻

STONE HEAVED a great sigh and left the past behind. He had a long climb ahead, and it would go better if his mind were clear. If the birds signified what he suspected, they would lead him to the Temple of The Librarian, held to be a myth by all those who had never been to this land and could not, as a consequence, fit their minds to its wonders.

He plunged into the jungle, moving easily at first between tall trees whose smooth trunks sprung upward for a hundred feet before raising limbs to the green ceiling. Here there was little undergrowth, and light descended in long-slanted beams, light of an almost palpable density, celestial lumber propped up against the trees as though awaiting its destiny in the frame of some magnificent cathedral. Then, as the incline rose, the sense of exaltation diminished and died. The venerable giants were replaced by shorter, gnarled trees and dank explosions of vegetation with mottled and weirdly shaped leaves. Stone's attention was drawn to a squat plant whose waxy leaves curved to form chalice-shapes filled with a pale green liquid. In one such goblet, a thick-bodied insect struggled to escape, its antennae waving frantically as it sunk beneath the surface. Stone turned away and pressed on. Lianas as thick as a man's thigh blocked his path. He unsheathed his machete and began to hack his way upward through florid, steaming vegetation and stubborn thickets that were armed with long thorns, and inhabited, as every swing of the machete revealed, by angry, stinging ants.

Stone proceeded with grim purpose. He would find the monster who had killed his mother and held him in long bondage. He would avenge an old wrong.

As Stone went on, the incline grew steeper, and he was forced to pull himself up, gripping the smooth trunks of the trees with one massive hand while battling the under-growth with the machete. The hours fell away as he fought the jungle, and the light of day retreated. Shadows grew and every yawning black hole that was born in the hollow of a stone or in the cleft of a lightning-savaged tree seemed filled with red eyes and malevolent movement, glittering black against black.

Then the rise ended abruptly, and the darkness gave way to a luminous sky. Stone found himself in a clearing where tall, silver grass undulated in a fair breeze. He stood up, only now aware that his climb had necessitated a crouched and crippled posture. Above him stars glinted like knives, like assassins attending the moon. He saw the waterfall tumbling from a stone cliff and only then heard it, although it made a roar that filled the air before entering the pool with a fanfare of roiling white spray. Stone hastened to the side of the pool and knelt amid the lichen-mottled rocks and thrust his face toward the clear water. Small angular fish exploded from his reflection; he drank. The water was cold with a brave taste of rock and metal. After the jungle, this place seemed a haven for gods, and Stone was tempted to spend the night here. In the morning, he would be rested and better equipped to deal with whatever awaited him.

But as he lifted his lips from the water, a small white object on the water's surface caught his eye. He reached for it, and something primal within recognized it with a thrill of revulsion. He lifted the wet, crumpled piece of ruled paper, pressed it smooth against his thigh, and read what the wretched student's hand had wrought:

GUILT IN THE SCARLET LETTER

BY NATHANIEL HAWTHORNE

by Harmon Perks

I read The Scarlet Letter *so that I could write this paper. I have picked as my theme* guilt.

Hawthorne was interested in how guilt reacted in people. He was especially interested in this aspect with adultery which is a sin that Hester Prynne and Arthur Dimmesdale completed. Arthur Dimmesdale is a minister, so the guilt is worse and causes a "scarlet letter" to appear on his chest. This is a symbol, but it looks like a red "A" and it might not really—

The writer had crossed out the next two lines with angry scribbles and then written, "*I hate this book I hate this book I hate this book I hate this book I hate this book I hate this book I hate this book I hate—*" before crumpling the paper and hurling it into the stream.

Stone uttered a powerful oath, one that he had vowed to use no more than five times in his life, honoring his mother by this frugality. He crushed the paper, his hand white-clenched as though it held an enemy's heart, and hurled it back into the pool. Confronted by such suffering, he could not wait until morning. He turned away from the pool and the surrounding glory of the meadow and plunged back into the jungle.

The darkness fought him with sharp spines, wet leaves, the resolute limbs of trees, spiderwebs, insects. Larger creatures followed him through the dark but did not attack, for Stone's bulk was considerable (he had fulfilled the promise of his birth-size), and no taint of fear could any beast detect, only the hot odor of rage and its hunger for release.

No starlight found him in the jungle, no hint of sky, nothing with which to fix a course, but his course was upward and he followed the ache in his legs, the route that bent his back.

He traveled for hours—three, by the feel of his calves. At some point, the anger engendered by the book reporter's anguish relented, and Stone regained his senses and understood that further effort might only take him away from his goal. So he found the blasted stump of a tree, hollowed like a throne, and he brushed out a nest of blind shrews (he recognized them by their fierce cries) and centipedes (their feathery feet), and wrapped himself in the rain poncho that bore the stamp of a warring nation two thousand miles to the north, a war whose outcome he no longer remembered.

He slept and dreamed or perhaps he did not sleep and only remembered, the images of his memory so fragmented and distorted that they bore the look of dreams.

* * *

"WE COME here from across time to find the ones who might save us," the Librarian told the newly enslaved. They were in the auditorium that echoed his voice and made his breath audible. The students sat in hushed rows as the monitors moved down the aisles with supple wands capable of raising a welt.

As always, the Librarian was dressed in the same uniform the students wore.

When Stone was a child, new to Knowledge Base #29, he thought nothing of this, but later he realized it was an affectation of humility where no genuine humility existed, for the old man was thin and sharp-featured, and his uniform was precisely tailored, creating an impression of elegance without extravagance. Those uniforms worn by the students were another thing entirely. They were made of some shoddy material, gray and shapeless as rags, the pants wide and overly long, inducing a loutish shuffle.

The Librarian told them, again and again, that they were the hope of the future. He told them that he was *from* a future that was in need of hope, for the greatness of Mankind resided in its knowledge. In that future that was the Librarian's present, knowledge had been disrupted. All literature, all science, all history had been blown into smoke by some dark magic.

Stone thought, *What is it worth if a sorcerer can banish it to oblivion?*

But the Librarian went on, as he always did. In the two months since his capture, Stone had already heard the story six times in its fullness, and every morning began with a shorter version as he and his classmates sang, "Lost Glory" ("Our grandeur mourning, we watch a savage dawn unfolding"). There was no forgetting that civilization was gone.

"I don't miss it," Stone told Stokey Bram, who immediately ran off and repeated that heresy to one of the headmasters, who came and punished Stone with some perfunctory swats.

The long and the short of it was this: what knowledge remained had wound up in books, those archaic rectangles of pulped wood. With those the world would be reborn to knowledge.

"My dad's gonna get me out of here," Stone told Stokey, and Stokey had replied, "I thought your dad was here. I heard—"

"He ain't."

"Well, he won't find you. Couldn't find you with a dozen bloodhounds."

"Why's that?" In truth, Stone doubted his dad would look much for him. They had never got along.

"This here school moves around. It's what you call mobile. Sliding in and out of space."

"Who told you that?"

"Nobody. But everybody knows it's so. Just look out the window, why don't ya? One day you got snow falling down on a lot of piney trees and the next day you got an alley full of garbage and cats. How do you explain that?"

Stone didn't try. He hit Stokey with his fist, a good whack to the temple, and when Stokey came around Stone said, "Go tell one of the headmasters I smacked you. You do that, and I'll smack you so hard you'll swallow your tongue and that will be the last of telling headmasters anything."

The logic of this was not lost on Stokey.

✱ ✱ ✱

ONE TIME Stone was reading about some made-up person who was wrestling and wrestling with his conscience because he'd killed somebody and couldn't make up his mind whether he should tell someone about it or not when any idiot with half a brain would know, with *no thought at all*, that telling was not a good idea and would only end in grief.

Stone was in a study unit, and he laid the book flat on his desk and thought, not for the first time, *If we are going to get knowledge, why can't we have more of the science and how-to knowledge and less of this literature?* But he knew the answer because it was another thing the Librarian went on about at every single rally and every single orientation. "It wasn't," the Librarian would boom over the speakers, "the lack of science that led to the end." It was the absence of compassion, the absence of empathy, the absence of *humanity* that brought civilization to its knees. So what needed to be stressed in this bunker where the flame of civilization burned with a small, hopeful light was *knowledge of the heart.* And where were you going to find that? In literature, of course!

Stone would have given a lot to trade *Crime and Punishment* for a book on how to make a small bomb using only kitchen and bathroom supplies. There was knowledge dying in the world for want of attention, and Stone felt for it.

* * *

IN THE morning a band of monkeys woke Stone, shouting and leaping from branch to branch. They were overly pleased with their agility and sought to taunt Stone, who threw a net over the closest imp and, as it fought to untangle itself, screaming like a banshee, silenced it with his knife. Stone was always in a black humor in the morning, and hungry to boot. He made a small fire, rousing it with a flint. He carried spices with him, and these he rubbed into the animal's flesh. The spices failed to improve the taste or Stone's mood. He recalled that in Zaruba he had heard a tribesman describe the ancient chief there as a man with "no more savor than a Bakalu." The chief had been a very old man covered in dust (whether by design or happenstance, Stone never discovered). Stone decided that he had just eaten a monkey of the Bakalu family.

He climbed the tallest tree and looked about him. The sun was out and already well-risen. He had slept later than was his wont, but that was one of his freedoms; he moved to no clock but his own.

He could see mountains in the far distance, bare stone wreathed in clouds. By his reckoning, the temple, if it had not been magicked away, was three or four hours' march ahead. As he watched, a flock of yellow butterflies floated over the trees, moving with a jaunty motion as though animated by music only they could hear. Then two loud explosions came from the trees and the butterflies wheeled away and half a dozen carrion birds flew out of the jungle, uttering their squawks and dirge-like cries.

So they are already shooing them off for the day, thought Stone. He fumbled in the pocket of his fatigues and produced the small gem that old N'Loopa had given him when they had both fought the wizard Mesu Pork, and he held the gem up to the light. Within it a red liquid flowed, always seeking the west, and by this he adjusted his course. His travel during the night had not been in vain; he was barely an hour from his destination.

II
THE TEMPLE OF THE LIBRARIAN

HE SPIED the golden domes and turrets and strangely angled walls long before the whole of the building came into view. In fact, it could be said that the whole building never did present itself to his eye, for the temple stretched out and back and into the jungle so that its limits were not easily apparent. Indeed, Stone could not tell if it were a single building or a collection of buildings.

This was nothing like Knowledge Base #29, which was gray brick and stolidly drab. The ornate structure he now beheld could only be a thing of Africa, brown and gold and shining and somehow *of the earth*, bathed in the blood and dust of this savage land. Stone did not doubt that mountains of bones lay beneath this labyrinthine structure. It might now be the refuge of the Librarian, but it had been raised by an older race.

Despite its remote location, Stone assumed the temple would have guards and perhaps sophisticated instruments for spying out intruders. He proceeded carefully, remaining within the trees and tangled vegetation that came within fifty feet of the walls of the temple.

He heard another explosion, and more of the brown, ungainly scavengers rose in the air. They were to Stone's right, coming up over a red and brown domed roof, and one of the birds landed clumsily in the branch of a tree just thirty feet to Stone's right. They didn't scare far, these creatures, being fearless or, more likely, addled by the promise of a feast.

Stone continued his slow progress around the building, staying in the shadows and moving cautiously, always assuming that someone or something watched.

He saw them then, and he felt a familiar revulsion and a sense of suffocation, as though he were imprisoned again in their company.

The green, gentle hill with its well-manicured grass and tamed fruit trees was littered with the bodies of students. Not a one of them moved. They sprawled, leaned against trees, sat with their knees crossed, and all of them were studying. Books held them in thrall, eyes were willed to pages. The students were of both sexes, sometimes together, but always locked in separate trances as though this learning, this *literature*, exuded mind-killing vapors that immobilized its victims. The frenzy in the loins to mate, even this proud imperative, the progenitor of wars and fine heroic deeds, was stilled by the paralysis of *study*. This was death's image, even if the breath still stirred within. Wasn't it enough to fool the carrion birds? And if the monitors failed to fire the guns when the birds proved too bold, would the birds move yet closer...and feed?

The mere proximity of these students chilled his limbs. A wave of nausea overcame him, as though a powerful vertigo spell had found its mark, and he remembered the dreaded books.

"Call me Ishmael," one book began, and Stone had thought, not a hundred pages through and dead sick of whales, *Call me long-winded.* But you weren't allowed to call it quits. They devised tests to see if you had truly read the thing, and solitary confinement awaited those who failed.

Damnable books: *The Iliad, Silas Marner, Vanity Fair...* The thought of Thackery...Stone almost blacked out. Sometimes Stone would have a vision of an old man lying in bed, eating chocolates from a box, obese and in failing health, and talking and talking, occasionally shaking an admonitory finger, smiling or frowning, lecturing, unaware that everyone had left, that no one *cared* what he was saying. A book was an old man, impotent and raging, or, worse, self-doting beyond madness, a prattling assertion of ego.

Sometimes, in the years of his imprisonment, Stone broke away from slumber in a blazing fever, grabbed from the nightstand something by one of the infamous Jameses (Henry or Joyce), flipped wildly through the pages—and, full of dizzy revelation, saw precisely what the writer was getting at. He would jump up and run down the halls, banging on doors, awakening his fellow students. Waving the book in the face of some sleep-dazed wretch, he would explain. Yes. He would explain until someone roused the house monitor and a couple of orderlies were summoned. They would tackle and sedate him.

* * *

"NONSENSE," STOKEY Bram told him on the morning after one such episode. "Weren't even words you were saying, just gibberish like."

"'Gibberish?'"

"Yeah, you know, like *bibble bleep bah jabber ho spinnish sputtle hoo!*"

Stone could never remember anything beyond the rush, that sense of having finally got it. Alas, it was a delusion, for when he revisited a book that made no sense prior to the episode, it was, again, an implacable wall. After one such episode, he reopened the Faulkner that had been the catalyst for his derangement and found it as impenetrable as ever. He might as well try to puzzle out the thought processes of a giant squid mulling things over at the bottom of the night-black sea. And he had thought he *understood!* He roared with laughter, laughter so violent that it convulsed his body, and he broke out of his restraints and ran down the hall and smashed through to the adjoining ward where suicidal young women who had recently read *The Bell Jar* moped around like swamp wraiths. It had taken five orderlies to subdue him.

❋ ❋ ❋

NOW WAS not the time for the past, and he knew it. But the students, the carefully composed lawn, the massive walls of the temple, all seemed to urge passivity.

He would have preferred to formulate a plan, and to wait. Patience might reveal the manner and placement of guards. But he could not wait. To remain here would be to surrender to inaction. He might never move again.

He moved. With a speed and agility that had kept him whole among jungle and desert predators (including the human ones), Stone raced over the grass and reached the wall, releasing the rope from his waist even as he ran, and threw the grappling hook high where it caught on the lip of an ornate ledge. To anyone watching, it might seem that he ran up the wall and disappeared by supernatural means.

In fact, as soon as he found the roof he threw his poncho around himself, and the poncho, made for a desert war (made as a hammer is made to recognize a nail), turned itself the mottled red and brown of the roof.

Under this camouflage, Stone crouched and ran to a small domed shed that protruded from the roof. Above him, he spied three evenly spaced watchtowers, each containing the tall silhouette of a guard whose right hand clenched a spearlike silver weapon. The door to the shed was locked but no match for Stone's resolution and the thick sinews of his arms.

It was dark within. Stone descended a short flight of stairs and discovered a large storage space filled with casks, crates, armor, rusting weapons of mass destruction, and boxes filled with books and ammunition. Stone's mercenary days were not lost on him, and he retrieved a fine silver sword that shivered when he pushed the button at its base. The blade seemed to undulate, an illusion created by twin blades moving with uncanny speed. This was a sword to cut through stone and steel and bone.

He made his way to the end of the room and yet another door. This door opened on a long corridor, and Stone stepped out. Brass torches that simulated fire ran along the hall in both directions. He heard voices to his right and moved toward them—it was not his inclination to hide—and almost immediately the owners of the voices rounded a corner and came into view.

He saw a teacher, dressed in traditional garb, a tweed jacket, elbow patches that signified thoughtfulness (thought required considerable leaning on the elbows), and an ill-groomed beard, brown and flecked with silver, which some called—it was all coming back to Stone—a tenure. The man was accompanied by five students, two male and three female, who stayed very close to him, almost hugging him, and bent low, a posture that allowed them to look upward into the face of their mentor who was short and yet, by his station, demanded upward gazes.

They all stopped abruptly, and one of the male students said, "Who's this, Professor?"

"I have no idea," the professor said, frowning. "He's not a level two, so he has no business here. Where is your uniform, young man?"

"I gave my uniform to a leper in Wantoga," Stone said. "Had he not been naked, he would have refused the gift, I'm sure."

"What's your name?"

"Stone. And yours?"

The professor smiled and looked at all his students. "Well, this fellow is grilling me like a first year, isn't he?" The students giggled, and the professor, easily encouraged, began to recite a cynical, archly insulting poem.

That is, Stone took the poem for an insult, but there was no way he could know for sure. He could never know what lay within a poem. The runic words, the incantatory rhythm, seemed a threat filled with sorcerer's guile, and a blinding red haze filled his eyes—this had always been so—and the madness of the warrior rose up, and he leaned forward and sank the humming blade deep into the man's heart.

Stone looked at the balding academic, lying in a pool of blood, his thinning hair an accusation (*You've killed a feeble foe!*), and thought, *He shouldn't have poemed me.*

The students fled down the hall. Instantly, Stone was restored to his senses. A loud ringing filled the halls, the same ringing that used to send every student into the pavilion back at Knowledge Base #29. Stone felt a need to go outside and stand in a line, but he was pleased to discover that this old imprinting no longer ruled him. He turned and ran in the other direction, spied a door on his right and wrenched it open. He ran quickly up the stairs.

The Librarian would be above him. The old man loved a view, loved to sweep his hands before a window as though petitioning the world, and he would be up there in some high vaulted room, up there minding the clouds.

Finally, Stone came to the topmost step and broke in another door. More than a dozen armed guards, bristling with swords, greeted him. Their faces were dark, glowering, their shoulders wide—formidable brutes, but not, Stone thought, bound by loyalty. He knew the mercenary's eye, having lived among them, and for all their love of money, they loved their own blood more and would bolt if the work of killing cost too much of their own red stuff.

"Good then!" Stone shouted. "Your numbers tell me that something of value must be lodged behind that door! Some treasure? Your master, I think."

He moved into them with a roar, his humming sword low. He crouched, lunged, moving with such speed that the gleam of his blade left a shining cross in the air, a swordsman's benediction. Stone stepped over the fallen bodies. Others filled the void immediately and died as quickly. Shouts and imprecations thundered in the hall. Stone's foes pressed forward with howling determination, thinking to overcome him with numbers, but their swords broke on his spinning one, and the swords that breached Stone's defenses (succeeding by sheer number) shattered on his desert armor (made from the hides of sentient lizards from the distant planet Celicus, where they basked and rolled in fire as cats will yawn and stretch in a sunbeam).

As Stone had guessed—*no, it was a certainty!*—they turned and fled.

With a wan smile, Stone watched the last of them round the corner. They could have killed him with their numbers, but each of them could not count past himself, an army of one, no army that.

❋ ❋ ❋

THIS LAST door would not be broken into by brute force. This Stone knew, but he had not come unprepared. He removed the gem that his old friend N'Loopa had given him, and he remembered his old friend's words, "This be *seek* rock, some say Eye of Old God called sometimes Abathoth. Can find your way on journey, sure, but more more power too. Find man or woman's heart. Find lost thing. Find hidden thing."

Stone held the gem up to the door, as one might hold a candle up to illuminate a murky corridor. The gem cast an eerie, greenish light that uncovered what cunning spells sought to conceal from human eyes. Upon the door, strange runes were drawn in a square, and, as Stone looked on, one symbol grew brighter, then faded as another underwent the same transformation, dark to bright then dark again. Some primal voice spoke to Stone without words, without sound, and Stone knew what to do. He leaned forward and touched each symbol as it shone.

When the cycle had completed, the door swung open silently. Stone entered the room with his sword held high. The Librarian was motionless, slumped forward on his desk, a small lamp illuminating his bald pate.

Stone thought to slay him in his sleep. The old man's power and cunning were not to be underestimated. And the advantage of surprise was not to be traded for some misguided notion of fair play.

Even as Stone thought this, the Librarian looked up.

"Son," the Librarian said, "your mother's been worried sick. Where have you been?"

Stone spoke, undaunted: "I have been many places. I have fought and reveled in lands beyond Atlantis and Mu, beyond the reach of your assassins. I have stood under a midnight sky where three moons illuminated the naked daughters of Lenthe, Goddess of Lust, as they danced their lascivious dances and fought for my seed."

The Librarian sighed. "Your mother went to bed in tears. I told her I'd wait up."

"My mother was killed by your minions when I was just a child. And I am no son of yours. I doubt my father is alive, for—"

"Yes, the mines of that small village you grew up in are dangerous." The Librarian shook his head, expressing fatigue, disgust. "It was a simple field trip to the Museum of Natural History, Edward. Mr. Miller was extremely upset when he discovered you'd slipped away from the group. I assured him that it has happened before and that you'd turn up. That assurance didn't keep your mother from hysterics. I finally talked her into taking a sedative."

"My mother is *dead*," Stone said. "And I have had enough of your words."

The Librarian smiled. "Do you intend to hit me with that umbrella, Edward?"

Stone's eyes rose slowly to his clenched hand. The sword was *gone*—and in his hand, instead: *a thin black umbrella!*

Stone felt the strength go out of him. The blue smoke that encircled him was not, as he had foolishly assumed, the familiar effluvium produced by the Librarian's pipe. No, this was some insidious vapor that distorted—

And then that thought was gone, and Stone lost consciousness before the floor smote his forehead.

III
REMEMBRANCE OF THINGS PAST

HE WENT to the classes and returned to his room. How long he had done this, he did not know.

"I think I'm overmedicated," he told the school's physician, who nodded and said, "Probably. In time we can reduce the dosage, but for now..." He shrugged. "Better safe than sorry."

They called him Edward, and he didn't like it. "Call me, Ed, okay?" he said.

So his fellow students called him Ed, but his teachers insisted on Edward, and he hated the name and imagined they called him that because they knew he hated it.

This day he lay on the bed and opened the new novel they had assigned him. *At least*, he thought, *it's a short one.*

It was about some teenager named Holden. It was "written" by Holden, although it wasn't really written by him. There was a writer out there who had really written the book, pretending to be Holden.

Ed hated this, hated the levels of the lie, the depth of dissembling. In the novel, this Holden kid calls everyone a "phony," and complains about everything and doesn't do much of anything, just drifts around, and talks about how he'd like to be the guy who stands around watching children play in a meadow where there's a cliff. This imaginary guy's imaginary job would be to grab a kid up if he strayed too near the cliff's edge. Only: *Why have children playing in such a dangerous place just so you could be a hero?* Ed thought Holden was a pain in the ass. But Holden wasn't real, and the true pain in the ass was this Salinger guy who wrote the book.

Here's this writer guy. You can see him making up this voice in his head, imitating the accent, the gestures, the slouch.

You can *imagine* him imagining this whiney teenager. Ed couldn't exactly explain why this was so enraging. This Holden Caulfield was a worthless waste of time, and that was bad enough, but it seemed a thousand times worse that someone had intentionally brought Holden to life. What an abomination: *a listless author giving birth to a listless teenager!*

That night Ed tossed and turned in his sleep and was harried by fantastical dreams that he could not remember, dreams that left him covered with sweat. In the morning, he resolved to stop taking his pills. He went to a drugstore on Livingston and bought a bottle of vitamin C pills that were white, oval shapes—just like the pills he swallowed each morning. He poured these pills into a plastic sandwich bag and walked down to the medical annex where Nurse Werther was drinking coffee and watching the news on the overhead television. She sighed the way she always did when anyone interrupted her, as though she wasn't being paid to dispense medications but did it out of the goodness of her heart, despite the ingratitude of those she served.

When she came back with the pill bottle, Ed pretended to stumble. He grabbed at the table to right himself, and Nurse Werther's coffee went over.

"Shaw!" she shouted. She ran off to get a paper towel, and Ed grabbed the bottle, turned away from the retreating nurse, opened the bottle and poured its contents into his left pocket. Another few seconds, and he had emptied the plastic bag's contents into the bottle and screwed the cap back on. Nurse Werther hadn't returned. When she did, and when she had finished mopping up the spilled coffee while sighing copiously, she watched Ed take his pill.

Tomorrow and the next day and the next day, he would dutifully come in and take his vitamin C.

❋ ❋ ❋

THREE WEEKS later, Ed finished the obligatory book report. His report began, "If I met Holden Caulfield in an alley, I would kill him with a rock," but he didn't hand that one in. He didn't want trouble. So he pretended he was one of the prissy girls in the class, and he wrote about how much he liked the book, and he used the word "alienation" because that was his teacher's favorite word that month.

He went to classes. Time turned the color of a rain-laden sky. People called him Edward, and it didn't bother him so much.

* * *

"MANY PEOPLE consider this the greatest novel of the twentieth century," the professor said.

Wonderful, Edward thought. He was in a different part of the university now, and here the level of complexity was deeper. Many of his fellow students never finished a sentence, so besieged were they by elaborate, subtle thoughts.

At least I don't have to read it in French, he thought, as he studied Volume One, which contained four novels, the first half of this imposing masterpiece. He flipped through the pages of the book. There were 1,141 of them. Many pages were flat blocks of small type with no indentions, no paragraphs. The translator was a man named C. K. Scott Moncrieff, and Edward wondered if that was a pseudonym but realized he didn't really care.

With trepidation that was immediately validated, he began reading the first paragraph:

> *For a long time I used to go to bed early. Sometimes, when I had put out my candle, my eyes would close so quickly that I had not even time to say, "I'm going to sleep."*

* * *

A FEW sentences in, and his brain already felt dull and heavy. His eyes traveled over several sentences before his attention kicked in again:

> *Then it would begin to seem unintelligible, as the thoughts of a former existence must be to a reincarnate spirit; the subject of my book would separate itself from me, leaving me free to choose whether I would form part of it or no; and at the same time my sight would return and I would be astonished to find myself in a state of darkness, pleasant and restful enough for the eyes, and even more, perhaps, for my mind, to which it appeared incomprehensible, without a cause, a matter dark indeed.*

* * *

EDWARD READ on. No one had to tell him that this Proust guy wrote while lying down. The convoluted sentences induced a fever state that destroyed his sense of time.

* * *

EDWARD STOPPED attending classes, but in this crowded university, away from the usual parental supervision, his absence was not noted, and he did manage to drop by the medical annex for his vitamin C dose, so Nurse Werther wouldn't raise an alarm.

He was free to dream. He lost all sense of the convoluted sentences, and they began to devour him. He could make no clear distinction between reading and staring at the ceiling. He had heard other students speak of this lack of clarity, the way the sinuous thoughts would turn to sounds, cadences that induced trance states. He thought he might die, but felt no sense of fear. He was interested only in describing this state with the longest sentence he could fashion.

He hadn't eaten in days, perhaps weeks. Could one not eat for weeks? He stumbled toward the bed and fell. He grabbed an end table to steady himself, but it accompanied him downward, and a drawer fell out, tumbling as it fell. The bottom of the drawer was revealed, and on it, lashed with silver tape, was a book. Edward peeled away the tape and studied the book, a paperback. The end table, which he had brought from home, was old, and the book had clearly been affixed to its hiding place long ago. He thought he remembered it, remembered reading it surreptitiously, late at night, the way one might remember eating a crumpet with some tea in some long ago past. He studied its garish cover, an oil painting of massive cavemen marching out of the mist of some brutal prehistoric dawn. A pale white woman is draped over the gigantic shoulder of one such brute. She is as white, *whiter*, than the moon above. She is naked.

Edward lay on the bed reading the book. Halfway through the first story, a sharp knife stabbed his stomach. He identified the knife: hunger. He ate the cheese and ham in the refrigerator, washing it down with six or seven beers. He ate a loaf of bread. He had bought these groceries some time ago. There may have been mold growing on some of the items, but he did not care. He was not fastidious.

He slept soundly and was roughly awakened by a man he felt he ought to know.

"You're alive," the man said. He was a big man, and his eyes burned with impatience.

"Who are you?" Edward asked.

"You know," the man said, and Edward was surprised to discover that he did know. This was the man who had made the sentences his slaves and so escaped the dust and tedium of West Texas.

"They said you were dead."

"They would say that, wouldn't they?"

Of course they would!

The man leaned closer, his eyes solemn, intense. "The real question," he said, "is who are *you?*"

Edward would have said he didn't know, but the answer was on his tongue when he opened his mouth. "Stone."

The man nodded and turned away. "I've taken the liberty of breaking this window. You're a sound sleeper." He waited, as though Stone might want to refute this. Stone said nothing, and the man continued. "I thought you might wish to leave without attracting attention." Then the man was in the window, a silhouette, and then he was gone. Without hesitation, Stone followed, leaping into the night, the star-bright air roaring in his ears like the welcoming roar of a vast crowd. The soles of his shoes slapped down on the asphalt parking lot, and he stumbled forward, but he did not fall. He looked around at the campus, the rows of stark winter trees against the mist-enshrouded lamps, the stately admin building to his right, dormitories one through eight receding in the distance like some trick of a mirror or too much to drink.

"Come on!" the man shouted. He was on down the path; another ten feet and he would disappear behind the tall evergreens that lined Burroughs Way. He raised his arm, and described an urgent arc. "Come on!" he shouted. "We'll be safe once we reach the jungle!"

And Stone knew he was right.

The Indelible Dark

E WATCHED THE car come down the mountain. The autumn trees were full of muted color, and black clouds rolled in the sky, restive monsters bloated with rain. The road unraveled in a series of switchbacks, and the car, black, shiny as a beetle, appeared and disappeared amid the trees.

Gravid raindrops began to fall, exploding on the road in front of him, and the boy closed his eyes and stood motionless. He could raise the temperature of his body by the power of his will, or, more admirably, he could acknowledge the discomfort and endure it. He preferred the latter.

The clothes he wore were designed to shed the rain before it reached his skin, and his hair was shorn so short that there was nothing to muss. He opened his eyes and waited: a proper schoolboy, not of the elite, but of merited parents, no scars, no admonishments scribbled on his face, his hands.

Now that the rain had asserted itself, there was nothing much to see. He hoped the car would not race by him, oblivious.

The car came out of the rain. He saw that it was bigger than the cars he had seen at Ashes Ville, and he suspected it might be powered by the blackoil that had burned the old world up.

The car slowed and rolled to a stop in front of him and the passenger door swung open. A black shaft—a weapon?—emerged, bloomed suddenly with a popping noise, and the boy stepped back, alert. An *umbrella*. The man beneath it was tall and seemed to vacate the car in stages.

"Stepped out for a bit of wet, did you?" the man said. His face was pale, unlined but ancient-seeming, smooth in the way that a river rock is smooth. Faded ink encircled his neck. He grinned, displaying a row of tiny silver teeth. "Where you bound?"

"George Washington City," the boy said.

"Well, fancy that! Same as ourselves. Come on. In you go." The man ushered the boy into the passenger seat, closed the door, then opened the rear door and, folding again, knees and elbows like some intricate device, shut his umbrella with a fierce shake and settled in the backseat.

The boy could sense no danger in the man behind him, no psychic crouch or killer's caution, which meant: a) that the man was no immediate threat or b) that the man was a grave threat, an assassin who could hide the subtle body language of intention. There was another person in the back-seat, behind the driver, and this other was seeking him with a bright, hungry intelligence that the boy perceived as heat on the back of his neck.

He did not turn and stare. He suspected that the scrutiny was meant to be felt, and he did not wish to dignify it with a response. The boy turned his head slightly and regarded the driver. The man was a menial, an Albert or a Jorge, and possibly dangerous but predictable. He wore a gray uniform, and a hat, too small for his head, intentionally comic, demeaning, as was the present fashion in menials.

They drove on in silence, through a blur of colored trees, the world under glass and melting. Sometimes the beauty of the natural world felt like an assault, and his defense was a memory of burning cities, streets littered with rotting bodies, hulking scavenger machines that spoke to each other in bursts of static and feedback howls. The memory was not his own.

The one who studied him spoke, instantly revealing her gender. "You are a Cory," she said. He turned now and saw a girl with silver-blue eyes and short-cropped red hair, intricate ink scrolls crossing her forehead like a veil.

"My father was Andrew Cory," the boy said. "My name is Mark."

"I've never met a Mark. I hope you aren't vicious or sly. Can I trust you?" She offered a quick smile, tilted her head, studied him. She looked a mere girl, her slight body enfolded in shimmer cloth, moth-themed, green wings that seemed to flicker in the dark-blue shadows of the fabric. Her face was pale and perfect and her mouth, lipstick-shaped to mirror moth wings, revealed the giddy fashion sense of a child.

He shrugged. "Why would you need to trust me?"

"I don't," she said, frowning. "But I was hoping you'd say a simple 'Yes'."

"Why?"

She turned away and glared out the car's window at the roadside flora. Here the bright orange of maples pushed to the front, easily upstaging the purples and dark greens of the false birches and dog pines. The man behind Mark spoke: "What she's hopin' is that you aren't a bomb."

"Of course I'm not!" Mark said, turning to look again at the tall man whose eyes glittered with madness or amusement.

"You don't have to be offended, boy. There's more than a few of your kin who walked into the thick of crowds, yanked their little peckers and blew themselves and everyone around them all to fuck."

"You are speaking of an old protocol," Mark said.

"It puts my mind at ease, hearing you say that. You surely have an honest face."

The girl spoke: "Solomon, be quiet. He's not a bomb. I'd know if he was." She leaned toward Mark and touched his shoulder. "My name is Mary Constant," she said. "My people fight against Lethe's Children."

"We all did," Mark said. "The LC won."

"That is what they would have us believe. But imagine a world without them."

"I thought pirates had no politics," Mark said.

"Pirates? We are no pirates."

"The scrollwork on your face is pirate. This is your longman here, with a rope tatt round his neck and the augmented smile. You could be costumed revelers, I guess, but you aren't."

"Why not?" asked Mary Constant. She had taken her hand from his shoulder and it lay in her lap with the other. She gazed down at her hands as though chastened.

"I know the smell of pirates," Mark said. "I bet you stole this vehicle, and I wouldn't be surprised if its former owners are dead."

Mary Constant looked up and frowned. "They are dead, but it was none of our doing. And, if we are what you say we are, why shouldn't we kill you and be done with it?"

Mark said nothing.

The girl said, "We are not any pirates. We are revolutionaries."

* * *

OKAY. THIS isn't one of those metafiction things. I hate it when an author intrudes, when he tries to ingratiate himself with his readers by pretending to be some sort of regular guy who is just trying to tell a story and hopes you are enjoying it. Here's what I mean: for years I lived in South Austin (the authentic, slacker heart of the city), and every day, mired in traffic, I would be forced to contemplate a giant billboard advertising life insurance. On the billboard, a smiling man in a suit held a telephone receiver to his ear while above him these words demanded attention: WHY BUY LIFE INSURANCE FROM A STRANGER WHEN YOU CAN BUY IT FROM ME, JOHNNY GARCIA? Johnny looked a little shifty to me, something larcenous in his smile and the black mustache that presided over those paper-white teeth. And, try as I might, I couldn't remember meeting the guy.

I, dear reader, am not presuming we are friends. And here's the best news: you'll never have to read this. Back in 1973 an innovative teacher named Peter Elbow wrote a thin, brilliant little book entitled *Writing Without Teachers*. Mr. Elbow discussed the process of writing and suggested that a writer might consider writing a rough draft that contains reflections on the piece being written, random thoughts, a poem, anything that would create momentum. All of this peripheral writing would enliven the writer's brain and when this chatter was later deleted it would, nonetheless, have imbued the final draft with its intellectual and emotional energy.

I've been having some problems with this nascent novel, so these are my mental stretching exercises.

My name is Joel Sherman, and I am typing this in my bedroom/office here in the Paris Apartments in Austin, Texas.

I came to Austin in 2002 when an ex-girlfriend impulsively invited me down here after her marriage fell apart. Elaine and I got along brilliantly for about eight months, and then we didn't get along at all, and I left the house but not the city.

I moved into a large, ramshackle house in Oak Hill, sharing it with the landlord and an ever-shifting mélange of university students and guys in bands. That's where I resided until recently.

I logged many years in that house, knocking out my series novels, vaguely aware of the melodrama that surrounded me. These transient young people, filled with hope, horniness, desperation, ambition, sundry drugs and alcohol, were volatile and unpredictable but easy enough to ignore. I assumed my ship would be coming over the horizon any day, and I'd be able to leave (maybe a movie sale, maybe an inexplicable surge in the popularity of private eyes whose eyes are very red) so I felt above the fray.

I considered myself and my landlord, Maxwell, rock-solid. We weren't close—I would never, for instance, have thought of calling him Max—but we would occasionally share a couple of beers and discuss the collapse of civilization. Maxwell was twelve years older than I, and somewhat morose. He wasn't one for sharing personal details, his sorrows being couched in elliptical language. He explained the failure of two marriages as "hegemony issues."

It had taken me a few years to establish this relationship with Maxwell. He rarely spoke to the other tenants unless they were late with the rent. So I should, perhaps, have been the one to investigate when my housemates approached me in a ragged delegation and asked what the racket was all about. One student maintained that the incessant construction noise robbed him of thought. All my sympathy went to any robber who got away with that kid's thoughts. I told them that our landlord was no doubt embarked on some major home improvements, and it was his house so he was within his rights. I recommended patience—and earplugs.

Two days later the noise ceased. We all moved warily, aware that it could resume at any moment. I think we spoke in whispers, although that may be a storyteller's embellishment. I remember at breakfast we all shared our observations: of the lumber and machinery delivered to the backyard, of the way it seemed to magically evaporate, and of our own creative relationship to the enigma of its use. What was Maxwell fashioning? Surely he intended to show us. It was not uncommon for days to pass without anyone laying an eye on Maxwell. His living area (which included a kitchen, living room, bedroom and bath) abutted the garage where he parked his aging Mercedes, so he could come and go at will without being seen. An unobtrusive landlord is usually a boon, but we were eager to see the results of his industry.

My bedroom was directly above Maxwell's, and in the general course of events, I never heard him. His home project altered that for a spell. I would have been justified in approaching him and asking that he curtail his zealous banging and sawing when 10:00 p.m. came round. That wouldn't have been asking much, but I understood creative passion and how the muse shouldn't be constrained by clocks. I worked at night myself. So I did not disturb him, and I was pleased when relative silence was regained without my intervention.

It was a little after ten in the morning, and I was sleeping soundly when I was jolted out of sleep by a single loud resounding *whump!* as though some fairy-tale giant had slammed a castle's giant-sized door. I had no recollection of a dream, but I felt an inexplicable dread. I lay there for a while and tried to will myself back to sleep. I failed and got up, pulled on a pair of trousers, and walked out into the hall where several young men and a waifish young woman I'd never seen before were milling around. I started down the stairs, and they followed. Being the oldest tenant (oldest both in tenancy and in years-on-the-planet) I led the way.

I knocked on Maxwell's door, but no one answered. The door wasn't locked, so I pushed it open, raising my voice to carry his name into the room. The door opened onto his bedroom—I knew this, of course, having been invited over to his living space many times—and the bed was empty and made. I had never seen it unmade. There was a minimalist, military feel to this room, everything in its place. I walked across the room and passed through the open door and into the living room.

I could feel my young roommates crowding up behind me: ragged breathing, a nervous squeak from the girl.

We stopped and stared.

I don't know what they were experiencing, but, while horror was surely the dominating emotion, they may have felt admiration for the craft involved, the care, the attention to detail. I know I did.

I had never seen such a well-wrought gallows. There is something about a solid-built thing. In the rigor that has fashioned it, there is love. I could smell the sawdust in the air although the room had been swept and everything was neatly put away. If a single detail could sum it up, I suppose that would have to be the banister that rose parallel to the nine steps leading up to the platform. Some would argue that on this very short walk to oblivion a banister was superfluous, but this wasn't about utility. The banister was there for its simple line: its dignity.

The room was awash in morning sunlight, which spilled from the skylight and the glass doors that led to the patio. Maxwell himself, revolving very slowly, his body half-hidden under the platform where the rope had halted his brief and sudden descent, wore a dark blue suit, a white, hangover-bright dress shirt, and a red-striped tie. He had thoughtfully powdered his face so that his countenance wouldn't look garishly engorged, and he wore sunglasses with a strap at the back so that they wouldn't go flying off and reveal eyes that bulged and made one think of trashy horror flicks.

He'd thought of everything. There was a piece of typing paper affixed to the lapel of his suit. It didn't look like anyone else could be relied upon for clear-headed action, so I carefully ascended the steps to the platform—without using the banister so that the inevitable police investigation could not accuse me of contaminating the scene (I've seen my share of television). I leaned forward and peered at a single line of 12 point Times Roman. He had signed his name, Maxwell Armour under the line of type.

This is what he left behind: "To my friends: My work is done. Why wait?"

None of us could think of what work Maxwell referred to. Someone suggested the gallows itself—which *was* imposing—but that was too reductive to make sense.

I learned later that his words were not his own. They were the words of the famous founder of Eastman Kodak, George Eastman. Maxwell had stolen Eastman's last words, which plagiarism rendered them, I thought, more poignant.

We all of us went to the funeral, where, surprisingly, a large contingent of relatives awaited us. They sobbed in an inconsolable fashion, and a beautiful young woman in a gray business suit became hysterical. I learned that she was Maxwell's daughter by his first wife. Who would have guessed that Maxwell could inspire such powerful emotion? I talked to the beautiful daughter and shared my thoughts on the craftsmanship of her father's final project, but she was too agitated to take any comfort in my words, and, indeed, glared at me as though I had said something reprehensible.

❋ ❋ ❋

THE HOUSE was put up for sale, and we were all obliged to move out. I guess I wasn't aware, when I moved to the Paris Apartments, that most of the residents here are old folks, many of them retired. Thanks to this older demographic, the management schedules activities such as day trips to the restaurants in neighboring towns, bridge games, visits from a podiatrist, group exercise and lectures on nutrition. I don't attend any of these events. I am of the opinion that the less contact you have with your neighbors the better. I don't have time for their stories. I've got my own, after all.

My first novel, *Fat Lip*, was written when I lived in Fairfax, Virginia, and it was a minor success (by which I mean that it continued to generate royalties after the paltry advance paid out). My hero was a private detective named Hoyt who was allergic to lies. I was thirty-one when I sold that novel, and I've written eight more novels (sequels, because my agent says that most bestsellers are sequels although not all sequels are bestsellers), and a couple of dozen short stories. If you have read anything I've written you may have spent some time in a psych ward. That observation is based on the fan mail I receive, and I feel privileged to have such resilient readers.

Now, at forty-two, I live on the second floor in the central court of this two-story apartment complex. In order to reach my apartment door, I have to walk up the outdoor stairs and past my neighbor's door. In the long summer my neighbor, Vernon, will be sitting in a sturdy wrought-iron chair, one of two that preside over an infirm iron table, small and round, that someone has painted white with a brush (Vernon?). Vernon will sit there reading the newspaper, smoking a cigarette, and/or spooning something food-like into his mouth from the pot it was cooked in. He never deviates from his dress code, which consists of blue flip-flops and tiny cut-off jeans. His immense belly eclipses his vestigial shorts, and I can't be the only person who assumed on first encountering Vernon that I was in the presence of an extremely sweaty nudist practicing the tenets of his sun-worshipping religion.

Vernon's primary activity is surveillance. He studies the courtyard below, with its mimosa trees, its sidewalks, and its rectangles and circles of grass, which, despite the sprinkler system, have turned a mottled yellow and brown as the result of a record drought. He searches the courtyard for signs of life, generally people although I have seen him address a lone cat or dog with considerable animation. He is always talking, which is an edge he has if you are hoping to dart past him. When a resident or maintenance person or postal worker comes within range, Vernon can easily address that person (already having, as it were, a running start).

In the history of humankind, those members of the tribe who could not utter an interesting sentence developed other ways of stopping and holding their fellows. Vernon has all the inherited moves of this evolutionary byway. He can speak at great length without pausing to breathe. He can fix you with his eye, he can call upon your sympathies as a fellow human being, he can ask questions that require a response. If the recipient of his discourse attempts to flee, Vernon can raise his voice, instinctively gauging the exact number of decibels required to compensate for the increased distance, which suggests to the reluctant listener that flight is futile. And, of course, Vernon has the gift of obliviousness, the belief (shared by academics and members of 12-step groups) that his thoughts are inherently interesting.

I have come to terms with Vernon. I have learned to race by, to feign talking on a cell phone, or—if time is not an issue—to peer from between my mini-blind slats, waiting until he makes one of his brief but frequent retreats into his apartment.

I don't want to hurt his feelings. And I don't want to enrage him, to antagonize him in any way. I'm not sure what he is capable of, really.

Now where did that come from? I wasn't expecting that sentence. Maybe this free-writing stuff is like fooling with a Ouija board. Time to get back to the real story.

✱ ✱ ✱

THE RAIN stopped and the last watery light departed with the clouds and left a residue of stars. The car rolled on and Mark slept, not wholly lost to his physical self but maintaining a shadow sentry, a psychic construction similar to the created self he could summon under interrogation. He was aware of the driver, the girl and her longman as gray shapes on the other side of his dream. Well. Not *his* dream.

It was a bequeathed dream, one of his father's memories, filled with such love and rage that it left no room for private dreaming.

In the dream he was kissing her, his fingers lost in her black and bloody hair: this rough and terrible kiss, with its need to hurt, to invoke a scream.

But the dead are mute.

He lifted his head, blinking up into the cold light that came from the tunnel's painted walls, a varnish of glowing life, part of the outlawed orgtech that the rebels took for their own. He turned his gaze back to the pale face cradled in his hands and panicked. Her left cheekbone was oddly sunken, her bruised eye a red and angry slit beneath a purple lid, her other eye beautiful and terrible and abandoned. "*Mother*," he whispered, and in that word was also lover, wife, warrior, comrade.

A strong-fingered hand clutched his shoulder, and the longman's voice, eroded by the narcobugs that slept in pirates' lungs, croaked in his ear: "Easy. Don't spook! What generation are you anyway? Could be you've been copied one too many times."

Mark said nothing, feigning stupor.

"Let's stretch our legs," the longman said, stepping out of the car. Mark followed, prepared for an assault, perhaps even welcoming such, for he had been reduced to confusion and disquiet by the dream, and a fight's present tense would be bracing. How often in the course of his training had he been awakened by some physical confrontation? As the teachers were fond of saying, "Sleep deep and you may sleep forever."

The car had stopped in a pool of moonlight beyond which pine trees presented a monochromatic wall. The rain was elsewhere, only recently departed and leaving in its wake an echo of its passing, the patter of raindrops still ticking amid the trees.

The man called Solomon walked away from the car, down the side of the road in the direction they had come, not looking back, and Mark ran to catch up. They walked until the car was out of sight. The wind pressed at their backs, a cold ghost, its breath sour and importunate. Above them the pale moon floated like something that had recently drowned and owed its buoyancy to the gases of decomposition.

"You are leaving that girl in the car," Mark said. "Isn't that unwise? The LC could be nearby."

Solomon stopped. He turned and smiled his moon-sparkled smile. "They could be. Life's no picnic anymore, unless you live in a rich fief where all the cooterments of civilization make for a nice dream. On the road, it's dangerous, although the LC don't have the patience for an ambush. I'm not over-worried about Mary. If something comes along, she'll waken and deal with it. Don't underestimate that girl, boy. You'd be no match for her in a mix-up."

"Is that what you wished to say to me beyond her hearing?" Mark said.

"No. I wished to *show* you something." He was still holding the folded umbrella in his right hand and with a flourish revealed its role as a flashlight. The wide beam illuminated a tangled wall of dwarf oak and thorn-laden jacketbush.

"Here we go." The pirate took a long stride into the trees, and Mark followed. A path had been machine-burned, leaving a flat wall of vegetation on either side, truncated branches, everything split and blown away by brute force, and leaving an odor Mark knew— "blood-and-razors" his brothers whispered. His heart sped up on the insistence of some dead soldier's encounter with this same stink. An LC trail, but old enough to allow the surrounding woods some tentative regrouping, a toadstool here, a burst of yellow-green ferns leaning out and looking both ways, some small reckless purple flowers raggedly running across the path toward the safety of the other side.

Mark hesitated, and the longman, turned and said, "Let's not be coy. It's what you came for."

Mark shook his head. "No. I sought a ride to George Washington City. That is all."

"My friend, I don't wish to call you a liar, but the alternative is to call you a fool, and I don't think you are short on brains. We are all rolling along on the tracks our masters fashioned. Let's make the best of it. I suspect you were sent here to see this."

Mark thought this might very well be true. He could not see the whole design. No one could.

"All right," Mark said, "Show me what I am destined to see."

Solomon laughed. "That's the spirit!" He turned and set out again, Mark following.

* * *

SO LETHE'S Children are vicious little child-like creatures with a single day's worth of memory and very mutable swarm behavior. What the reader doesn't know is how closely Mark is related to these goblin-like children. These creatures were created to repair a damaged earth, to terraform it, and their common father is Andrew Cory. Mark Cory doesn't know that these creatures are kin.

And Mary Constant is my wife—or rather the ghost of my wife and this is not something the reader needs to know. It is something *I* need to remember.

Just thinking out loud. It has been a few days since I last wrote anything. What have I been up to? I don't know how it is with other writers, but writing often feels like the only time I have a self that can answer that question.

Growing up in Virginia, I had a friend, Artie Modine, whose father was considerably older than the parents of my other friends. Artie's dad always wore a suit—that's how I remember him, in any event—and was losing his mind in spectacular ways. "He got hit with Al's Hammer!" Artie would say and laugh. Artie and his dad weren't close. One time, Artie told me, he and his sister and his mom were waked in the middle of the night by a racket (glass breaking, metal screaming, a big hollow booming). *What the fuck?!* they all wondered (or maybe just Artie), and they followed the noise to the basement and there was Artie's dad, squatting in his underwear and watching the dryer spin. He'd stuffed it full of soda cans and bottles and coat hangers and trash and turned it on, and he was grinning like he'd won the lottery.

Not long after that, Artie's dad went into a nursing home.

Artie said that after his dad lost his mind, his dad was always punching buttons, flipping switches, working the remote on the TV without any plan. "Like he just wanted to make the electricity do something, anything." Artie had a theory about this: his dad had lost control and maybe thought he'd punched a wrong button somewhere, like when you accidentally change the television channel and can't get cable anymore so he was trying to push a button that would set everything right again.

That's sort of what writers do, isn't it? They try to restore order via narrative.

If you happen to say, "I try to restore order via narrative," in front of a bunch of people (say, during a book signing) you will immediately be identified as a pompous asshole. Just assume your book isn't great literature. It's going to be hard to avoid puffing up, and I suppose you could forgive yourself because you are, after all, only human—although, is that a good excuse? Hitler was only human. Charles Manson was only human. Every day humans are doing really awful things to other humans. So "only human": not a good excuse.

I've been thinking about this because my latest novel, *Heat Rash,* is now in stores, and BookPeople, a large independent bookstore that has always been welcoming (one of the staff even feigning knowledge of my series) arranged a signing. There were maybe twenty people in attendance; I recognized some of them from a writing group I sporadically attended.

I am proud to say that I did not talk in an exalted way about this humble comic crime novel. *Heat Rash* takes place in the midwest in the whacky world of little girl beauty contests. A tiny Madonna-pretender is murdered by an equally petite Lady Gaga imitator, or so it would seem. But the whole setup rubs my sleuth, Hoyt, the wrong way, and since he is already in the midwest (see: *Wasted in Waterloo*) why not take the money that the diminutive Lady Gaga's wealthy parents press upon him?

I read the part where Hoyt wonders about kid beauty contests and how such events might attract pedophiles, and he gets a brutal beating for thinking this out loud in a local bar. Hoyt gets beaten up at least once in every one of the books, and some insight always arises in the aftermath of a beating.

I signed six books, which isn't bad, although one of the books I signed wasn't written by me. I didn't have the heart to tell the woman that I wasn't Lawrence Block. I signed it "God Bless you, Larry Block."

I wound up getting cornered by an older gentleman who said he was writing a memoir and didn't read any fiction because life was short. *Not short enough*, I was thinking by the time I escaped the harangue.

Now that I had signed all the books—BookPeople buys a bunch, and if you sign them all they can't send them back—I wandered around the book store. I can't go into a book store without looking around—and buying a book. In these digital times, these ghost times, every lovely artifact, every physical book with its analog soul should have someone who will cherish it.

In the philosophy section I saw a book that had been dropped on the floor. I picked it up and recognized the title: *A Savage God*. The book was written by A. Alvarez, and I remembered reading it in college. Its subject was suicide (Sylvia Plath being a sort of template for that) and, as I recalled, it discussed suicide as a legitimate choice as opposed to most modern thinking in which depression, a result of unfortunate brain chemistry, is the engine that drives suicides.

Since I had found the book on the floor, I felt obliged to honor its in-my-path significance. I bought it. In college the paperback had probably cost me a couple of dollars at a used bookstore; the reprinted trade paperback cost $13.95 and, as was often the case, I suspected it would wind up on a shelf without being read again.

* * *

I DIDN'T feel like going back to my apartment, so I drove north on Lamar, then over to Guadalupe and The Drag. Every university town has something equivalent to The Drag, a four- or five-block ecosystem for young people of the college persuasion. I like the energy, all these kids heading somewhere with backpacks, iPods, tattoos, exclamatory hair, smartphones and bottles of purified water (including *smartwater*®, recommended, perhaps, by their smartphones).

I ogled the co-eds and may have been guilty of a thought crime since some of these kids were no doubt underage (although a skilled thought-policeman would surely be able to read the nature of my thoughts and see their essential innocence).

I was thinking about what a world with thought-police would be like when a cluster of homeless people caught my eye. The last of the day's light was being consumed by street lights and neon signs, but these folks were illuminated by the light from a sign advertising vinyl records (the latest thing: like big, two-sided cds). There were plenty of cars on The Drag so I was moving at about five miles an hour, and I had ample time to ascertain that my mind wasn't taking some vague likeness and photoshopping it into someone I knew.

A skinny guy with a guitar hanging from his neck by a rope was leaning forward, eyes squinted to improve his concentration, a sort of fierce hunger manifest in every angular bone of his weedy body. Two ragged teenagers, a girl and a guy (both with exploding hair, geysers of hair) were sitting on the concrete with their legs pulled up, chins resting on their knees, backs against a wall covered with faded posters advertising defunct bands. Their mouths gaped open as though they had just witnessed a spectacular fireworks display.

I saw an ancient man whom I had seen all around Austin (sleeping on a bus stop bench, moving with a steady gait across some armageddon of a construction site, shouting with his head thrown back under a sky the color of a dead catfish), a man with a long brown beard and a wrinkled overcoat and the high seriousness of a prophet born at a time too narrow and petty to contain his truth. He too was entranced, his eyes wider than I'd ever seen them.

What was it that held their attention? What mesmerizing event was this? Who was so riveting?

Vernon.

Yes. My neighbor Vernon was speaking to them. He wasn't wearing his stay-at-home outfit. He wore khaki overalls and a long-sleeve gray garment that might have been the top half of winter long johns. It was ninety-five degrees, starting to cool down, but he was still over-dressed. Aside from his disorienting attire, he was the Vernon I knew. He stood still, his arms at his sides, somehow robbed of all vitality, while his mouth shaped words and loosed them into... well apparently into the enraptured minds of his indigent audience. When I listened to Vernon, did I have some equally entranced expression? It seemed unlikely.

I drove home thinking, "What the hell?"

* * *

MARK CONSULTED the semi-Q that vibrated in his temple and learned that he had traveled for fifty-two minutes, an unpleasant trek whose destination remained obscure. He had no reason to trust this pirate, but if Solomon intended any harm, it would be a waste of time. Mark knew he was worth very little in terms of information, a link in an encoded chain, and his death, even his dissection, would instruct no one.

In any event, he didn't think the pirate was scheming against him. He wasn't sure what—

In front of him, Solomon suddenly crouched. Without looking over his shoulder, Solomon patted the ground next to him, and Mark came forward and they both looked down at the valley below.

The crowd within Mark noisily urged flight, but he quelled their voices with a warning. "I can be rid of you for good," he thought, and the voices settled into a fluttering of moth wings. He added, "And you're no help if you hide."

Every nest differed, because Lethe's Children were not inclined to do the same thing twice. They were busy as bees but not as consistent. And not much smarter, according to some of the scientists who studied them. What the LC was was *flexible*.

They had swarmed this old NewMeriCo fortress, and they'd left some of the company's biggest weapons intact because Lethe's Children just didn't seem to care about these killing machines. They had no fear. Although they screamed when hurt, they didn't avoid pain. *Good soldiers!* Mark thought. Mindless idiots: good soldiers.

These soldiers looked like children—from a distance. Up close, they looked creepy and terrifying. Unless you were observing a dead one or one strapped on a board—and alone they didn't last long—you wouldn't know just exactly what they looked like because they were very, very fast. The way their alien-attributes entered your consciousness was subtle: a moan that rose to a scream. Better to see a monster at once, a full-blown horror, than have it enter your mind as a guest, something familiar, and transform into a goblin.

War Solutions, Inc., one of the bigger weapons manu-facturers, created drones that could track them despite their speed. There were a hundred ways to kill the LC. They were, in truth, flimsy creatures. But they existed in vast multitudes and the killing machines grew mired in pale goblin bodies and then the LC decided to shift behavioral gears and bring some new horror forward. And most of the human world, barred from the fortresses, the shielded cities of the elite, crouched in small villages preparing for an attack, practicing with their weapons, while Lethe's Children were playing elsewhere. Later, on a whim, the LC would come and kill the big, irrelevantly brave humans.

Mark watched Lethe's Children closely, hardly breathing, looking for some pattern, some weakness, as though they had not already been under the world's scrutiny for years. Mark had never seen them firsthand; all his memories were hand-me-downs, and, beneath his revulsion and fear, there was still some satisfaction to be had in acquiring a memory born of his own experience. He just needed to live to keep it.

Lethe's Children scrambled up and down the altered shell of NewMeriCo. Scientists had discovered that each creature had between three and ten instructions that governed its behavior. As with the social insects, fairly sophisticated swarm behavior could be created with a set of limited protocols. What was unsettling was the constant reprogramming that occurred, apparently somewhere deep in the hive, as though some greater intelligence existed and could make administrative decisions. No such central intelligence existed in an ant colony, and ants were already the most successful insects on the planet. What if the LC were something more?

They move so fast! Mark thought. They were excavating a hill next to the fortress, running as though some project deadline were rapidly approaching. When they encountered each other they would kiss or slap each other, the slapping behavior being elaborate like a vid his teachers showed him of long-ago humor for long-ago television...*slapstick* someone said...yes, the stooges, three of them: Curly and Mo and another one.

A hand clutched Mark's wrist, and he almost screamed. It was Solomon, and the pirate handed him digi-wraps, which Mark slipped over his eyes to look where the pirate directed.

There was some beast, a black, bulky thing—a gorilla? No there were no gorillas here, this was a shambling, shabby thing a—yes!—a bear. Not a grizzly, a smaller bear, but bigger than Mark.

Lethe's Children were tormenting the bear, prodding it with sticks, throwing stones at it, rushing in to bite a leg, a buttock, genitals. Another LC, smaller than the general lot, jumped on the animal's shaggy back and bit it on the shoulder. The bear was not defenseless, and with a roar it flung the creature off and swiped at it with a massive paw. Something rolled beyond the frenzied circle, and Mark turned to let the digi-wraps call it into focus. It was a head, still animate, mouth open and making an ululation which rendered the brothers within Mark crazy and incoherent.

Now the LC were on the bear, and the animal collapsed under their numbers and grunted and coughed and something dark—blood—seeped out beneath the awful writhing of these small, idiot monsters.

Mark thought he might be sick despite his high marks in self-mastery. A hand fell on his shoulder and he heard the pirate's voice: "I think they wanted our eyes on the show," he said. "And it's too late now."

Mark turned, pushing the digi-wraps aside, and beheld the grinning faces, and noted a detail no one residing in his mind seemed to have logged: the creatures had three thin tongues that slipped like a black tide between their blood-red teeth.

* * *

STRANGE TIMES. I'll cut to the chase here. Yesterday, I came out of my neighborhood grocery store at about one in the morning. I like to do my shopping when most citizens are sleeping. There is a downside to that, but there's a downside to almost everything. In the case of late-night grocery shopping, the problem is this: now that the crowds have thinned out, the shelf-stocking begins in earnest. There are boxes and giant pallets all over the place. You can't push a cart down most of the aisles, and you are forced to dart in and out of narrow spaces like some marginal scavenger in the end times. In this predawn state, when few humans are around to enrich the ambience, the lights cast a gray-green pall that wouldn't be out of place in the world's worst zombie crack house, and the electricity is more apt to snap at your hands (despite the cart's rope-like wire that skids along the store's floor to prevent just this from happening). If you decide to tell your cashier (average age: 14) that you are getting electric shocks, he will look at you with new wariness and say "Whoa," or something equally unhelpful.

So I came out of the store and watched a nightjar swoop after bugs drawn by the parking lot's many lamps. This was not a bat, it was a nightjar. You might think that I don't know what I'm talking about, but in this instance, I do. Consider that a preemptive strike against your incredulity.

I unlocked my car with my remote. I was six feet from my car when, out of the shadows, a large shapeless person appeared. His silhouette and lurching gait suggested a man who was sleeping outdoors, and when he came under the street light I recognized him. He was the ancient bearded prophet who I'd seen listening to Vernon on The Drag.

"Hey," I said. He had the reek of someone marinated in cheap wine and boiled under a bad year's vicious sun. He was shabby and sick and wore unsnapped rubber boots that wouldn't be seeing any rain any time soon. He wore one glove, and that gloved-hand clutched half a scissors, which glittered ominously as though recently sharpened.

"What do you want?" I asked.

He frowned, possibly interpreting this question as a trick. He said, "Don't want nothing. Don't fear nothing. Don't—"

He staggered forward and tripped, his clumsiness resulting in a swift lunge that neither of us had been expecting. I dropped the plastic bag—a jar of pickles burst, releasing a sweet and sour smell—and I staggered back, banging against my car. My attacker lay on the ground, muttering. I opened the car door, ducked my head, and turned in the driver's seat. I slammed the door and drove away.

When I got back to the Paris Apartments parking lot, I noticed that I still had the half-scissors. My stomach had claimed it, and it was sticking out of my t-shirt. My heart sped up when I realized the blade was firmly embedded in my stomach. Beyond a certain muted discomfort, I felt okay, but I knew that didn't signify anything. Maybe I was in shock. I was pretty sure it should hurt *a lot.* I parked my car, and thought, "I should probably drive to the ER," but I didn't. Moving carefully, I slowly marched up the stairs to my apartment. Vernon was not in sight, and since he would engage me in some inane conversation even if I told him I had just been stabbed, I was glad he wasn't around. He was a night owl, too, and so it was just luck that I dodged him.

The reek of pickles entered my apartment with me, and I realized that the cuff of my right pants' leg was soaked in pickle juice. I sat on my sofa and studied the scissors. Should I call an ambulance? Probably I should, but— I gripped the scissors' handle and slowly pulled the blade out. It came out as clean as it had gone in. No blood? I was expecting a great dark patch to bloom on my shirt, a malignant Rorschach test whose interpretation was easy. But nothing happened, and when I lifted my shirt up, my stomach, though larger than I would have wished it to be, was unsullied by any wound.

I don't know how someone else would have dealt with this anomaly, but I was exhausted. I lay down on the sofa and immediately fell asleep.

✱ ✱ ✱

ALL MY life, I've felt that some reckoning awaits me. For the longest time, I assumed that everyone felt that way, but they don't. Say the phrase "existential dread" to most folks and they'll draw a blank. Some folks will say, "I studied that in college. Camus, Sartre, those guys, right?"

I was always a morbid kid, I guess, although I only know that in retrospect. I can remember when I was maybe seven or eight, me and Artie and Susan Randall and her kid brother Pie and a gawky kid named Hoot who lived in a haunted house, we found a dead cat by the side of the road. I told everyone that we could all be like that in less time than it took to spit, just as dead, because we were made of the same stuff! I told them I'd seen a television show about the human body, and it wasn't good news, we were built out of jelly-stuff and baloney-like valves that opened and closed but couldn't do that forever and a heart that beat like a moth against a screen door and germs that swam in all the juices inside us and a brain that looked like a lot of grubs stuck together or maybe one of those popcorn balls people make at Christmas and everything depended on everything else, which was supposed to be wonderful according to the television scientist but wasn't when you thought of all the things that could go wrong, and if you took your eyeball out and put it on the curb in the sun, it would dry up right away like a grape on a hot skillet because: *we were just like that dead cat.*

Susan Randall hit me with her lunch pail, and I still have a tiny pale scar on my chin. I went to her funeral in high school; she'd jumped off the Skyway Bridge that stretches across Tampa Bay. She was on vacation with her folks, and they found a note. Her boyfriend had dumped her for a girl named Lily Fields who was cute in a way that I knew was going to go bad and it did. I saw Lily at a ten-year high school reunion and she was already looking puffy and clownish against her will. Her boyfriend wasn't there, but they had both shown up for Susan's funeral, clutching each other in an erotic fit of bereavement.

In college, I was friends with Leslie Heckenberg—and we were just friends, no sexual entanglement. She was pretty, but I wasn't attracted to her for whatever reason (pheromone mismatch maybe). She was the funniest, smartest person I knew.

She could talk for hours about life's various hideous aspects. She had some hilarious rants. There were other days, however, when irony deserted her and in a harrowing monotone she would talk about the utter failure of her existence. She began going into hospitals for depression. She got some electro-shock treatments and cheered up for a while but then plummeted into some dark hallucinatory hell and took a lot of pills and left a message on her landlady's answering machine—it was a Friday and the landlady wouldn't be back until Monday—saying: "By the time you get this I will be dead." And she was.

A friend of mine said, "Well, she's been talking about killing herself for years, so maybe congratulations are in order. She followed through. You've got to admire that." And he added: "I'm sure you helped her along; you've always been sort of...I don't know...pro-death?"

* * *

OF COURSE I thought about killing myself. To some extent, it was peer pressure—one time I made a list of friends and acquaintances who had offed themselves, and it came to fourteen names—but I also fancied myself an intellectual, so I had to reflect on Camus's famous utterance: "There is but one truly serious philosophical problem, and that is suicide. Judging whether life is or is not worth living amounts to answering the fundamental question of philosophy."

My father and older brother were hunters, and on my sixteenth birthday I was given a shotgun. I had decided, years earlier, that I was never going to shoot at anything that couldn't shoot back, so my father and brother continued to hunt without me, but I did, on occasion, go off into the wilderness with my weapon and contemplate blowing my brains out. However, I had never liked Hamlet's overwrought vacillating, and when I saw the same behavior in myself, I stopped entertaining thoughts of self-destruction. I figured I'd know if I were ready to end it all. Hamlet never figured it out. He was killed when Laertes stabbed him with a poisoned sword, and consequently never had to answer Camus's ultimate question: why proceed?

I dreamed that Vernon was in my apartment last night. I woke to the sound of a match being struck. I was instantly alert and upright, peering into the dark to where a cigarette's red ember hovered.

"Who's there?" I said.

"Oh, good, you're up," a voice said, someone sitting in the big, multi-colored armchair I'd gotten for free when a couple I knew grew rich and needed more sedate decor. The lamp on the end table clicked on, and I saw Vernon. He was wearing a suit, which may have been his usual visiting attire for all I knew. He held a small black derby, balanced on his knee, while he held his cigarette with his other hand.

"No smoking in here," I said, the sort of thing anyone might say in a dream when more pressing issues are at hand.

"Nothing to worry about. I have disabled the smoke alarm." He gestured toward the ceiling, and, sure enough, the smoke alarm was dangling there, clearly deprived of its 9-volt battery.

Vernon leaned forward and said, "I want to apologize for Truthman's behavior."

"Who?"

"Truthman." Vernon chuckled. "He says an angel on fire gave him that name, and it burned away his memories of his parents and whatever name they might have pinned on him."

"Well he stabbed me with a scissors," I said.

"I did not encourage that at all."

I remembered. "I saw you talking to him. You put him up to that, didn't you?"

"I did not. I was just discussing the nature of free will with Truthman and some of his cohorts. He is not a sophisticated man, and he came to the conclusion that he should kill you."

"What for?" I asked.

"To prevent your doing more harm in the world."

I was starting to get angry.

"Who are you? This isn't the Vernon I know. That Vernon is...well...a boring idiot...a monologist...a nuisance...but I can't imagine him breaking into my apartment in the middle of the night."

Vernon nodded. "Yes. That Vernon utters 'polite, meaningless words' as the poet Yeats would say. I have been in a disguise, and you have told me much about yourself."

I knew I had told him nothing.

He read my expression and answered it. "But you have. It is what Yeats said, again, 'Too long a sacrifice can make a stone of the heart.'"

"What sacrifice are you referring to?"

Vernon sighed, put his cigarette out by scrubbing it against the bottom of his shiny black shoe, and stood up. "Your compassion. We've had this conversation many times before, but you don't remember. You were hell bent on not listening. You used to be what we call a karmic facilitator, for want of a better name in this sad fleeting world, but you are retired now. I should have retired years ago, myself.

"We are night people, you and I. We are more comfortable in the dark, and the dark has entered our blood. The indelible dark. Ring a bell? It should, you're the one who coined the phrase. Well, you are my last case, and I can't say a lot, so you'll have to listen as hard as you can. You are not responsible for the people you killed, but you killed them all the same."

"How come I don't remember this entire secret karma-agent thing?" I asked.

Vernon shrugged. "When you retire, you get a choice. You can remember, or not."

"And I, of course, chose to forget."

"Well, most people do. It's what I'm choosing. And, any-way, on some level, you didn't forget, did you?" Vernon looked around the room as though he might be forgetting something.

He said, "You might decide that you need to leave this world, that your staying in it endangers others. There is a young woman you spoke to several months ago at her father's funeral. Earlier tonight she was lying in her bathtub. The water was warm, and she held a razor in her right hand and she knew that the surest cut was lengthwise and she had been drinking, wine, quite a lot, and she was confident she could do this thing that would separate her from her pain, but, reach-ing out for the wine glass, she knocked it to the floor, and it shattered, and she got out of the tub and cleaned the mess up—fastidious woman—and the water went tepid and the impulse toward oblivion was lost. She went to bed, wrapping herself in blankets, crying until the alcohol pulled her into sleep. Tomorrow is another day, and she can kill herself then."

Vernon paused, but it was clear he had more to say. How could this be the same man who had never, as far as I knew, uttered a single word worth marking? I was breathless now, waiting for him to speak.

"You may discover—I suspect you already have... Did Truthman's scissors make you bleed? No. I thought so. You have been given a kind of protection for your service. But there are ways for you to forsake this life, and though I can't direct you, I can urge you to reflect. Think of that young lady, your late-landlord's daughter... Our world has a fondness for the circular. That is karma, after all. Meditate on karma, my friend. The dark gets on us, and it's indelible and we pass it along. You carry the suicide virus in your heart, and any chance encounter can infect others."

He lifted his hat, positioned it over his head with both hands, then tapped it smartly with the fingers of his right hand and disappeared (confirming his dream status should I have had doubts in the morning).

* * *

I CAN'T meditate. I can't think. I've been walking around the room in an agitated state. A minute ago I spied a copy of *The Savage God* on a bookshelf next to *The Bell Jar*. This is the old, battered copy of *Savage* that I purchased long ago. I guess I wasted $13.95 on the new copy I bought on impulse. Maybe BookPeople will give me my money back.

I was thumbing through this old copy, and I came upon something Mary (not the child of my sf novel, which is, I think, going to be a short story, not a novel) no, Mary my wife, something she wrote, something Mary whose eyes were silver-blue, whose hair was red, who thought she might save me but knew nothing of the indelible dark wrote in one of her goofy editorial moments. She had a fondness for these brief annotations. I don't remember seeing this one before.

This is what she wrote in *The Savage God*: "Oh Joel! Coals to Newcastle, I guess! Love forever, Mary."

What can a writer do? Well, I can finish this damned story. Although other things are more pressing now.

Here's a synopsis to make quick work of it:

* * *

MARY ARRIVES to save Mark and Solomon from Lethe's Children. They do not attack Mary. She is a god to them. They lead her to a vast computer, the ancient machine that alters the child-goblins' primitive instructions.

Being a god in a science fiction story is often bad news, and since this story is more Edgar Rice Burroughs than Kim Stanley Robinson, Mary is in grave danger. She is the new genetic material that the monstrous machine requires to write new diversity into its hapless children. Mary has already suspected this, and she is willing to make the sacrifice in the interests of a better world, but—

* * *

IN THE shadows of the underworld, Mark watched the door slide open and Mary, accompanied by half a dozen of the LC entered. The door began to slide closed again, and Mark realized that it was a vast steel wall that *revolved*. This was no simple door that might be broken by brute force; this was a slow-turning wheel that might roll round again in a hundred, a thousand years.

* * *

AGAINST ALL odds, promising vengeance if Mary's salvation proves a lost cause, Mark and Solomon battle their way over the wall and through jungles and treacherous cities. Solomon is wounded several times, and a cybersyncOrgbot whom Mark has befriended keeps creating artificial bits for Solomon, bits that will come in handy later.

Maybe it would end like this:

* * *

MARK WASN'T too late. He hadn't raged at her and stalked off and stayed at a friend's house and returned late the next night, still drunk, to find her dead, the bath water red, her face like porcelain, her lips the faintest blue.

* * *

OH MARY. I should have been your champion. And I failed you when I thought I was only failing myself.

I think I know what Vernon was getting at. I think I know how to remove the curse that lies on that young woman's heart. I'm going to drive out to Oak Hill, fingers crossed, my equivalent of a prayer. I still have my key to the house. I think Maxwell's masterpiece will still be there. Wouldn't anyone hesitate to destroy something built with such rigor, such care?

This time I will use the banister, running my hand along its smooth, lovingly-sanded surface—and though I walk through the valley of the shadow of death, I shall fear nothing: for there are no shadows in the dark, and the daylight ghosts won't follow me there.

The Dappled Thing

W HEN *HER GLORY of Empire* rolled out of the jungle and stopped at the edge of the black river, two dozen green and yellow parrots exploded from the trees. Sir Bertram Rudge, unsealing the topside hatch, emerged in time to see the birds blow across the river like gaudy silks, but the sight stirred no aesthetic shivers within his stout frame. He and his team were heading into the wild heart of the jungle, and he had no time for beauty's wiles. This savage land had swallowed Wallister's party, which included Lord Addison's granddaughter, Lavinia, a girl of twelve when Rudge had last seen her and now, by all accounts, a willful and beautiful young woman who had shocked high society and sundered a dozen foppish hearts when she left London to cross the Atlantic on the *Cloud King*, a chartered zeppelin, in the company of Henry Wallister, famous explorer, member of the Royal Geographical Society, and, according to Lord Addison, a thorough scoundrel.

"Lavinia's a good girl," Lord Addison had declared. "Spirited, not utterly without brains, but a fool for a rogue like Wallister." His Lordship, face red, eyes maddened by the hearth's fire, fixed Rudge with a wild stare. "Bring her back to me, Bertie. By force, if you must."

* * *

WITH THE opening of the hatch, a railing of gleaming steel pipes rose up from the silvery surface of the great sphere and snapped into place with a hydraulic exhalation. Rudge gripped the railing and leaned out to study the river below. Here was a test he didn't relish.

"Hot down there!"

Rudge turned at the voice and saw that Tommy Strand, the expedition's naturalist, had come up from below and was wiping his face with a cloth. A hank of his blonde hair fell forward and, in profile, he looked like an addled cockatoo. The day was dying, and a large bird swooped low over the river. This inspired Strand, who spread his arms wide, something a cockatoo might do in preparation for flight, but this flight, alas, was merely verbal. He recited:

"I wandered lonely as a clown
Whose heart of red is filled with rue,
When all at once I saw an owl,
A bird of nighttime, nocturnal,
Up in the sky and all a-hooting,
A lovely balm for my heart's soothing."

Why, Rudge wondered, were supposedly educated young men so often inclined to declaim in meter? Rudge recognized the quoted poet, the insufferable Wadsworth, one of the fashionable Lake Poets (although where, one might ask, were the corresponding numbers of River Poets, Pond Poets, Bog Poets?).

Strand continued to bellow out Wadsworth, and Rudge unfurled the rope ladder he'd brought from below, secured it to two of the steel posts, tested his knots with a yank, and methodically descended the ladder. He was huffing a bit by the time his boots met the mud, but still—and the thought pleased him—steady on his legs, hale and hearty (by God!) in a world where so many of his old comrades were content to drowse in armchairs, poor old sweats muttering about some bloody wog, some worthless *apke wasti*.

On the ground, where a fishy smell contended with the green odor of rotting vegetation, Rudge walked to the very edge of the water and looked down. He saw no piranhas, no fer-de-lance, no giant anaconda, no cunning crocodile. The only animate life he observed was the vile cloud of black flies and mosquitoes that rose up from the mud to greet him. He tried to ignore them, as he had done in a younger life in another jungle, but the years of his retirement had drained some of his stoicism. He swatted and cursed the mindless buggers, then turned to regard the rescue vehicle.

Her Glory of Empire was a vast silver sphere, easily big enough to contain several row houses, and it burned in the twilight, pink and gold, with an authority that reduced the surrounding elements (the clutter of greenery, the outlandish verdancy of the jungle) to a shadowy backdrop. The machine was presently feeding, a strange business that Rudge found endlessly fascinating. Great mechanical tentacles, armored like the carapace of a millipede, stretched to the tree tops, clutched branches, and broke them with its segmented strength or severed them with small spinning blades. The thin, tapered end of a tentacle would wrap itself around a leafy bundle and carry it to an open hatch that glowed with ruddy light. The furnace within could devour any sort of vegetation by subjecting the green and unpromising material to a series of processing containers—rather like the multiple stomachs of a cow—before turning the altered material into a blazing motive force.

Her Glory of Empire was the fevered brainchild of the eccentric and fabulously wealthy Hugh Edmonds, whom

Rudge had met only once, briefly, when Lord Addison had driven Rudge to Edmonds's estate. There they had found the estate's master in avid conversation with one of his gardeners.

Since Edmonds was a notorious recluse, Rudge's friends would ask what the man was like, and, in the privacy of his club, Rudge would respond by saying that the man was well-spoken, erudite, somewhat small and frail with an unusually large penis, a description that gave some people pause. One had to understand that Hugh Edmonds was a devout Christian who believed that hiding one's nakedness was "giving in to the serpent." He never wore clothes while at home.

Edmonds was a self-taught scientist, a not uncommon condition among English madmen of independent means, and had been the architect of this immense traveling rotundity, discovering new principles for the science that informed it, and offering detailed instructions for its manufacture.

The machine had not been designed expressly to rescue Lord Addison's granddaughter, but providence had nicely timed its completion to correspond with that task, and this was its maiden voyage.

Rudge watched as the furnace hatch closed. The several tentacles retreated into the body of the sphere, and iris-like portals closed behind them. Rudge turned his back on the vehicle and regarded the sunset. *I'm too old for this*, he thought.

* * *

WHEN RUDGE climbed back down into the bowels of the vehicle, he found Mallory already strapped into the pilot's chair, checking the various gauges and wrestling his arms into the appendage lacings. A red-faced, whiskered man, Mallory was always slightly damp and became quickly soaked with perspiration when exerting himself. He wore—and apparently slept in—a dirty linen outfit that looked to be of some unknown military lineage, with mud-spattered puttees wrapping his calves and even his forearms, as though he had planned to mummify himself but had been distracted by other, more pressing matters.

It was hot in the enclosed space, and only two of the duct fans were running. Rudge could hear the furnace rumble and the hiss of pipes as valves obeyed the engineer's commands.

This circular floor space, with its bolted chairs and equipment, comfortably accommodated its five travelers. Had the expedition contained twice that number, it would have been crowded indeed. Returning with Wallister's group might prove difficult, Rudge thought—if, of course, Wallister and his party were still alive. Rudge was not a pessimist, but he'd lived long enough to know that hope had to be kept on a short leash.

Six weeks ago a column of smoke had drawn the attention of the denizens of a nearby mission, and after a day's trek into the forest, the mission's priest and his companions had come upon a clearing and the fire-ravaged remains of a zeppelin. Since the skeletal frame was still intact, the priest concluded that the conflagration was not the result of a crash. No charred corpses were discovered amid the airship's remains. Various scorched artifacts revealed its identity as that of the luxury cruiser *Cloud King*. All of the passengers were missing, their whereabouts a source of much conjecture. Perhaps Wallister's group had found refuge with one of the tribes to the north of the Negro, although the priest thought it more likely they had been captured or killed by hostile, deep-forest denizens he referred to as the Yami. "Crazy peoples," the priest had said. "Eat you up. Of your head, they make a jar."

Rudge had heard stories of the Yami or a similar tribe inhabiting the same region. These natives of the deep rain forest filed their teeth to points, fought constantly with neighboring tribes and with members of their own tribe, and taught their children violence—a young boy who beat his sister was praised. They ate the dead.

* * *

"**ALL RIGHT**, then," Mallory said, his voice returning Rudge to the moment. "Here we go."

The machine began to rumble and shiver as Rudge took his seat and strapped himself in. From his position behind the engineer, Rudge could see the panel of instruments and the glass portal that offered a view of weeds and mud and the river beyond.

The outer shell, the hull, began to move and the rat-scrambling sound of the steel brushes that generated a weak Faraday Effect as they spun between the inner and outer shells set Rudge's teeth on edge. Now the view portal flickered, no longer a direct view of the landscape beyond but an ever-changing image retrieved by mirrors from ports that opened and closed as the behemoth rolled forward.

The floor swayed some, like the deck of a ship in open sea, but it was marvelously steady considering that portions—and sometimes the entirety—of the outer hull was moving, a gleaming, rolling monstrosity that thundered down the muddy bank and into the rushing black water. Directly, water spit and hissed from the two open fan ducts, and Jon Bans, the fifth member of the crew, slapped the portals closed with a curse, his tall, seaman's frame contorted over the walking cage that allowed him to move easily across the floor. Rudge felt his lungs contract in the visceral certainty that the meager bubble of air that now sustained them beneath the river would be breached by black torrents.

The weak radiance created by the Faraday Effect made blocky shadows of the men within. The view portal was useless now, and they would have to depend on the compass and the questing touch of mechanical tentacles to guide them to the other side.

"I'm sending some air tubes up," Mallory said. He pulled several levers and a hollow clattering announced the rise of the tubes. He studied the dials, then nodded. "That should do her." He turned his head and shouted to Jon Bans. "Open four, five and six above and the furnace feeds."

The fans spit briefly and then the cool air above the river blew through the cabin, and Rudge felt the tightness go out of his chest.

Now they moved without the rolling hull, dragged forward by grapples and propelled by bundles of uneven, jointed pipes that sprouted from the base of the vehicle to produce a slow, lumbering motion, a falling forward, then catching, then falling again that translated to the ship's floor as a lazy, rocking-horse gallop.

In the blackness, time congealed. Rudge became convinced that they were making no progress at all, that they were stuck in mud, rocking back and forth, like some poor idiot who has lost his way in the night and seeks to console himself by hugging his knees and aping a pendulum or the clapper in a bell.

Something exploded, echoing in his skull. Booming, scratching, rending sounds sent Rudge's heart racing as he imagined some monstrous water beast attempting to rip open this hard-shelled egg and lap up the life within.

"It's all right!" Mallory shouted. "It's a submerged tree."

Stolid Mallory, sweat beading on his forehead, moved his arms as though fondling a ghost, and external tentacles obeyed his pantomime. The vessel clambered against the current, and the sunken branches grasped for them with a scorned lover's desperation. Rudge tried to picture it: a drowned tree wrestling with a mechanical squid whose belly was full of people (soft flesh over breakable bones) and all in black murk, an invisible battle raging, meaningless and unimaginable to some beast or savage gazing at the river's roiling surface.

So Sir Bertram Rudge contemplated the unutterable strangeness of his situation, and this acknowledgment of his insignificance and vulnerability calmed him, as it always did at such times.

✳ ✳ ✳

THEY LUNGED and grappled, fought to escape, were hopelessly mired, and then, in an instant, as though the struggle had been a game, a tug-of-war with a giant who had abruptly lost interest and abandoned his end of the rope, they were free and rising into shallower water, and aground again.

There was little light in the sky by then, but they traveled on, not wishing to camp too close to the river. That night, all but Mallory pitched their tents outside the vehicle and slept swaddled in mosquito netting, weapons by their sides. They might have been safer within *Her Glory of Empire*'s armored orb, where no wild beasts could find them, but, for the moment, their hearts were done with dank, enclosed enterprises, and they preferred to take their chances on the ground.

Snug in his tent, Rudge reached out to douse the kerosene lamp and a small round object bounced twice as though dropped from the ceiling. Rudge jerked his hand back, wary of spiders and other stinging, biting vermin. Leaning forward, he saw a tiny pale frog. He moved his hand slowly over it—with no thought except to test his reflexes—and snatched it. He slowly uncurled his fingers and looked at the pop-eyed creature. It was walnut-sized, its skin transparent so that you could see the organs within. Turning the creature toward the light, Rudge could see its tiny beating heart, the twist of its intestines (like a water-drowned worm), and its fragile green bones. Rudge leaned forward, stretched his arm out and under the tent flap, and opened his hand. The creature leapt away, and Rudge pulled his empty hand back inside the tent and lay down again. *You are far from green England's cozy hearth*, he thought.

* * *

IT WAS the dry season, a relative term, and Rudge cursed a so-called *dry* season that could grow mold on a man's skin and generated a pale mist in which monsters seemed to lurk.

Their progress through this world was loud and violent. *Her Glory of Empire* was not designed for stealth. It moved by thrashing and sawing its way through the jungle, pulling trees down or climbing them like an ungainly spider until they bent beneath its weight. Sometimes monkeys would scream from the trees, following the vehicle for days, hooting with outrage or, perhaps, a kind of carnival glee, delighting in destruction, as Rudge had seen men do in the frenzy of war.

He was fascinated with *Her Glory of Empire*, but there was something about the machine that he distrusted. It was, Rudge thought, against Nature, by which he did not mean that it was some kind of Devil's work, but that, being fashioned by immutable physical laws, and, consequently, itself a creature of Nature, its destruction of the natural world seemed a perversity, a subverting of those laws God had stamped on His Creation. Rudge could not have explained this to anyone, and if, somehow, he *had* managed to voice his reservations, no one would have taken him seriously. They would have been amused, would have seen him as some foolish old codger at odds with inevitable change.

Well, he was old and set in his ways. Maybe that was all there was to it.

On the eleventh day of travel beyond the site of the burned zeppelin, they had a bit of good luck. They came upon a small village of round huts, a village they might have passed if the cacophony of their passage hadn't attracted the natives, who were friendly and showed some acquaintance with civilization, even to the point of wearing clothing and emulating Jesus by pushing thorns into the palms of their hands. Rudge's manservant, Jacobs, had a gift with languages, or, more precisely, communication itself. A small, swarthy man, Jacobs possessed a gray explosive mustache that suggested belligerence, but he was, in fact, as calm as a cat, and capable of getting the meaning from any human being with vocal chords.

After talking at length to the village elder, Jacobs was able to relate the good news. Wallister's party had passed this way heading north. "He says he warned them about the Yami, but they seemed unperturbed on that score," Jacobs said. He added, "The old fella says he thought they might have been earth or water spirits because they didn't know things that even a child knows."

Rudge asked what that would be.

"He said they didn't know that they could die."

* * *

THE NEXT day, they ate lunch in a small clearing with a bright stream running through it. The stream was bordered by thin pale-green trees and lush black-green ferns. When Rudge went off to relieve his bladder by the edge of the forest, tiny blue butterflies fluttered around the stream of his urine and settled on the wet grass as though he were spilling a rare elixir. When he returned, Rudge found Tommy Strand sitting by the brook. Strand started declaiming immediately, as though Rudge's presence required it. It was another poem:

"Glory be to God for dappled things,
For skies of couple-color as a brinded cow,
For rose-moles all in stipple upon trout that swim;
Fresh-firecoal chestnut-falls, finches' wings;
Landscape plotted and pieced, fold, fallow and plough..."

It went on like that for a while. Rudge thought the verse was apt enough: a jungle was definitely dappled, light tumbling through the leaves, water, always moving, the light within it alive, mottled and animate. But it was a stretch to compare the sky to a cow. Poets often did that: started out well enough but then let go of the reins, let language get the best of them in their zeal.

Strand said the poem was by a fellow named Manly Hopkins. Rudge didn't think of poets as being all that manly, except for that Kipling fellow who had some grit in his lines and knew how to tell a story.

* * *

ANOTHER NINE days of travel were consumed in slow progress northward. The jungle was crisscrossed with a hundred nameless tributaries, none deep enough to require harrowing underwater descents but the sum of them creating a daunting maze that made *Her Glory of Empire*'s steady compass-guided route seem arbitrary and futile. Morale was suffering, and the spongy, sodden ground—dry season, indeed!—required that Rudge and his men spend their nights within the vehicle. In this forced, uncomfortable proximity, it was no surprise that Jon Bans and Tommy Strand got in a scuffle, nor was it any surprise that the older, hard-muscled sailor won. The manifestations of Strand's defeat were minor (a bloody nose, a black eye, a swollen lip) but Rudge couldn't let the fight pass unremarked. He tried to sort out the altercation's cause.

Apparently Strand had objected to the way Bans had referred to a woman, calling her, among other things, a "doxy." Bans, in his defense, said that the woman he was referring to was his own wife. He loved his wife but felt that he was better acquainted with her than some young dandy stuffed full of fairy dust whose sole knowledge of women came from reading love poetry (which, everyone knew, was designed to seduce women not to portray them accurately) and who had no business, in any event, instructing a man on the proper way to describe his own wife.

When the two cooled off, Rudge sat them down and addressed them solemnly. "I will not tolerate fighting," he said. "We are on a rescue mission, and personal differences must be put aside." He added, wistfully, "There was a time when I could have had the both of you shot." There: he was getting nostalgic again, an old man's affliction.

As more days passed, the sun began to send long shafts of light down through the trees, yellow light like celestial grain pouring from some angelic silo, and Rudge felt that God was surely in His Heaven and looking out for those denizens of His most cherished island, dear emerald England.

God does not, however, wish anyone to lie too easy in his hammock, complacency being a sin that can easily escalate into pride. The next day, around noon, just after he'd finished his lunch and was folding his tarp, Rudge looked up to see a man, naked except for a black patch above his groin, poised between two trees not ten yards away and staring at Rudge over the sharp stone point of an arrow.

Civilization had dulled Rudge's survival instinct, and, instead of taking immediate evasive action, he shouted, "I say!" and might have added something equally inane like "That won't do!" The arrow snatched the folded tarp from his hands and pinned it to a tree.

The old warrior within him was roused by the attack. Rudge knew better than to turn and flee and take an arrow in the back. He charged the man and slapped soundly into him before the savage had another arrow notched. Down they both went. Rudge was roaring now: "Bloody bastard!"

The savage was not a big man, but he was strong and feral-fast and hissed like a snake and his body was slick with sweat or animal oils, and Rudge couldn't pin him. Rudge had knocked the man down, and they both rolled on the ground, thrashing amid the wet leaves and mud, and doing this for an inordinately long time, exchanging blows, making pig noises and grunts of menace, and then the savage was on top of him, his knees slamming into Rudge's chest and Rudge couldn't catch his breath, and he saw that the hand raised above him held a sharp killing-stone, and Rudge raised his forearm to block the blow.

* * *

THE MAN leaned back slightly. Rudge could see the swollen scars that marked the man's cheeks and the way his eyes suddenly widened, and Rudge felt his own lungs gasp for air as the weight of his attacker seemed to lift.

The savage uttered a sharp cry, bird-like and quick, and he floated away, rising up into the trees, squeezed magically small by perspective, twisting and kicking and howling now, and Rudge saw the thick, gleaming coil that encircled the man's chest and fell away like a burnished silver vine, and he swung his head to follow the arc of the silver cord, his eye still sorting details while the logic of what he saw lagged behind. The great sun-struck curve of the shining mirrored orb showed his own reflection, and he saw where the tentacle protruded from the vessel, and his eye traced it back again and up to where the man squirmed high and small in the canopy of trees.

In an instant, Rudge understood what had happened. Mallory had witnessed the attack from within the vessel and had acted quickly, sending a segmented tentacle stretching to the edge of the clearing to snatch Rudge's assailant and haul him skyward.

As Rudge sorted this out, he was surprised by a hand on his shoulder. It was Jacobs. "Are you all right, Sir Bertram?"

"Yes," Rudge said, getting to his feet and brushing muck from his thighs. "Bit out of breath, but—"

He was interrupted by the body that came crashing and tumbling down from the trees to land on its back with a wet smack on the forest floor. Mallory had either released the man or the man had wriggled out of the tentacle's grasp without reflecting on the consequences of that maneuver.

The man's eyes were open as was his mouth. He was dead and wore a dumbfounded expression, as though the other side was not at all what he expected.

"Sir!" Jacobs said, and Rudge looked up to see more naked men, armed with spears and bows and arrows, moving out of the trees and into the sunlight.

"Over here," another voice shouted, and Rudge looked over his shoulder and saw Jon Bans and Tommy Strand. Jon Bans was aiming an ancient Enfield Musketoon at one of the natives, but Rudge felt that the odds of Bans killing anyone other than himself were slim. Rudge had examined the moldering gun weeks ago and pronounced it worthless. Tommy Strand was holding Rudge's own Lee-Metford, a fine bolt-action rifle that Rudge trusted with his life. He did not, however, trust the abilities of the feckless naturalist who was presently holding it. Rudge wondered how many savages Mallory could wring the life out of with his mechanical tentacles.

But the savages seemed uninterested in Rudge or any of his comrades. They surrounded the dead man and began talking and grunting and slapping each other on the back. One of the men threw his feet up in the air, threw his arms wide, and sprawled on his back to the accompaniment of loud hoots and grunts which Rudge identified as expressions of mirth.

"These boys have a hell of a sense of humor, don't they?" The man who had just walked out of the forest and uttered this remark was dressed as though for tennis, or, perhaps, croquet. He was smoking a cheroot with an insouciant air, and a black-rimmed monocle was screwed into his left eye.

"Wallister!" Rudge blurted. He'd never met the man, but his likeness was famously familiar.

"I am," the man said. "I don't know who you are, but I bet you are looking for Lavinia. There's always someone chasing after her."

* * *

THE YAMI village was less than a mile away, and Rudge and his men accompanied Wallister on foot. Mallory followed behind in *Her Glory*, maintaining a distance of several hundred yards so that the falling trees and flying branches that were an inevitable byproduct of the vehicle's progress wouldn't maim anyone. The natives walked ahead of Rudge and Wallister.

"Didn't know that fellow was going to try to shoot an arrow through you," Wallister said, as they pressed on through the jungle. "I wouldn't have stood still for that if I'd seen it coming. Sorry though. I should have been paying more attention." He shot a glance at Rudge. "Although you know how to look out for yourself. I can see that. That was quite a trick with that machine of yours. Never seen anything like that."

They were silent for a while, and then Wallister said, "Lord Addison sent you, didn't he?" and Rudge nodded and said that Lavinia's grandfather had been concerned for her welfare, and that Rudge had volunteered to find her and report on her safety. He'd become, of course, much more worried when he and his men came upon the burned out shell of the zeppelin.

Wallister was surprised to learn that the zeppelin had burned—"wasn't burning when we set off," he said—but he didn't seem particularly upset. He had a cavalier manner that suited his heavy-lidded eyes and too-full lips, and the slightly vexed expression of a man often misunderstood by his inferiors. He moved through the jungle with a twisting of hips and shoulders that suggested a man wending his way through a party crowd with the bar as his destination. Rudge better understood Lord Addison's antipathy for Wallister and, consequently, felt less ambivalent about getting Lavinia back to England and her grandfather by whatever means necessary.

Their arrival at the village was heralded by a dozen or so small children, who ran down the path to meet them, silent, swift, pale creatures, weaving and darting and ogling the new intruders and then running on down the path to where *Her Glory of Empire* was shaking the jungle and throwing up debris. They would flee it, then stop, turn, and run toward it, stand wiggling and flapping their arms and uttering rude noises, then flee again.

When Rudge and his companions arrived at the village, they found every man, woman and child who had not set out to greet them, the lot standing in a fleshy mass of expectancy, and, as Rudge entered the clearing, the crowd parted to reveal a hut from which a young woman emerged, a strikingly beautiful girl with raven hair that fell loosely from under a pith helmet decorated with pink and purple orchids. She seemed dazed by the sunlight; she brought a hand to her throat, and her eyes widened, blue eyes that pierced old Rudge's memory and brought her name to his lips, reflexively. Could this vision be the precocious twelve-year-old he had known so long ago?

But before her name could pass his lips, a voice shouted in his ear: "Vinia!" And he saw Lavinia's eyes grow yet wider, impossibly large, and she began to run toward him, and he felt something like pain—perhaps acute embarrassment at an old man's fancy—when he realized she was not running toward him but toward the man who had just raced by Rudge to close the distance in mere seconds, take Lavinia in his arms and spin her in the air while she laughed with that merriment that only the young have access to.

Tommy Strand and Lavinia Addison hugged and kissed, sobbed and laughed, aware perhaps of their audience—as the young so often are—and portraying two besotted lovers with a skill well beyond that of the most accomplished thespians.

* * *

IT WAS the evening of the next day. The sun was still in the sky, but, in less than an hour, it would slide precipitously into the water. Rudge stood at the end of a ramshackle pier, which, he suspected, had not fallen into disrepair but been born in that state. A sizeable lake spread out in front of him, its mirrored surface full of the cloudy sky, not a dimple on its surface (curious, that). There was no sign of life at all, and a strange, dank odor filled the air. Nonetheless, Rudge was delighted to have evaded, if only briefly, the chatter of the Yami, their idiotic bluster and pomp. Primitive peoples did not inspire Rudge, who saw in them the worst aspects of human nature, reminding him that superstition, ignorance, violence, and cruelty were inherent human traits, first impulses, and that civilization was a cheap coat of paint over a rotten edifice.

He was not, he decided, angered by Tommy Strand's subterfuge. The young man was not a naturalist, a fact which should have been apparent from the beginning; he was, in truth, the feckless son of Arthur Strand, a powerful industrialist who had prevailed upon Lord Addison to take his son on board for this rescue mission. Neither Arthur Strand nor Lord Addison had any idea that young Tommy and Lavinia were enamored of each other—or had been until an unfortunate misunderstanding had led to a heated argument which had prompted Lavinia, obeying an impulse not uncommon in young people, to put an entire ocean between herself and her unhappy suitor.

She had quickly come to regret this. Wallister proved an unpleasant man, a "brute," (although he had not, according to Lavinia, indulged in any sexual impropriety beyond a certain sly familiarity and presumption). The jungle had failed to improve her disposition, and the insufferable Yami were the last straw, a noisy, foul-smelling lot who wore no clothes except—how stupid was this?—a small black patch to cover the navel, a kind of spiritual precaution, since demons tended to enter a person via this umbilical entrance. You were just asking for trouble if you didn't hide your navel under a mollusk shell or bit of sloth hide.

In any event, the lovers were reunited, and it looked like a happy—

The sky seemed to die and fall upon him. A cold fist squeezed his heart. He fell to his knees. Suddenly it was as though his body were fashioned from clay; surely this numbness heralded his death, and yet this mortal fear was nothing compared to an overwhelming sense of desolation. If he had been told that everyone he knew and cared for had died, hideously, that might have engendered such despair; a palpable evil, a malevolent spirit, had settled in his mind with the authority of truth, bringing with it a suffocating terror, a need to run, to flee, but robbing him of volition.

Somehow he managed to stagger to his feet and gaze down into the water from which this malign psychic force seemed to emanate. The water was clear, and he saw the lake's bottom, which rippled with shadows, black blotches that shifted and danced, as though cast by broad leaves shivering in a strong wind. He had thought the lake deeper, even here at the end of the pier, and this shift in perception created a kind of panicky vertigo. What did it matter how deep—? Then he understood. He was not looking at the lake's bottom; he was gazing down upon the back of some unknowable beast. It was gliding under the water, a vast, translucent creature, shapeless, or shifting in shape, a kind of ovoid whale-sized jellyfish. The mottled, black shapes within it pulsated and moved, and these black undulating inkblots were not organs beating to some animal pulse—how Rudge knew this he could not say; but know it he did—they were mouths opening and closing to reveal a terrible hunger, more ancient and ravenous than any jungle beast or mythical monster.

Rudge did not know if he walked or ran or crawled back down the pier and over the ground and back to the hut. He had some memory of falling upon his blankets and being seized by a deep and unrelenting lethargy, which a scientist of the mind might have identified as a strategy of the subconscious designed to defend the self from a horror it found untenable.

In the morning, when Jacobs brought him his tea, Rudge came awake, groggy but in full possession of the previous night's horror.

❋ ❋ ❋

THE OLD man could speak English, having spent four years in a mission before deciding that one god was not enough for a jungle life, and now, having heard Rudge out, he nodded.

"This in-the-lake thing big. Very big, very bad. It not live here. It from some other. It splash into this world and very angry, and it kill-kill everything thing and eat up everything. Mostly, it stay in the night, wait for the night when the sun is shy. We Yami, we try to kill it. It eat up Yami. Ha ha!" The old shaman laughed and slapped his thigh. "We stick him with spear. We stick him with arrow. He eat up spear and arrow and Yami!" The old man glowered, as though suddenly struck with the seriousness of this Yami-eating business.

"It make slave of some Yami. It catch Yami and make him fetch food and trick other Yami to lake, but it take Yami soul to make of him slave, and we see that. We say, 'That man, he have no soul,' and we kill him."

The Yami were not fools. They had discovered several things about the beast. It could not travel on land, and its substance, its flesh, was, consequently, trapped within the lake. It needed to eat, to feed, and it had done that until there was nothing left for it to eat. No birds, no fish, no frogs, no turtles, nothing. It would die in its dead lake.

"We kill it with nothing," he said, his smile revealing half a dozen ragged black teeth.

Rudge was about to ask something about the Yami slaves when a series of high-pitched screams made him leap to his feet and run outside.

The screams were coming from the lake, and as soon as Rudge rounded a gnarled clump of trees, he understood what was happening. So much for the shaman's assertion that the creature shunned the daylight. It was, no doubt, growing desperate.

Wallister and Lavinia were both kneeling on the end of the pier, clutching the weather-battered logs and desiccated vines that comprised it. The pier had been ripped from the shore and was moving out into the lake, riding the back of the beast, a raft surrounded by white turbulence and leaving a wild, frothing wake.

Rudge saw Tommy Strand running toward the lake. He stood on the edge, preparing to dive in and swim valiantly after his beloved, but a shout stopped him, and Rudge turned too, and spied Mallory, standing atop *Her Glory of Empire* and urging Strand to hurry.

Mallory disappeared before Strand reached the vehicle, and a silver tentacle reached out and lifted the young man up to the hatch. Rudge marveled at Mallory's skill. He was an artist with old Edmonds's invention.

Her Glory rolled into the lake and water rollicked all over the banks and then, amid several flying tentacles and the ball-ended air tubes, it disappeared beneath the surface. The steady progress of the bobbing tubes was all that marked its journey. Those air tubes gained on the floundering pier, and suddenly a tentacle reached out of the water and encircled Lavinia's waist. The girl screamed, no doubt thinking the beast had her, and continued to scream until, suddenly, she fell from the tentacle's clasp. The tentacle sank beneath the waves, and so did Lavinia. On the bank, Rudge shouted, appalled, crazy in his helplessness. Then Lavinia's head and shoulders broke the surface, and Tommy Strand could be seen behind her. Lavinia's eyes were closed, but Tommy had his arm around her and was in no danger of losing her. With strong, purposeful strokes he drew her to the shore.

Rudge turned back to where the pier now lay motionless in the middle of the lake. Wallister was nowhere to be seen, and *Her Glory of Empire* had failed to resurface.

Time passed. The crowd of naked men, women, and children, silent at first and keeping a cautious distance from the shore, began to talk excitedly and gesture among themselves.

Rudge spied Tommy and Lavinia on the shore to his right. Tommy had an arm around her shoulders and she was sitting up, coughing. Rudge was about to set off in their direction when a great funnel of water erupted and *Her Glory of Empire* rose up, all twelve of its tentacles thrashing, shimmering in the blazing sun, seeming to dance upon the water. It was up and on the shore in an instant, and then it was among the Yami who screamed and fled in all directions. The machine snatched them up, each tentacle moving of its own accord, independent of all others. Mallory's skill was nothing like this. Men, women, and children were tossed in the air, slammed against tree trunks, torn to bits by tentacles that sliced them with gleaming blades. An old warrior's head bounced at Rudge's feet. He jumped back as it rolled past, blood splattering his boots.

And then this great machine stood tall on six tentacles, in defiance of all engineering principles, and Rudge saw the slumped form of Wallister, sodden and surely lifeless, bound by several coils of a single tentacle, and the machine, moving with an unholy ease that suggested a decisive intelligence, darted into the jungle, parting trees and brush in a welter of sound and fury—and was gone. In less than five minutes, its progress could no longer be marked by the noise that accompanied it, although Rudge could still discern the cloud of dust and twigs and leaves that rose above it.

As he walked to meet Tommy and Lavinia, Rudge saw, on the lake's bank, a litter of pipes and seals and broken gauges, the mechanical guts of *Her Glory*, instruments of no interest to the creature that now wore the vehicle like a suit of armor.

* * *

ALL'S WELL that ends well. That's what Rudge told himself on his return to England. And certainly Lord Addison was pleased to have his granddaughter safely home.

But what is the end? When, six weeks after his disappearance, Wallister walked out of the jungle, miraculously whole, was that the end? When the great explorer abandoned his travels and devoted his fortune to industry, was that the end? When a factory in Sheffield began producing great hollow steel orbs that dwarfed the men who made them, and when the public learned that these were the prototypes of a new and glorious engine based on Hugh Edmonds's invention, what was one to make of that?

People said that Wallister had changed, was serious, almost solemn, and the flamboyance that had delighted the public and annoyed his fellows was gone for good. Was there anyone in England who could discern the absence of a soul?

Rudge would have liked to know if these manufactured steel casings awaited cunning furnaces and engines and navigational devices. Or did they await creatures in need of external skeletons? If these empty spheres were waiting upon the latter, then that, Rudge thought, might well be the end.

Usurped

1.

THEY WERE DRIVING back from El Paso, where they had been visiting Meta's parents, when Brad saw something shimmering on the road, a heat mirage or, perhaps, some internal aberration, those writhing, silver amoebae that were the harbingers of one of his murderous migraines.

Meta had insisted that they turn the air off and roll the windows down. "I love this desert air," she had said, inhaling dramatically.

"Nothing like the smell of diesel fumes at dusk," Brad had responded, only he hadn't. He was thirty-six years old, and he had been married for almost half his life, and he loved his wife, loved her enthusiasm for the flawed world, and understood how easily, how unthinkingly, he could curdle her good mood with his reflexive cynicism. Besides, the trucks that had heaved by earlier were gone, as was their stink, and the two-lane highway he presently followed was devoid of all vehicles and had been ever since he'd abandoned the more straightforward eastbound path.

Having satisfied himself that the cloud was illusion, a trick of nature or his mind, he no longer saw it. Such is the power of reason.

And then, like that, the wasps filled the cab. Incredibly, amid the pandemonium and his panic, he knew them instantly for what they were, saw one, red-black and vile, arc its abdomen and plunge its stinger into his bare forearm, a revolting, indelible mental snapshot. A whirring of wings, wind buffeting his ears, thwack of bodies, one crawling on his neck, another igniting his cheek with bright pain, and Meta shrieking—and he made a sound of his own, an *aaaaaaaaghaaah* of disgust— as he wrenched the steering wheel, and the Ford Ranger leapt up, surprised by his urgency, and twisted, exploded, a series of jolting explosions, with the sky and the earth tumbling in ungainly combat.

✳ ✳ ✳

HE BLINKED and a hundred thousand stars regarded him. He lay on his back, unable to summon full consciousness, resistant to what its return might mean. Breathing was not easy; the air was full of razors. He rolled onto his side, slowly. Mesquite and cacti and unruly juniper threw tortured shadows across a flat, moonlit expanse that stretched toward distant mountains.

He raised himself on his elbows; a knife-thrust of pain took his breath away, and he was still, waiting, as a deer might freeze at the sound of a predator. He slid his right hand under his t-shirt, and he found the source of the pain, more than he wanted to find, ragged bloody flesh and the broken spike of a rib.

He stood and might have thought to rejoice that he had no greater injuries, that he had, miraculously, survived the wreck, but he couldn't imagine more pain; he had a plenitude of pain, a surfeit. Meta might say—

Meta!

He saw the Ranger then, lying on its side, the passenger door gone and the windshield gone, a bright spume of pebbled glass vomited into the sand in front of its sprung hood. "Meta!" he shouted. "Meta!"

He limped toward the vehicle. There was something wrong with his left knee, too, as though his kneecap had been replaced with a water-filled balloon.

She wasn't in the Ranger, wasn't under it either.

Moonlight painted everything in pale silver, revealing detail in every shadow, a hallucinatory world, too precisely rendered to be real. Brad moved in slow, widening circles, calling her name. Finally, he turned toward the road, approaching a thick-trunked live oak, solitary and massive, its thousand gnarled branches festooned with small, glittering leaves. The tree, he saw, had claimed the passenger door, which lay, like a fallen warrior's shield, close to the oak's gashed trunk.

And here, Brad thought, *is where she was thrown.*

Maybe he would discover her on the other side of that thick trunk, her body hidden in some declivity, invisible until you stumbled on its very edge.

But there was no hollow to hide her body, nothing. And after he had climbed to the road, looked up and down it, and crossed to gaze at another stark vista that revealed no trace of her, he accepted what he'd already known. She wasn't here. He would have known if she were nearby—because he was connected to her, more than ever since the onset of her illness. He had always had this psychic compass, this inexplicable but inarguable ability to know just where she was in the world.

In their house in Austin, he always knew what room she was in. If she was down the street visiting a neighbor, Brad knew that, too—and knew *which* neighbor. If her car was gone, he knew where she had driven to (the library, the grocery store, the YMCA at Town Lake, wherever), and he realized, one day, that he knew this whether or not she had told him.

Once, when they were kids, nine-year-olds, Meta had gone missing. It was dark outside, and Meta had failed to come home. The neighborhood went looking. Brad set off on his own. Under the luminous summer moon, he ran past the elementary school, past the creek where they hunted frogs and crayfish, across old man Halder's field. He found her at the abandoned barn. She lay next to a rusted-out wheelbarrow, one of her legs crimped oddly under her. That she was alive filled him with wild relief and the terrible knowledge that he could have lost her forever, that the world was a monstrous machine, and anyone in its path could come to mortal grief. She frowned at him, pale blue eyes under tangled red hair, and said, "You were right about that rope," and they both gazed at the tire, on its side in the dust. Until recently, the tire had been an integral part of a swing.

"Why did you do something so stupid?" he had shouted, and she had begun to cry, silently, tears falling from her eyes, her lips parted, lower lip trembling, and he thought, *I'm an idiot*, and he realized that he would marry her one day, if only to keep an eye on her, to protect her (from evil, which ranged across the world, and from his own desperate love, half-mad and hiding in his heart).

Standing on the road, he remembered that he had a cell phone and, after retrieving it from his pocket and turning it on, he remembered why the cell phone was no cause for rejoicing: no signal, no help.

He turned away from the empty road and studied the mountains. They were purple and black and seemed closer now. Could she have walked to the mountains? And why would she do such a thing? Surely the road was more likely to bring rescue.

He thought of Meta, conjured her, carefully visualizing her blue eyes, curly red hair, and high cheekbones (sown with a constellation of freckles that refused to fade, a last vestige of her tomboy childhood). Ordinarily, imagining her calmed him, relieved the stress of a bad day at the office, an unhappy client, the black dog of depression, of fear, but now, with Meta missing, her image failed to console, only exacerbated his dread. Her face shimmered, faded, was gone, and he realized that the mountains were glowing, exuding a pulsing light, a mottled purple hue that filled him with inexplicable disgust and panic and despair.

He felt consciousness receding like a tide. He leaned into oblivion, seeking refuge from the horror that assaulted him.

2.

HE WOKE to white light in a white room. He was propped up in a hospital bed, his left leg encased in an elaborate cast and suspended artfully from stainless steel scaffolding. A large, ridiculous bolt pierced the cast in the vicinity of his knee, like an elaborate magic trick. Breathing, he discovered, was difficult—although not, he decided, impossible, not worthy of panic—and gazing down at his chest, he saw what looked like duct tape, yards of it, binding swathes of surgical gauze and cotton around his ribs.

He remembered the damage then, remembered the wasps.

A woman stepped into the room and said, "Where's Meta?"

It was Gladys, Meta's mother, dressed in khaki pants and a white blouse, filling the room with willed energy.

Where is— Before Brad could speak, someone to his right spoke.

"She went to the cafeteria to get some coffee." It was Buddy, Gladys's husband. He had been sitting silently in a chair, dozing perhaps. He was a stern, formal old man (much older than his wife), bald with tufts of gray hair sprouting above each ear. Querulous, nobody's buddy: Buddy.

Before Brad could assimilate Buddy's statement, Meta appeared in the doorway, behind her mother. She was holding a cardboard carton containing three styrofoam cups with plastic lids. Her eyes widened. "Oh," she said. "Brad."

Gladys turned. "Oh my," she said.

Meta put the carton down on a dresser top and came to him. There were tears in her eyes, and she was smiling. Brad felt as light as dust, mystified, out of context. Wasn't Meta the one in hospital beds? Wasn't he her visitor, her caretaker, her terrified lover?

"Where have you been?" she said, laughing, running her hand through his hair.

And wasn't that *his* question?

* * *

META TOLD him he had been unconscious for two days. They sorted it out, or rather, they did their best to make sense of what had happened. Wayne County's sheriff came by the hospital, and Brad and Meta told him what they could remember.

The sheriff was a big man with a broad face and a mournful mustache. He was slow, his bearing solemn and stoical, as though he'd seen too much that ended badly. He introduced himself by taking his hat off and saying, "Mr. and Mrs. Phelps, my name is Dale Winslow, and I'm the sheriff in these parts, and I'm sorry for your misadventure," and he pulled up a chair and produced a small notebook and a ballpoint pen from his breast pocket.

He told them what he already knew. A local named Gary Birch had been driving back from a visit to his ex in Owl Creek when he'd seen a woman out on the road. He stopped and got out of his car. He could see she was bleeding, blood on her face, her blouse, and, when he came up to her, he could see the Ford Ranger on its side maybe fifty yards from the road. It didn't take any great deductive powers to figure out what had happened. Here was a woman who had flipped her truck; she was in shock, couldn't make a sound. Gary told her to hang on, and he went down and looked at the Ranger, checked to see that there wasn't a gas leak, took the keys out of the ignition. He didn't see anyone else, but he wasn't looking. A fool thing, not to look, but it didn't even enter his mind. He wanted to get her over to the hospital in Silo. For all he knew she might already be as good as dead and just not know it. That happened sometimes. Gary had heard about such things from his dad, a Nam vet. A fellow could say, "I'm okay," when he wasn't nothing but a disembodied head, although maybe that one was just a story.

Meta, it turned out, had sustained no serious injuries. She didn't remember anything about the accident. She didn't remember the wasps in the truck, didn't remember Gary stopping for her and taking her to the hospital. At some point, in the ER, she'd started screaming for Brad, and a nurse, Eunice Wells, who'd worked the ER for twenty-some years, put two and two together, got Sheriff Winslow on the phone, and hollered Gary Birch out of the waiting room. "This is Eunice Wells," she told Winslow. "Gary Birch just brought a woman in here for treatment. He found her on Old Nine where she'd flipped her truck. Sounds like there's someone still out there. I'm gonna give the phone to Gary, and he's gonna tell you just where you gotta go."

Which Gary did. Sheriff Winslow found Brad lying by the side of the highway, as inert as yesterday's road kill, a dark lump next to a creosote bush. He might have been a sideswiped deer or a sack of trash that fell off someone's pickup on the way out to the Owl Creek dump. Likely Winslow wouldn't have noticed him if he hadn't known where to look.

Brad asked about the wasp swarm. Was that sort of thing common around here?

Brad thought he saw something flicker in Winslow's eyes, something furtive. The sheriff closed his eyes, and when he opened them, whatever had been there was gone. The man just looked tired. He said, "It's hard to say what an insect will do. I haven't heard of anyone running through a patch of wasps, but termites will swarm. And you can get locusts out of nowhere, like a judgment." He shrugged. "I'd thank the good Lord you're alive and put it behind you."

Good advice, but not easy to follow. He was in the hospital four more days, foggy time, nurses in and out of the room, Meta sitting in a chair, sometimes holding his hand in hers. He would wake as though falling into freezing water, his heart clenching like a fist, nightmares leaving a coppery sediment in the back of his throat. He had no memory of the dreams, only a sense of diminishment and hopelessness. He would look down and see his hand resting in that other's hand, and his eyes would trace the route of that hand to arm, to shoulder, to neck, to that lovely face, and slow seconds would fill with disquiet before he realized he was looking at his wife, at Meta. He, who had always been able to find her wherever she was in the world, could no longer sense her presence when she sat beside him holding his hand. He said nothing of this to Meta; it frightened him too much. This disoriented state might, he reasoned, be the result of the pain medications they gave him, and as he tapered off, his sense of his darling's spiritual weight, her certainty in his world, would return.

The day before Brad was to leave the hospital, a wizen man with a close-cropped gray beard came to visit him. The man wore a light blue shirt, tan slacks, and a brown sports jacket. He was pale and sickly looking, wearing glasses with thick black frames, glasses that a younger man would have worn for comic or ironic effect. He introduced himself, and Brad said, "So, how am I doing? Do I still get to leave tomorrow?"

The man frowned, perplexed. "I don't—" He realized his mistake then and said, "I'm sorry. I'm not a medical doctor. That's what I get for calling myself a doctor in a hospital. I'm a PhD. I taught at Baylor but I'm retired now."

It was Brad's turn to look stumped. Dr. Michael Parkington introduced himself again. He said that he was writing a book on the desert and was particularly interested in unusual anecdotal material. He'd heard about Brad's encounter with a swarm of wasps, and he wondered if Brad would mind telling him about it.

Brad had nothing better to do—Meta was seeing her parents off at the airport and wouldn't be back for hours—and he was interested in what this man could tell him.

Parkington asked if it would be all right if he recorded Brad's recollections of the accident, and Brad almost said no, which was irrational, of course, but he would have preferred an undocumented chat. He'd heard his voice on a recorder once, and his voice sounded thin and full of complaint. But he said, "Sure," and the professor turned on a small, cell-phone-sized recorder, and Brad told him everything he could remember, ending with, "I got woozy standing out there on the road, and I just passed out, I guess."

"How many times were you stung?" Parkington asked.

Brad shrugged. "Maybe half a dozen times. I don't know. It's hard to keep count when you're flying through a windshield."

Parkington smiled ruefully. "Any welts? Any swellings or discolorations?"

Brad looked down at his forearm where he'd seen the wasp sting him. Nothing. His skin was smooth, unblemished. He lifted his hand to touch his cheek. No soreness there, and, shaving for the first time that morning, he hadn't noticed any redness or swelling.

"No," he said, slightly puzzled. "I didn't even think to look."

Parkington turned the recorder off and put it in his pocket. "I want to thank you for your time, Mr. Phelps." He stood up.

"Sure. How many people have you interviewed?" Brad asked.

The professor sat down again. He took his glasses off, rubbed his forehead, and put the glasses back on. "I'd appreciate it if you wouldn't say anything to Sheriff Winslow about my coming by."

"Why's that?" Brad was starting to feel a little miffed. He hadn't wanted that recorder running, and he should have trusted his intuition, because…well, here was this guy getting all circumspect, enlisting him in some local intrigue.

"Winslow thinks I'm trying to stir things up. Truth is, he thinks I'm a crackpot," Parkington said. "He'd be pissed if he knew I'd come out here." He looked at the doorway, as though expecting the sheriff to come walking through it on cue. He made a decision then. Brad could see it in the way he straightened his spine and narrowed his eyes. "I haven't been entirely candid with you."

The man leaned over and fumbled in his briefcase. "I've already written a book," he said. He retrieved a book and handed it to Brad. Brad knew a self-published book when he saw one. The title was set in a lurid, old-English typeface: *Haunted Mountains: Atlantis in the Desert* by Michael Parkington, PhD. Translucent ocean waves were superimposed over a photograph of a desert panorama, mountains in the background. This computer-manipulated image, murky and lurid, offended Brad's artistic sensibility while managing to instill a queasy sense of dislocation.

Brad looked up from the book in his hands and said, "And what, exactly, haven't you told me?"

Parkington nodded his head. "I didn't tell you that after interviewing some other people who encountered hostile swarm phenomena, I've come to the conclusion that these people were *not* attacked, not physically, in any event. I believe they all experienced a psychic derangement. I'm telling you that I don't think you were attacked by wasps, Mr. Phelps. I think you were the victim of an induced hallucination."

Brad sighed, disgusted. "The last week hasn't been one of my best, but I think I know what I saw." Brad held out the book, but Parkington smiled and shook his head.

"You keep the book. Maybe you'll want to read it sometime. You know, not a single wasp was found in your vehicle, which is what I expected. I've documented *five* other cases of people being attacked by swarms, all within a half mile of where you were found."

Brad was silent.

Parkington held his hand up, fingers wide, and lowered each successive finger as he ticked off an attack: "Birds, bats, rattlesnakes, ants, and—my favorite menace—moths. In all but one case, the subjects were driving down Route 9 when they were attacked. The drivers were all forced to abandon their vehicles as a result of an onslaught of bats or flying ants or sparrows or moths, and all of the attack victims seem to have lost consciousness for some period of time. Your adventure was the only life-threatening encounter, although any of the attacks could have resulted in a fatal accident.

"I might add that I know about *these* attacks because other travelers along that lonely stretch spotted the abandoned vehicles or the confused, semi-conscious owners and stopped to offer assistance. It seems reasonable to assume that some other drivers suffered swarm attacks during times when traffic was sparse, came to their senses, shrugged off their weird adventures, and drove on."

Parkington said that there was one man who was *not* in a car when attacked. A man named Charlie Musgrove was on foot when he found himself surrounded by rattlesnakes. Musgrove maintained that he was bitten by five or six of the creatures, but a sample of his blood revealed no toxins, other than the alcohol he habitually imbibed.

"He's a local, a homeless alcoholic," Parkington said, "and not a credible witness, but I'm inclined to believe him, because he was in the vicinity of the other reported incidents, and his account is consistent with them."

Parkington said that, in every single one of these reported attacks, no sign of the attacking creatures was found, no birds, bats, rattlesnakes, ants or moths. And in the case of the birds, the driver was adamant in her description of their thrashing and banging around in the car, feathers flying everywhere, much avian carnage, so one would think that the most cursory forensic examination would have produced some corroborating evidence. Nothing could be found. "I'm guessing Sheriff Winslow hasn't told you any of this."

"He hasn't," Brad said. "Probably because he is a professional and understands that it is not his job to share bizarre theories with someone who has just been traumatized by a near-fatal accident. Now my meds are kicking in, and I'm going to close my eyes and get some sleep. Thanks for the book."

And Brad closed his eyes, and when he opened them again, it was dark outside his window, and Meta was sitting in a chair with the book on her lap. She looked up, smiled, and said, "It says here that during the Permian age this whole area was under an ocean. That was 250 million years ago. Who gave you this book?"

"The ancient mariner," Brad said.

3.

THEY DROVE back to Austin in a rented Honda Accord. Meta did all the driving. Brad remained bundled in a semi-fog of pain meds, and a substantial cast girded his left leg. He'd been instructed in the use of crutches, but they were of limited utility thanks to his ravaged rib cage. A folded wheelchair, which would be his primary mode of transportation for the next six weeks, lay in the car's trunk.

Once home, Brad called friends and family, quickly wearied of telling his story, and cast a forlorn eye on the upcoming weeks of recuperation.

On the positive side, he accompanied Meta to an appointment with her oncologist who was pleased to tell them that all tests were negative; there was no trace of the cancer that had short-circuited their lives for the last year and a half. They had celebrated that night, with champagne and sex.

The sex had not been entirely successful. Brad had been struck with the intense conviction that, should he experience an orgasm, it would kill him; something vital to sustaining his life would be seized and devoured by his partner's need. This thought robbed him of an erection, but his failure to achieve orgasm was, paradoxically, a great relief, as though he had survived a brush with death, so it wasn't the *worst* sex he'd ever had, but it didn't bode well for his erotic future.

Brad called work and had to talk to the insufferable Kent, a completely insincere creature, ambitious and feral, who assured Brad that he could avail himself of as much time off as his recuperation required. "I got your back, Brad-O," he said, which didn't cheer Brad at all. And yet, Brad felt no urgency about returning to work. Work felt like some remote, arcane endeavor, the rituals of some strange religion in which he had, long ago, ceased to believe.

Having plenty of time on his hands, Brad read Parkington's book, *Haunted Mountains: Atlantis in the Desert*. The bulk of the book, after its author had argued unconvincingly for a sunken Atlantis near the town of Silo, presented the usual lost civilization stories. The only part of the book that was interesting (and poignant for the insights it offered) was Parkington's revelation that his own father, a lawyer and amateur paleontologist, had encountered an Entity (his father's word) while camping in the mountains outside of Silo. Parkington's father referred to this alien visitation as a "remnant manifestation," and had embarked on a book about this visitation. He believed that there was an alien enclave established under the mountains in a "waiting configuration," that would transform the world when its time came round.

The author's father disappeared in 1977 after a sudden decline in his mental state, characterized by paranoia, hallucinations and a fervid hatred and fear of Christian doctrine. On more than one occasion, the man had entered one of Silo's numerous churches during a Sunday service, wild-eyed and disheveled, and beseeched the minister and his congregation to "be silent and know that the only thing that hears you is monstrous and indifferent to prayers." Much of the man's rant was in an unknown tongue, and he was committed to private mental asylums on two occasions, but he was never at such places for long, because he grew remarkably calm and rational after a brief period of confinement. When he disappeared, he left a note for his son, which, Parkington writes: "I destroyed after reading, or, rather, after I had read as much as my sanity could bear."

It was this last part of the book that spoke most directly to Brad, because it explained the author's attempt to find some explanation for his father's last years. The book Brad held in his hands was an artifact of two generations of pathology, and, as such, it was sadder and more profound than its cliched, sensational subject initially suggested.

There was no mention of the swarm attacks, and Brad assumed that such attacks were a more recent phenomenon.

＊ ＊ ＊

BRAD'S HEALTH improved, and he ceased to rely on the wheel-chair. The cast came off his leg, and his ribs were protected by a more flexible, shower-friendly fiberglass cage. With the help of a cane—he'd never had any success with the crutches, which promoted a form of locomotion too unnatural to be taken seriously—he was able to hobble to the kitchen and back to the bedroom, exhausted at first but slowly regaining his stamina, reclaiming his will.

He had much time for solitary reflection, because Meta, on his urging, had returned to her job at UT's library. In the evenings, she'd talk to him about her day, her voice his only window on a larger world.

Brad found his attention straying from her words. His mind, his heart, was otherwise occupied: he was wait-ing (every day, every hour, every second) to feel, again, her presence. Since the accident, she had turned invisible...*and* opaque. Both words described her, despite their warring definitions. She was a ghost in his mind when out of his sight. His psychic compass could no longer find her. She could be anywhere, pursuing any activity—and he imagined her in the strangest places: curled amid warm towels in a clothes dryer; hanging upside down in a closet; smiling with her eyes open while underwater in the upstairs bathtub—and when she was in front of him, he did not know her. She seemed to study him with cool interest and an absence of any binding emotion. Even her voice had altered, and he found himself marveling at how skillfully this woman reproduced his wife's sounds, failing only in recreating certain resonances that were within the province of her soul.

He should have been afraid, but he was not, not, that is, until he received a call from Sheriff Winslow who informed Brad that Michael Parkington had left Silo, abruptly and without notice. The date of his departure was uncertain, since he kept to himself. Only when Parkington failed to show up on the first with the rent check did anyone (*i.e.*, his landlord) evince interest in his whereabouts.

Brad was wondering why he had been called, since he had only met the man once, but the sheriff must have been anticipating this question, because he answered it before Brad asked.

"I called because we don't know whether the man is dead or alive, and he may be dangerous." Winslow explained that, on entering Parkington's apartment, they had immediately been confronted with a wall of photographs and newspaper clippings, and while the bulk of these items had yet to suggest anything relevant to the man's disappearance, the investigation had discovered an interesting and disturbing connection between four people (one woman and three men). These people were all the subjects of hometown newspaper articles (newspapers in Newark, El Paso, Phoenix, and Santa Fe) and had all, prior to the appearance of these articles, been interviewed by Dr. Parkington.

"We also discovered a small digital recorder and listened to your interview," Winslow said.

"I still don't understand why you called me," Brad said, mildly irked, again, for having allowed Parkington to record him.

"Those newspaper articles are about people who have disappeared. They are the people Parkington interviewed. Since they all disappeared between one and four months after he interviewed them, and since he took the trouble to track those clippings down and stick them on his wall, it is likely those vanished folks are connected, in some way, to Parkington. I wanted to call and give you a heads up, in case he comes knocking on your door. You might not want to open it."

"You think he killed those people?" Brad had difficulty envisioning a homicidal Parkington.

"I don't know what to think. Do you?"

Brad didn't, and he promised to call if Parkington showed up in Austin.

After he replaced the phone in its cradle, he went to the refrigerator and got a beer. He drank half of it and decided to call Meta at work.

"She left early today," someone told him. "A couple of hours ago, I guess."

Brad sat in a kitchen chair and drank the rest of his beer. He had no idea where she was.

But he did. He realized he did know. Not in the way he had always known, not with that magical (gone and now precious) lost sense but with the new cold logic that had replaced it. She was on her way to Silo, the town where it had all unraveled and where, now, some accursed force awaited her.

He set off at once, driving toward Silo, stopping every hundred miles or so to empty his bladder and take on gas and supplies (which consisted primarily of beer and snacks). He wasn't up for such a trip, not fully recovered from the accident and emotionally exhausted by Meta's betrayal, her retreat from his love and protection into the arms of some monstrous Casanova from Atlantis—and, yes, he admitted that he now swallowed Parkington's nutcase scenarios, and they went down easy; there was something out there in the mountains—*under the mountains*—that had reached out and wrecked his marriage and was now dragging Meta toward its lair.

But he was exhausted and would be no good at all unless he rested. So, on the far side of midnight, miles away from morning, he pulled into a rest stop and turned the engine off and slept.

The sun was up when he woke, and it was late afternoon when he drove down Silo's Main Street. It was a lean town, not given to airs, saturated with the sun's weight, sidewalks cracked by time, two old men on a bench in front of Roy's Restaurant, the Silo Library next door, then a barbershop called Curly's Quick Hair. Brad parked in front of a bar, B&G (which he knew, having eaten lunch there with Meta on a therapeutic outing from the hospital, stood for Bar & Grill, minimalist humor or the lack of it).

Brad wasn't a drinker, and his overindulgence of the day before was now taking its toll. So he went into B&G and sat at the bar counter. He ordered a beer and a fried egg sandwich from the barmaid, a middle-aged woman of undecided hair color with a tattoo on her shoulder that said "Dwayne" over a heart. Under the heart, clearly the work of a less skilled artist, it read: "Stinks." It made Brad sad, that tattoo. He thought of the entropy inherent in all relationships, and he ordered another beer. He considered a plan of action.

He didn't have one, he realized. No plan of action. The certainty that had brought him here had drained out over the miles, and he was left with a panicky sense of abandonment. Who did he know in town? No one. Well, Sheriff Winslow, but what could he say to him? Nothing relevant. He'd sound like a madman.

Am I? he wondered. But it was the truth itself that was mad, and how could it help but irradiate him, taint his own sanity?

His musings were interrupted by the barmaid, shouting "Musky! Hey Musky! Wake up! Come on. I got a couple of beers for you if you take out the trash."

She was leaning over a man and shaking his shoulder. He stirred, raised his head like an ancient bloodhound scenting a rabbit, and said, "Trash." He was a bearded man with a pocked face and heavy-lidded eyes stained yellow, the same color as the bar's smoke-saturated walls, and he had been sleeping in a corner booth, the only other patrons an elderly couple who were dancing to tinny sounds from the jukebox, the sort of music you could make with a comb and a piece of wax paper.

Brad watched the man lumber past the bar counter and through a door that must have led to the alley in back. Brad called to the barmaid, and when she came over, he asked her who she'd just been talking to.

"You mean old Musky?" She looked a little incredulous, a little suspicious. "Musky?"

"That's his name?"

"It's what he answers to, yeah. Why you want to know?"

Brad hesitated. "I thought he might be somebody I heard of recently. But I believe that person's name was Charlie."

"Ain't nobody calls him that anymore. But that's what he was born. Born Charlie Musgrove, the light of his momma's eye, and as full of promise...you won't credit this, cause he looks about a hundred years old now, but we were in high school together."

"What happened?" Brad said.

"Shit," the woman said. "Ain't that what the bumper sticker says? Shit happens. He drank up all his opportunities cept the opportunity to drink more." She backed up and narrowed her eyes. "Why you want to know about Musky? What makes him any of your business?"

Brad explained, starting with the wasps that had attacked him and his wife in the desert. He did not mention Atlantis under the mountains or the alien theft of his wife's soul, however. He did tell her how Charlie Musgrove figured in the narrative.

"Rattlesnakes!" she said. "You want old Musky to tell you about them rattlesnakes that tried to get him!"

"Yes," Brad said, not wishing to explain, in detail, what he really wanted.

"Hell, he's been hard to shut up on that subject. You won't have any trouble there. If you say the magic words, you'll get an earful. I guarantee it."

"What are the magic words?"

"Can I buy you a beer?" she said.

4.

"TURN HERE," Musky said. They followed a winding road into the mountains. The car leaned upward, as though the stars above were their destination. Musky took a swig from the beer bottle and lurched into song again: "Away in a manger no crib for his bed, the little Lord Jesus was wishin' he's dead. No..."

It hadn't been hard to elicit the rattlesnake story from Musky—who hadn't responded to Brad's initial *Charles Musgrove?* query—and Musky had a few things to say about Michael Parkington. "That fellow told me I didn't see no rattlesnakes, said I *lucinated* them. I didn't tell him I'd read that fool book he wrote. Yep, found a copy in a dumpster, autographed to Cindy Lou with his cell phone number, but I guess that didn't work out. That book was a lot of crap, all that Atlantis stuff."

"You don't believe there is some alien force in these mountains?"

Musky finished the beer and threw the empty bottle out the window, which made the Austin-environmentalist in Brad cringe when he heard the shattering glass. "Oh, there's something awful and ancient in these mountains. My grandfather knew all about it, said he'd seen it eat a goat by turning the goat inside out and sort of licking it until it was gone. He said it was a god from another world, older than this one. He called it Toth. A lot of people in these parts know about it, but it ain't a popular subject."

He opened another beer and drank it. "Anyway, I think those rattlesnakes were real."

They bumped along the road, flanked by ragged outcroppings, shapes that defied gravity, everything black and jagged or half-erased by the brightness of the car's rollicking headlights.

"Okay! Stop 'er!" Musky said. Brad stopped the car. Musky was out of the car immediately, tumbling to the ground but quickly staggering upright with the beer bottle clutched in his hand. Brad turned the ignition off, put the key in his pocket, and got out.

Brad followed the man, who was moving quickly, invigorated, perhaps, by this adventure. The incline grew steeper, the terrain devoid of all vegetation, a moonscape, and Brad thought he'd soon be crawling on his hands and knees. Abruptly, the ground leveled, and he saw Musky, stopped in front of him, back hunched, dirty gray hair shivered by the breeze.

"There's people who would pay a pretty penny to see this," he said, without turning around. Brad reached the man and looked down from the rocky shelf on which they stood. Beneath them, a great dazzling bowl stretched out and down, a curving mother-of-pearl expanse, a skateboarder's idea of heaven—or imagine a giant satellite dish, its diameter measured in miles, pressed into the stone. No, it was nothing *like* anything. He knew he would never be able to describe it.

He felt a sharp, hot ember sear into the flesh immediately above his right eyebrow, brought his hand up quickly, and slapped the insect, crushing it. He opened his fist and looked at the wasp within. Its crumpled body trembled, and it began to vibrate faster and faster, emitting a high-pitched *whirrrrr*. It exploded in a purple flash that left an after-image in Brad's mind so that, when he turned toward the sound of Musky's voice, part of the man's face was eclipsed by a purple cloud.

"I always bring them up here," he said. "Toth calls 'em and I bring 'em the last lap."

"You brought my wife here?" Brad asked.

"Nope. Just you. She wasn't savory somehow. She had the chemicals in her, and it changed her somehow. Wouldn't do. Mind you, I ain't privy to every decision, I just get a notion sometimes. I think she was poison to it, so it didn't fool with her."

"But it changed her," Brad shouted, filled with fury, intent on killing this traitor to his race.

"It wasn't interested."

Brad's cell phone rang.

"You get good reception up here," Musky said.

Brad tugged the phone out of his pocket, flipped it open. "Hello?"

"Brad?"

"Meta?"

"Where are you honey? I've been trying to call you. I've been going crazy. I called the police. I even called Sheriff Winslow, although why—"

Brad could see her standing in the kitchen, holding the wall phone's receiver up to her ear, her eyes red and puffy from crying. He could see her clearly, as though she stood right in front of him; he could count the freckles on her cheeks.

Her tears, the flush in her cheeks, the acceleration of her heart, he saw these things, saw the untenable vascular system, the ephemeral ever-failing creature, designed by the accidents of time.

He was aware that the cell phone had slipped from his fingers and tumbled to the stony ledge and bounced into the bright abyss. He leaned over and watched its descent. Something was moving at the bottom of the glowing pit, a black, twitching insectile something, and as it writhed it grew larger, more spectacularly alive in a way the eye could not map, appendages appearing and disappearing, and always the creature grew larger and its fierce intelligence, its outrageous will and alien, implacable desires, rose in Brad's mind.

He felt a monstrous joy, a dark enlightenment, and wild to embrace his destiny, he flung himself from the ledge and fell toward the father of all universes, where nothing was ever lost, and everything devoured.

The Unorthodox
Dr. Draper

1.

RACHEL PHELPS WAS trying to explain something, but Dr. Draper didn't have a clue what. He prided himself on being a good listener, capable of temporarily banishing the analytical impulse for a more receptive, open-minded state. He'd had his own practice for fourteen years now, and about midway through that first year of private practice, still giddy in his self-employment, no longer a servant to that stultifying HMO, he'd decided to trust more in his intuition, to color outside the lines of traditional psychotherapy. So, over the years, he had slept with a couple of his patients. He often made patients sing (primarily Broadway show tunes) while he pounded away on an old Steinway, his playing exuberantly bad. Sometimes he would start a session with a new patient by shuffling a deck of cards, fanning the cards on the coffee table, and saying, "Pick three cards." The new client would pick the cards, and Dr. Draper, a big, rotund man with a close-cropped silver beard that looked as soft as goose down, would let a silence fill up the room. He would hunker down (suggesting a sumo wrestler in an abundant blue suit and unfortunate gift-given tie), frowning, hands slapped on his knees like skull caps. Time would pass. He would lean forward and say to his cowed client (who sat there staring timidly over the top of his cards), "You think this is magic? You think this is a fucking parlor game?" Then he would jump up and shout, "I can't read your damned mind. If you can't tell me what cards you're holding, I can't help you!"

Just recently, he had taken to asking patients if they'd rather swim through shit or vomit. It was a question Ernie Bates had asked Draper in the fourth grade, and Draper had been unable to answer it. But those were the best questions, he now knew, the ones that made a person uncomfortable. An absence of ease could precipitate a breakthrough, a revelation. Since he had just initiated this new technique, his results were inconclusive; time alone would tell if the shit/vomit question was a keeper.

In any event, it wasn't a question for Rachel Phelps, whose discomfort index did not need to be artificially boosted.

"It's a situation," she was saying, and Dr. Draper was aware that he had missed something. Or maybe he just had the *sensation* that he had missed something, because Rachel Phelps's verbal narratives were like tumbling rivers, often diverted by silent rocks or a detritus of disclaimers, commentaries, footnotes, reservations, apologies.

She would knead her temples with the fingers of both hands and look at the ceiling and make tentative spoken stabs at some elusive truth ("…it's rather a difference…I mean a context…or maybe analogy is better…although, no, I suppose an analogy would have to be a falsehood because…"). Dr. Draper had been seeing Rachel for two months now, and he knew she was an extremely intelligent woman, educated and articulate...well, not *exactly* articulate if that meant easily conveying meaning via language. Her speech might be described as *hyper-verbal*. In the manner of, say, Henry James or Marcel Proust or, more recently, David Foster Wallace, she was capable of some seriously convoluted sentences, and, unlike the aforementioned literary giants, many of her sentences failed to coalesce, and she lost them before they ended.

It was as though whenever Rachel attempted to delineate the nuances of her thoughts and emotions, the circumstances of her life, her spiritual condition—she believed in God, but it was not that simple—and her reflections on free will, the bounty of her internal landscape easily defeated her ability to describe it.

After eight sessions with Rachel Phelps, Dr. Draper still could not say with any certainty *why* she had sought him out. But he was glad she had come, and he wanted to help her. He enjoyed looking at her, loved the profile of her face, so earnest, so delicate. She could have been an actress, finding her niche in elegant period dramas where the whiteness of her skin, her neck, the curve of her eyebrows, and her large dark eyes, would indicate fragility and vulnerability, qualities Draper associated with more genteel times. He would have liked to have sex with her, but, alas, he was fairly certain that physical intimacy was not the solution here. He *never* slept with a patient simply because he desired her. To do so would have been unethical. Dr. Draper was unorthodox, most definitely, but he had his standards and shunned any behavior that would have compromised his notion of himself as a man of good character. The women he *had* slept with as part of their therapy had been singularly unattractive.

The timer on the end table next to the armchair chimed musically, and Dr. Draper said, "Where does the time go?" which made Rachel's eyes widen and gave Draper the distinct impression that he had frightened his client, who had, possibly, interpreted this commonplace utterance as yet another difficult question she would be required to answer, a question she had, perhaps, already devoted many solitary and unhappy hours contemplating.

Dr. Draper stood up, smiled reassuringly, and extended his hand. "I will see you next Friday at eleven, Ms. Phelps." His smile elicited one from his client.

"Yes," she said. "I think I can see progress, or not so much progress, as, I think, more...how would you say it?... *congruent* patterns, clarity, as though I were coming out of a fog, or, more precisely, as though the fog were passing me, blown by a wind, you being, of course, the motive force... although I also feel as though I *am* the fog itself and that clarity, consequently, would be the absence of self, a death, so..." Her voice dimmed and died, and she pursed her lips and shook her head, confused, discouraged, exasperated. It was an eloquent and complex expression, and Dr. Draper couldn't help putting a comforting arm around her shoulders as he led her out the door into the waiting room.

"We *are* making progress," he said. "In the early stages of therapy, my clients often experience a period of greater confusion, which is frustrating, of course, but that is what precipitates a breakthrough. You'll see."

He closed the door and went back to his desk and found the file for his next client, Adam Rhodes, a small, wretched man whose wife had left him. Rhodes missed his spouse's constant verbal assaults, and Dr. Draper would spend the first fifteen minutes of the session berating the man before getting down to core issues.

* * *

THAT NIGHT, while watching a television reality show in which contestants with various terminal illnesses tried to schedule expensive surgeries without health insurance, Dr. Draper turned and said to Mr. Trip (his cat), "I think we need to investigate her world. What do you think?" Mr. Trip was upside down on the sofa wrestling with a small stuffed dog, and he stared at Draper with an expression that a poet might describe as wild surmise.

Draper hadn't wanted a cat, certainly hadn't *needed* a cat. And this was a very fluffy, cow-dappled cat (white with black splotches), and not what Draper would have chosen even if he had been in the market. But when it was clear that Angie was dying, when they moved her into hospice, she said, "Brother, there's just one thing I want you to do."

"Anything," Draper said.

"I want you to look after Mr. Trip. I know that you are terrified of responsibility, and that you have never had a pet, but I don't want to die and go to Heaven and, a couple of days later, find Mr. Trip there and learn that he's been eutha- nized because my brother refused to look after him."

"I'll take care of him. No problem, Angie. Anyway, you are getting way ahead of yourself because you—"

"I'm in fucking hospice, brother. Take care of Mr. Trip when I'm gone."

"Sure." He'd nodded his head. But he had been worried. Cats were notoriously delicate, weren't they? And how long did they live, anyway? This one was already two years old; maybe it was on its way out. Draper knew he was going to have to do some reading on the subject. And what if Mr. Trip didn't like him?

"Do I let him inside?" Draper asked.

Angie had rolled her eyes. "He *stays* inside. I can let him out sometimes in my neighborhood, but the streets are too crazy where you live. He's strictly an indoor cat, okay?"

"Okay." *Trouble,* Draper thought, but it had worked out great. It had only been three weeks since Angie's death, and already Draper and Mr. Trip had settled into a routine. The cat was kind of a comfort, in fact.

Dr. Draper used the remote to turn the television off. He lifted the phone and placed it in his lap. In his billfold, he found the business card for Caine Investigations ("Sink or Satisfy Your Suspicions!" the card declared) and he methodically punched out the number.

"Yeah?" a voice answered.

"Is this Milton Caine?"

"If it isn't, I don't know who is. So, how about you? You got a name?"

"This is Dr. Draper. You've done work for me in the past."

"Sure. You're the shrink, right?"

Dr. Draper might have sought a different detective agency—he didn't like Caine and resented the man's manner, which was overly familiar—but Caine was a loner, and Draper liked that. The fewer people who knew that Dr. Draper occasionally had his clients investigated, shadowed like adulterers in a contested divorce, the better. Draper could argue, eloquently, that a doctor of the mind needed an objective view of his patient's environment (just as a physician needed to see an x-ray to confirm a patient's conviction that a rib had been fractured), but he didn't fancy explaining that to a panel of his peers. Caine got the job done and didn't ask any questions.

When the phone conversation ended, Draper placed the receiver back in its cradle on his lap and said, "I know it's an invasion of privacy. But I feel some urgency here. I believe I'm witnessing the erosion of a personality." The doctor turned toward Mr. Trip, but the cat had slipped away, leaving a stuffed dog, feet in the air, a moronic smile on its upturned face. Suddenly weary, Draper called it a day and marched off to bed.

✷ ✷ ✷

ON THE next Friday, Dr. Draper's ten o'clock appointment (Mrs. Fritz and her ancient Maltese, Scout) ran over the hour. Mrs. Fritz had declared that Dr. Draper enjoyed seeing her dog more than he enjoyed seeing her, and Draper had agreed, since that was clearly *not* the response Mrs. Fritz desired, and he wished to lead her toward an acknowledgement of her unhealthy desire to elicit praise via manipulation. Mrs. Fritz did not wait to learn the lesson behind Draper's words. She stood up, said, "Fine! You can have him!" tossed Scout in the air and left the room in a rush, the heavy scent of her perfume lingering like the smoke from a pipe bomb packed with potpourri. Draper, lighter on his feet than his bulk might suggest, fielded the dog effortlessly, but by the time he had calmed the dog and carried it into the waiting room, Mrs. Fritz was not in evidence. He had his secretary call a cab so that the dog could be returned to his mistress—Mrs. Fritz would be regretting her fit as soon as she calmed down—and when he returned to his office, Rachel Phelps was already sitting on the sofa.

Dr. Draper closed the door to his office and went to sit in his armchair. "Well," he said.

Rachel offered a tentative frown. "I think someone's following me," she said.

Dr. Draper said nothing, moving his eyebrows interrogatively.

Rachel Phelps chose and discarded words with growing frustration: "rat-like, but not really, not *looking* like a rat, but more like the dream a rat would have of being a person, and the suit a rat might choose, like brown paper grocery bags, oh, and a mustache that, well, if you met the man you might say, 'I see you've got a mustache,' because ignoring it would be impossible, worse than, you know, acknowledging it…" Rachel went on at length, trying to describe the man who shadowed her, and, judging by her frown, convinced that she failed in the attempt. Dr. Draper, having the advantage of knowing Milton Caine, was impressed with her powers of observation.

Dr. Draper suggested that she might be mistaken. Perhaps no one was following her. He was surprised when Rachel said, with more conviction than usual, "No. I know when they follow me. I am like a mouse that knows the shadow of the owl because the mouse must be quick or she is dead." That would have been a good time, Draper later thought, to ask who "they" were, but he pressed on in his efforts to soothe her with his calm demeanor, the lulling rhythm of his words. Soon she was nodding her head, admitting that she might have been mistaken. "I know I imagine some things. I have thoughts that are not mine…and I have thoughts stolen, too, thoughts I cannot speak but which I know *were* there, because I sense the hollow, the absence, that their theft has left."

She eventually calmed down and the session ended. She was the last patient for the day, since Adam Rhodes, the harried ex-husband, had decided he was making progress and that verbal abuse every other week would be sufficient.

Now, lying on the office couch, his hands folded on his stomach, Dr. Draper exhaled (a weary fluttering of his lips) and thought, *I have been bitten in the ass by my own methodology.* Poor Rachel Phelps had wasted her entire session in the work of repairing emotional, mental, and spiritual damage, and the engine of that damage was none other than her own therapist!

"I am a bad person," Draper told the ceiling fan. He had defrauded her, really. He was no better than Microsoft Windows, causing a crash to sell you newer crashing software. He would not charge her for this wasted session he decided.

He did not enjoy self-loathing—not when there were others he could blame. He hauled himself off the sofa with a sort of lumbering, exaggerated effort, fixed himself a small tumbler of rum and coke and drank it. Then he called Milton Caine and got a stupid answering machine message, a recording of a song, something about not having any Caine on this Brazos, then Caine's voice directing the caller to leave a message.

Dr. Draper left a chilly message in which he used the word "ineptitude" and also the word "dumb-ass," which he immediately regretted but which was there on the machine anyway.

2.

"IT'S TIME and a half on Saturdays," Caine said. "And I don't work at all on Sundays, because that's the Lord's Day."

"I didn't realize you were a religious man," Draper said. They were in a bar called Fat Sammy's on the city's seedier east side. Milton Caine was eating chicken fingers, sticking them into a little pot of honey mustard, swirling them around and biting them with unwarranted ferocity, as though they still had life enough to elude him. His mustache had acquired a yellowish hue, and his pebble eyes were sly as a feral pig's.

"I'm a Christian and I ain't ashamed of it," Caine said. "You head-shrinkers..." Caine waved a chicken finger at Draper. "Sigmund Freud was a demon, you know. One of Satan's own minions, sent to tell the world that a man wasn't anything more than flesh and blood and a hard-on. Sent to make a man despair."

"At time and a half," Draper said, "why don't we leave Freud in his grave and move on to your investigation of Rachel Phelps? I trust you have given some thought to the message I left on your machine, so you can begin by explaining how Miss Phelps spotted you following her."

"That's unfortunate," Caine said. He chewed on the last of the fingers in the manner of a man whose thoughts have spoiled his appetite. "Maybe I could have been more careful. I keep forgetting that the folks you want me to tail are jumpier than average. What you call paranoid, right?"

Draper said nothing. Was Rachel Phelps paranoid? Was a mouse in the shadow of an owl paranoid?

* * *

AS LONG as the meter's running," Caine said, "I thought we could take a little drive." They were standing outside Fat Sammy's on the covered porch, rain hustling across the parking lot. It was almost Christmas in Austin, a time of uncertain weather and colored lights thrown into the trees with sad abandon. "There's somebody you should meet," Caine said.

So Caine drove, an old rust-ravaged Lincoln that had a tendency to lean into the ditch like a drunk nodding off, waking with a start, and nodding off again.

"Careful," Dr. Draper said, but his heart wasn't in it. He was not a native Texan but had moved south to escape the frigid Wisconsin winters, and when the cold found him anyway he felt hunted, betrayed.

They wound their way through residential streets. "He might be drunk," Caine said. "It's his natural state. He's disabled APD, got wounded on the job when a crazy man got the drop on him. The crazy guy was fixin' to kill your client." Caine turned to smile at Draper. "That got your attention, didn't it?"

Caine made a sharp left, drove halfway down the block, and pulled up in front of a small wood-frame house with a screened porch.

"Here we are," he said. Yellow light from within the house leaked through slats in the blinds that masked a small window. The porch light wasn't on, and there weren't any Christmas lights. The whole neighborhood seemed to be suffering some kind of yuletide anhedonia. The house across the street had a life-sized plastic Santa that had fallen on its face, arms spread like a luckless drunk, and the house on Draper's right sported a nativity scene featuring a small, wet dog on a chain. The dog was clearly assaying the donkey role, but his performance was marred by the fervor with which he gnawed on a bone...*no*, Draper amended, *make that a doll's plastic leg.* Most of the houses in the neighborhood were small, with the occasional newer, larger, assertively-modern structure signifying the beginning of the end for the ramshackle dwellings that might still be foolishly dreaming of a new coat of paint, a new roof. All the big new houses were decorated with tiny white lights, the shameless minimalism of people with money.

Caine and Draper got out of the car and walked along the curb—there were no sidewalks—and followed a rock path to the screen door. They walked across the porch, Caine knocked on the door, and a voice from within shouted, "It's open!"

* * *

AFTER THE introductions, and after Milton Caine had produced from somewhere within his brown raincoat a bottle whose contents, distributed into three squat tumblers, filled the room with a smoky, cough-syrupy effluvium, Earl Walsh, their host, raised his glass and said, "Here's to your health, gentlemen." He chuckled, shook his head. "Feeling healthy?

I used to read these autopsy reports, and I'd read, 'healthy lungs, healthy spleen, healthy liver,' and I'd think, 'Now *there's* a healthy dead man!'"

"Have we come at a bad time?" Draper asked.

"We live in a bad time," Walsh said. "I don't see a better time up ahead. And Mr. Caine here says I'm being paid for this interview. Money is always timely."

Their host was a narrow-faced man with gray hair that had receded to the back of his head; his eyes were hard, as were the shadows under his cheekbones, but his mouth was soft and red. He wore a long-sleeve red flannel shirt. The left sleeve was empty past the elbow.

"Don't care for Christmas," he said. "Your man Caine started asking me questions, and the next thing I knew he'd marched me down memory lane to the mouth of Hell. What do you think about that?"

Draper knew that wasn't a question to be answered. He leaned forward and conjured a listening aspect, second nature after all these years.

Walsh fumbled a cigarette pack out of the pocket of his flannel shirt and shook the pack and caught a single cigarette on his lip, and a match flared and he sucked in smoke and blew it out his nose and grinned like a Doberman, pleased with his one-armed dexterity. Draper could imagine a younger man, decked out in a cop's authority, confident, maybe arrogant.

"Thing I hate about Christmas," Earl Walsh said, "is all the goddam lies, Santa Claus and that shit, and the baby in the manger and knowing all the blood and suffering that's to come."

"Everybody's got an unhappy Christmas," Caine said. "It's Rachel Phelps that Dr. Draper is interested in. What we talked about."

Walsh nodded without turning to look at Caine. He studied Draper, eyes squinting through the smoke rising out of his nostrils.

"Well, that's it. It was Christmas the first time our paths crossed, me and Rachel Phelps."

✳ ✳ ✳

THIS WAS back in 1974, and Walsh and his partner, an older man that everyone called Geronimo although that wasn't his name—and damn if Walsh could remember what his real name was—were dispatched to some apartments off Chicon called The Pines.

It was late afternoon, dusk, and the apartment manager was out in the street when they pulled up. "They always fighting," he told Walsh and his partner. "'I kill you! I kill you!' they shout. Kill each other, fine by me!" The Pines was a two-story apartment complex, shabby, cheerless, painted the color of an overcast sky: a hollowed-out rectangle with a courtyard in the middle where a swimming pool lay covered over with a tarp, like a trap for drunks. Wind-tossed plastic bags clung to brown half-dead shrubs that sheltered empty beer cans and wine bottles. A couple of busted patio chairs lay where they'd fallen during happier times. Geronimo had been to visit the Petersons before. "A nasty pair," he said, adding, "And they hate cops more than they hate each other. So be careful. Don't stand between them."

The door of the Petersons' apartment, which was on the second floor overlooking the courtyard, was closed. The officers couldn't hear anything within, and Geronimo banged on the door with his fist. "Police!" he hollered. "This is the police." No answer, no sound from within. His hand went to the doorknob and it turned. He pushed the door open.

Walsh saw his first on-the-job dead person then, Jeri Peterson, known to her acquaintances as JP, lying on her face in a puddle of bright-red blood, her gray sweatshirt splotched with blood, like some Rorschach test for serial killers. It was a small apartment. Walsh could see across the living room to the kitchen. They shouted some more, waited, and went in cautiously. An open door on the left revealed a single bedroom and two closets facing each other in a narrow hall that led to a bathroom. The place was in disarray, the mattress pulled from its frame, a shattered television; blood was splattered on the carpet and walls. But George Peterson wasn't there. He'd ended the argument with his wife, settling it for all time, and left before the police arrived. No one had seen him leave, but then, no one had seen him enter and it was even possible, although unlikely, that someone else had ended JP's life.

Walsh waited in the living room, while his partner went down to speak to the manager and call in backup. Homicide would handle this one, and they were welcome to it, Walsh thought. He tried not to look at the dead woman, tried to envision the room as it had been before violence erupted, back when it was just two people's idea of bargain-basement interior decoration. There was a Christmas tree in a corner, sitting in shadow, festooned with ornaments, and under the tree were wrapped packages, a teddy bear—

The teddy bear moved, and Walsh's heart jumped. *Jeezus!* What an imagination. The teddy bear's arms jerked up and down, flapped ineffectually; its fuzzy legs kicked. *Shit!* Walsh's heart did its own jumping around, but he made himself walk to the stuffed animal and kneel down in front of it. It wasn't moving. There was a window half-hidden by the Christmas tree, and it was dark out now. Rush hour traffic hissed by on the overhead Interstate, and the cars' headlights cast shadows of the tree's ornament-bedecked branches. This crabbed, stuttering light explained the illusion of motion. Walsh clutched the bear, stared into its button eyes, its cross-stitched mouth, and didn't scream when it bucked in his hands. He'd seen what he'd seen, and he'd known it wasn't any damned shadow trick no matter what bill of goods his reason had tried to sell him. He found the zipper in back and pulled it down.

"I was shaking so hard," Walsh said. "I peeled that teddy bear pelt off her, and there she was, turning blue, duct tape sealing her mouth, and when I pulled it off she didn't scream, just made this heart-breaking tiny noise that I can't describe—I can't even think about it—and I just stood there holding her like an idiot until other cops started coming into the room, and I made a beeline for Shirley Banks, from the lab, because she was a woman, and I just handed the baby to her and she took it. And that was my first meeting with your Rachel Phelps."

Back then, she wasn't Rachel Phelps. She had no name, no history. She was not JP's child, that was a certainty; four years ago, a botched abortion had ended JP's parenthood prospects (and just as well). No one in the apartment complex, no one among JP's friends (consisting primarily of whores, pimps, and heroin addicts) could recall an infant or even the mention of an infant.

George Peterson might have been able to shed some light on the mystery, but he turned up dead in a dumpster two days after JP's murder. He was missing his head, but his tattoos (pornographic and poorly executed) were unmistakable. There were no wounds (headlessness excepted) on the body, and the cause of death could not be determined with any precision. He could have been shot in the head, bashed in the head with a tire iron...any of a number of assaults to the brain could have finished George Peterson, although the exsanguinated condition of the corpse suggested that the removal of the head itself, achieved with some very sharp blade, could have done the job...provided, of course, that the assailant had access to a guillotine.

"Homicide figured it was some kind of drug thing, some gang thing," Walsh said. "But that wasn't exactly science. You just figure, when some marginal dopers go down in a lot of blood, it's about street finance, retribution for some failed scam. Usually there is talk, though, and there wasn't anything out there, not a peep from a perp."

Earl Walsh took a long drink from his glass and said nothing. He set the glass down very slowly and looked at Draper and said, "Never did solve that one. And we never did figure out where Rachel Phelps came from. She and her sister just materialized out of thin air."

Draper widened his eyes. "Her sister?"

Walsh smiled, pleased with the effect. "That's what I said."

Walsh elaborated. He had already left the crime scene, so he didn't learn that another infant had been found in one of the closets until the next day. Smaller and weaker than Rachel but clearly her twin, the child had died on the way to the hospital.

"Like everything else, there was a mystery around that, too, her death that is," Walsh said. "The thing is the ME, old Carstairs, no fool, said Rachel's sister couldn't have been alive when they found her. Her lungs, her heart, other organs weren't fully formed. She couldn't have caught a breath in this world. But the officer who found her, young fellow, can't recall his name, said he guessed he knew what he saw. He said she didn't make a sound, but she was all atremble, and her eyes were open and seeing the savage world when he lifted her out of a cardboard box full of dirty clothes and hauled her into the light."

As the old cop talked, Dr. Draper felt his concentration waver, in part, no doubt, a consequence of the strong spirits he was imbibing, but also, he thought, a consequence of fear. But fear of what? He had no idea. He looked away from Walsh and saw Milton Caine, sitting in a straight-backed chair, his arms folded in front of his chest, thinking Lord knows what.

Walsh seemed unaware of either member of his audience. "Rachel got her name from her adopting parents, Mr. and Mrs. Colin Phelps. Phelps owned a couple of car dealerships. He was a big, easy, likeable fellow, and his wife was a Hastings from Dallas. She had the seed money for her husband's ambition, but the man would have made something of himself no matter what. They were a good couple. Jo Phelps was just as regular and good-natured as her husband, and they loved Rachel. You can see it in an old home movie I watched, the child's ninth birthday party. She and all her friends are out on the lawn at a long table, and everyone is laughing, wild, high giggles from the girls, and Rachel Phelps looks like a movie star...by which I mean...I don't know. Emotions just seemed to light her up—happy, sure, it was her birthday— but all *kinds* of shadow-and-sun feelings racing through her, leaping in her eyes, as though she was more alive than anyone else but could make you come alive too, just by watching her. And her parents are standing off to one side, big and clumsy and so proud of their little girl that all they can do is smile like fools."

Draper knew, as he listened, that this moment of happiness would be followed by some dire event. He'd met the haunted adult.

* * *

IT WAS late when Caine returned Dr. Draper to his car. The car was alone in the parking lot, and Draper got out, walked to his car, got in and started it. He waved to Caine, and Caine nodded and drove away.

When Draper unlocked the door to his house, Mr. Trip meowed loudly but did not get up from his place on the sofa. The unprecedented lateness of the hour, this departure from routine, irritated the cat, who was used to a more ordered existence.

"Hey," Draper said, and Mr. Trip jumped down from the sofa and huffed down the hall, tail lifted high, without acknowledging Draper's presence. It struck Draper that Mr. Trip was putting on weight, kind of waddling, more noticeable in retreat, and Draper wondered if he should be buying diet cat food.

Draper went into the kitchen and fetched a beer from the fridge—he really didn't need any more to drink that night, but he reasoned that a beer was probably an antidote for the stuff he'd been drinking earlier, a sort of homeopathic remedy. He lay down on the sofa, grabbed the remote and turned the television on. An evangelist was telling his congregation that Jesus was coming back and this time He was hopping mad and He wasn't going to be all light and forgiveness and turning the other cheek. This time He was going to kick some backsides. "You know who you are," the evangelist said.

Dr. Draper carefully put his beer bottle on a coaster on the end table. He had never been married, and he knew that he could slide into slovenliness in a second, so coasters were one of his strategies for keeping slobhood at bay. Of course, coasters were no match for the second law of thermodynamics, and he knew he would someday succumb to disorder. Now Angie, she had all the energy; she could have given inertia a good run for its money. Angie.

✽ ✽ ✽

A GRAY, reluctant light entered the room and woke him up. He was still on the sofa. A yellow legal pad lay on his stomach. He studied the notes he had written. Could so much unhappy history belong to a single person? Was Rachel Phelps cursed? Had Walsh, for reasons of his own, fabricated this outlandish history of abuse?

Draper lurched off the sofa and into the bedroom where he lay down on the bed. Mr. Trip already occupied a pillow, sprawled in blissful oblivion, plump and assured in his cat-ness, paws tucked under his chin. They dispatched most of Sunday with sleep.

3.

ON MONDAY, Dr. Draper went to his office, told his secretary to cancel his afternoon appointments, and dutifully set about attending to the neuroses of his morning clients, suppressing an urge to shout, "What do you know about suffering? You pathetic piker! Have you been buried underground in a coffin? Have you been raped, repeatedly, relentlessly for years? Have you been tortured and despised? I don't think so!"

At noon he left his office and walked down Guadalupe to the main branch of Austin's excellent library system where he spent the rest of the day reading old newspaper accounts of Rachel's kidnapping. He'd heard Earl Walsh on Rachel's travails, but he needed the newspaper overview.

Rachel was a little over nine years old when she disappeared—taken from her home in the middle of the night—and she was discovered almost four years later when her kidnapper, a renegade Pentecostal full-immersion Satanist who called himself Joseph Hellblood (and was, in fact, John Spease, a 42-year old former postal worker with a history of violence and mental illness) was delivered to the emergency room of Plains Regional Hospital in Clovis, New Mexico. Among the decidedly scruffy followers who had brought their prophet to the ER, a pale, skinny adolescent girl stood out, in part because she possessed a remarkable ethereal beauty and in part because she had a rope around her neck, a makeshift leash held by a small boy who could not have been more than six years old. In the ER, a man who was waiting for an injured friend to be treated and released, spied this young girl and immediately identified her as Rachel Phelps thanks to a television true-crime show which, like all such shows, recycled cold cases every couple of years. Rachel looked much like she had at nine, malnutrition and psychic trauma serving as a poisonous fountain of youth.

In the years immediately following Rachel's return, several books recounting her ordeal were published. One such book, entitled *I'm Not Who I'm Supposed To Be* (supposedly the first words Rachel spoke to reporters on being escorted into court to testify against cult members) was on the library's shelves and Draper checked it out. The author of the book was Suzanne Gilroy, and she had, apparently, written a number of true crime accounts.

More books might have been written on Rachel's ordeal had the prophet and chief malefactor, Joseph Hellblood (aka John Spease) not died of his wounds the night he arrived in the emergency room, depriving the story of its villain. His followers, a pathetic bunch of lost souls, remained in thrall to their dead leader, and what they had to say (end-time zealotry and garbled Antichrist screeds) offered no insight into his nature. So the book Draper read felt somewhat anticlimactic, although in its loose ends, its mysteries, it possessed the unsettling power of a nightmare—and this despite the author's garbled chronology, little-did-she-know foreshadowing, and inclination to describe people by invoking the movie star they most resembled.

Several details stuck in Draper's mind. The stagnant, bad-smelling pond that resided in a slight declivity behind three dilapidated buildings on the commune's property was drained and human remains were found, so deteriorated as to be forensically mute but belonging to somewhere between thirty and forty children. The vagueness of that number—*thirty to forty?*—evoked a queasy revulsion and something else, too...although Draper couldn't make out the source of that secondary chill.

And there was also the matter of Joseph Hellblood's death, the cause and nature of his wounds. He was bleeding profusely when he arrived at the ER, and his followers attributed this to an attack by demons which he had summoned but been unable to control. They were stoic in this pronouncement. Their faith had its risks, and they were aware of them. Worshipping Satan wasn't for the faint of heart. And no, they hadn't seen the attack, but they had heard his screams and had prudently waited until they subsided.

The ER doc who'd seen Hellblood did not characterize the man's wounds as "demon-inflicted," but he did say the patient appeared to have been bitten repeatedly—the marks were undeniably made by teeth—and that these bites, and the subsequent loss of blood, were the cause of death. When the police entered the cult's compound, they found a fenced-in area containing forty-two dogs, some quite vicious, and it was generally accepted that these dogs had been the engines of Hellblood's death.

In writing the book, several years after Rachel Phelps had re-entered the world, author Gilroy interviewed a number of people, including the emergency room physician who had attended Joseph Hellblood. She asked if there was anything he could recall that he had not entered in the dictated report he'd made that day. He said that he had made a *point* of not entering an observation and that he remembered precisely what he didn't say.

"Which was?" Gilroy asked.

The doctor smiled, which the author read as "an attempt to make light of this observation or suggest that it was the conclusion of a young, inexperienced, and overly-imaginative resident."

What he said was, "I thought the bites were human. Some of them, in any event. Children, actually."

* * *

ON TUESDAY, Dr. Draper visited Austin's famous Claridge School where he was granted an interview with Dr. Harriet Gertz, who was Rachel's primary counselor for the four years Rachel attended the school. Gertz held a doctorate in child psychology, her particular area of expertise being trauma— and specifically childhood sexual abuse and the dissociative states such abuse often engendered.

The Rachel who returned to her parents was not the child who had been stolen away. Deeply traumatized, she had difficulty communicating with others and often went days without speaking. Her parents enrolled her in Claridge School, a therapeutic community where teenagers with various learning disabilities were mentored by a large staff.

Rachel seemed to be improving, although Dr. Gertz warned her parents that progress was a relative term. "I told them," said Dr. Gertz, "that their daughter might appear to be adjusting to her school, her classmates, and her home life, but her mental and emotional health might be something else again. Rachel was exceedingly good at mimicking the behavior of her peers and pleasing her teachers, but there were indications that her interpersonal skills were performances and failed to generate any emotional or spiritual growth."

"What were the indications?" Draper asked. He was seated in a chair in front of a large desk strewn with papers and books. The woman behind the desk wore a gray suit and glasses with black frames. She was in her mid-sixties, Draper guessed, and had a somewhat austere expression and bright blue eyes that seemed busy assessing him. There was a big window behind her, and Draper could see rolling hills and, to the east, lifted by fog, downtown Austin.

"She had her violent episodes, attacking another student or, more often, attacking some inanimate object. I remember she threw a desk through a window during her history teacher's lecture on the Holocaust. She might have been expelled—the administration was seriously considering it—but she was the daughter of Jo and Colin Phelps, and a generous endowment can cover a multitude of sins. And after a violent episode, she'd be a model student for months, would, in fact, grow agitated and tearful if someone referred to one of her destructive fits, claiming no memory of the incident and maintaining her innocence."

Draper sighed. "I have been seeing Rachel Phelps for several months now," Draper said. "Until recently, I was unaware of her past."

Dr. Gertz's eyebrows lifted. "Well. If I may ask: how did you manage that? Ms. Phelps is—here in Austin, certainly—a sort of celebrity. Everyone has an opinion regarding her, even if that opinion consists only in wishing the press would let the poor woman rest in peace. You didn't take a history?"

Draper was embarrassed. He'd feared this question. "Well, sometimes the facts lie, or, more precisely, sometimes the facts become a story that is truer to the story than to the life. I like to encounter my patients directly, without the distortion of a personal history with all its presumptions of cause and effect. Of course—"

"*To make of it a sort of game?*" Gertz frowned. She tilted her head back, as though to bring him into sharper critical focus. "To entertain yourself? Surely it is never in the patient's interest for her therapist to willfully court ignorance so that the therapist can fancy himself some sort of Sherlock Holmes who deduces everything from his client's manner and clothing?"

"I think—" Draper stopped. He felt his face flush. "I know," Draper said, "that her parents were murdered when she was nineteen." He did not tell her that he had only learned this relevant detail on Saturday night, when retired cop Earl Walsh told the story, nearly incoherent with alcohol and the memory of the day that had ended his career.

* * *

"**I HAD** a premonition," Walsh had said, leaning forward. "I told Danny Krenitz—and he's never forgot it—that we were in for something really bad, and he wanted to know how come, and I said, 'I know this house. It's Rachel Phelps's folks'. You know, the girl that got kidnapped by that cult?' It wasn't like I had any sort of specific vision. I'm not saying that. I just knew that I didn't want to go in that house. It was a spring day, around two in the afternoon, April and a pretty day and nothing, you know, ominous.

"I didn't recognize the address, so I wasn't aware whose house we'd been dispatched to until we got there.

"'Look,' I said. 'Let's go around the back. I don't want to just walk in the front door. You heard that voice.' The dispatcher had played the recording of the phone call, and Danny and me had both heard it. It was a man's voice, amped up on speed or something, all wobbly and loose and punctuated by gasps and sobs. He hollered: 'She ain't gonna get away this time. I'm sending her on to her Lord and Master. And as for her false father and her false mother, I have killed them only because they asked me to.'

"That's word for word what he said. I had the opportunity to listen to that recording plenty of times when I was writing my account."

So Walsh and his partner went around to the back. There was a big rectangular swimming pool full of blue water and chairs around the pool, white chairs and little round tables under yellow beach umbrellas. The grass was cut—not that long ago; you could smell the sweet bruised sap of it—and the cloudless sky wrapped the visible world like a blanket. Walsh said he could hear police sirens in the distance, heading his way, and the sound filled him with a desperate need to act. And yes, maybe he should have waited on reinforcements, but he didn't, and he couldn't say why except that the sirens sounded faraway, a ghost of authority, irrelevant to present dangers. He saw that the glass-paneled sliding door was open halfway, and he motioned for Danny to go around the garage side of the house to the front so he'd be ready if Walsh flushed anyone.

Walsh gave Danny time to get there, and then, crouching, he unholstered his gun and entered a long room with a pool table and walls of books, and on his right some big, black-leather armchairs and brass standing lamps and a low table made of dark wood. The smell of furniture polish hung in the air and some solvent suggesting scrubbing and moping. Three low steps flanked by a wooden railing brought Walsh into the living room with its white, just-vacuumed carpet. Walsh thought he hadn't missed the maid by much, and then he turned and saw he hadn't missed her at all.

The blast had knocked her down the carpeted stairs that led to the second floor; the carpet was red with her blood. She'd been shot in the chest, and all that was left of her t-shirt's white on black logo advertising her company was an "E" an "A" and an "N." Aside from a few flecks of blood ("like freckles"), her face was untouched by violence, pale, pretty, young, a student perhaps. Now she was none of those things. Youth and beauty were rendered irrelevant, like "healthy" in an autopsy report.

This would have been a good time to stay right where he was, but Walsh couldn't even hear any sirens now, and what he did hear, what seemed at first to come from within his skull, was a steady hissing sound which, as he climbed the stairs, grew louder until he identified it as the sound of a shower.

He moved down the hall, the gun held straight out in front of him.

"I would have shot anything that moved," he told Draper and Milton Caine. "I'd seen enough, and I knew that anything still alive in that house deserved killing."

At the end of the hall, a door was partway open. He moved quickly, crouched, and peered into the room. It was a bedroom. On the bed lay the bodies of Mr. and Mrs. Phelps. Not that Earl Walsh could have identified them as such. The task of identification was left for later—and for other officers.

A window was open, and Walsh heard the sound of the sirens again. They seemed no closer. Perhaps they were on some other errand. Walsh entered the room and stepped quickly toward the open door of the bathroom and the sound of the hissing shower.

"Hey!" The shout came from behind Walsh, and he spun, raising his arm to fire the gun, and he saw a skinny, naked man, grotesquely daubed with blood, wearing goggles, as though he'd been swimming in blood, with yellow teeth grinning through a bloody scruff of beard and a shotgun clutched in his hands. The explosion rocked Walsh as though every part of his body had taken the hit. Walsh slid down the wall as the man ran toward him, and Walsh understood that his life was draining away through the ragged end of his left arm where his hand had mysteriously gone missing, and the man was saying something as he eased the shotgun toward Walsh's head. Walsh still gripped the Smith & Wesson semi-automatic in his right hand, but, in that shattered instant, he couldn't have said what that meant or what use he might have put it to.

He was watching the man's lips move, the tongue writhing behind the teeth like some sea thing in its lair. A figure rushed past Walsh, and Walsh thought it was the angel of death, right on time, and maybe it was, but it had come for the man with the shotgun, and it raised a great silver cape which enfolded the man who half shouted and stumbled back, and the angel (naked, a naked woman) moved in a whirlwind of limbs and drove the entangled man toward the window, already open, and angel and madman, bound together by this shiny, flapping cloth, crashed through the window's screen that gave instantly without argument, and, in the act of tumbling into the oddly canted sky, were blotted from Walsh's consciousness by the sudden descending dark.

* * *

"**IN CASE** you were wondering, I didn't die," Walsh told Dr. Draper. "Thanks to Danny Krenitz who studied to be an EMT before he became a cop."

The arriving officers found a naked dead man in the backyard, sprawled on a shower curtain as though thoughtfully providing for easier cleanup of his messy demise. The man was later identified as Howard Morell, another disciple of Joseph Hellblood. Morell had been in prison in Gatesville when Mr. Hellblood met his end, and Morell had vowed to carry on his work. That consisted of finding Rachel Phelps who should have killed herself the moment her husband and master had died. Morell wanted to correct that oversight. He'd failed, but he had tried. Danny found Rachel Phelps bound and gagged in the bathtub. She was nude, and her feet had been pulled up toward the ceiling by a rope and pulley so that her head rested flat against the bathtub's bottom. The water was almost over her head, her dark hair swirling around her face as water rushed from the shower head, and Danny was afraid she might already be gone, but when he pulled the gag from her mouth she coughed and her eyes opened, and Danny said, "It's all right, it's all right!" as she fought to get away from him, still bound, shaking her head violently from side to side, closing her eyes again, saying with every cell of her being that it was not all right, had not been all right, and would never be all right.

After the ambulance left, taking Rachel and Earl Walsh to Brackenridge Hospital, Danny went back upstairs to the crime scene and peered into the bathroom. There were puddles of water on the linoleum and a small, ragged swatch of silver plastic hanging from a shower ring: all that remained of the curtain that had been ripped away.

After Walsh had told his story, Draper asked what he thought had happened. Walsh had raised the stub of his left arm and said, "I got my arm blown off by a psycho. R.I.P. to my police career. And—regarding what I guess you are really asking—I saw the angel of death and she looked a lot like Rachel Phelps."

* * *

"**GIVE RACHEL** my regards when you see her again," Dr. Gertz said, pushing her chair back and rising from behind the desk, signaling that the interview was over. "Tell her I'd love to hear from her."

"I will tell her. I hope she calls you." Dr. Draper stood.

Dr. Gertz smiled ruefully. "She won't call."

"How can you be so sure?"

"She's not a woman who revisits the past. In fact, maybe there is something to be said for your ignorance-is-bliss approach. You haven't scared her off."

Draper didn't know what to say to that, and so he moved toward the door of her office and opened it. He turned back then, "I am properly chastened, Dr. Gertz. I plan to treat Ms. Phelps's condition with the rigor it deserves. To that effect, could I ask you what your diagnosis was?"

Dr. Gertz put a hand on Draper's shoulder and smiled, the warmth there again. "Dissociative Identity Disorder. What else? It's controversial, but not in Rachel's case. I urge you—regardless of whatever opinion you have formed regarding DID—that you give it serious consideration."

"I will," Dr. Draper said. And, as he drove back to his house, he decided he would give Dissociative Identity Disorder some serious thought. He would begin by discovering just what the hell it was.

When he unlocked the door, Mr. Trip didn't come running to meet him. This was odd, because Mr. Trip was generally highly sociable and liked watching the news with Draper. Draper would drink a beer and scratch the cat behind the ears and occasionally explain to the cat why some politician was a particularly odoriferous piece of shit.

Draper went looking for Mr. Trip and found him in the hallway closet amid a nest of old sweaters so clotted with cat hair that they would never again be worn—for he feared taking them to the laundry he frequented, rightly fearing the wrath of old Mr. Lee, who would have looked upon these sweaters as attempts to sabotage his expensive machines.

"Hey," Draper said, reaching into the closet and scratching Mr. Trip's head. "How are you doing?"

The cat licked Draper's hand, a sign that he was not sulking over some real or imagined slight, but he made no move to leave the closet.

"Okay, see you later," Draper said, and he watched the news alone. He decided that if Mr. Trip was still holed up in the closet tomorrow, Mr. Trip was going to the vet.

Before Draper retired for the night, he filled a bowl with water and brought Mr. Trip some of his favorite cat treats.

Draper was in bed by ten and fell asleep immediately, but he woke with the distinct impression that someone was speaking to him. He sat up and turned on the bedside lamp. No one was in the room, but the bedside phone's answering machine displayed a blinking "2" in red. The phone's ringer had been turned off, and the speaker phone volume was set to 1. Draper turned the answering machine's volume up, pushed the message button and listened: 1) "This is Milton Caine. I am quitting this case, Dr. Draper. I believe that your Ms. Phelps is a wanton servant of evil, a jezebel who draws men to her so that the devil can steal their souls. We been looking at this from the wrong end, thinking she's the innocent victim. It ain't that way at all, not close.

"I believe my soul is in jeopardy. I've been thinking black thoughts of lust and mayhem, and it is all on account of this surveillance. I've been thinking what I might do to her, how I might stop her from stealing another man's soul. I never did tell anyone this, but I killed my ex-wife Denise with a shovel back in '94, whacked her on the back of the head with it. We'd been divorced for eleven years, and she didn't see it coming. Anyway, that's nobody's business, and I expect you to appreciate the confidential nature of that statement, one professional to another. I'm just telling you so— There she is in the window, bold as brass! Pray for me!"

And 2) "Dr. Draper! I am...I don't know...this is Rachel Phelps? Tentatively. I mean...I am very dispersed. But here... well, in my parents' house which is, of course, now mine...I am, I would say, followed. But...here, I will say it...more *stalked* (to say it aptly) by that rat man! By which I mean, I see him outside in the cold and rain...and it is fear that I most experience...although there is more than one kind of fear, don't you think? But I think...Help! Could you come to here and help me?"

✳ ✳ ✳

IT WAS raining again and late, after 3:00 in the morning, and it was, Draper realized, Christmas Eve—well, technically, Christmas Day—and he was driving to Rachel Phelps's house in a state of dread. He had called 911, and the operator had assured him that a police cruiser was on its way to investigate the prowler report, but Draper felt that the future had already unfolded, dire and inevitable, and this was the same queasy feeling that had announced itself in his stomach when his sister had phoned him to say, "I've got a new doctor. He's an oncologist."

So he wasn't surprised when he located the house and saw no evidence of police. He navigated the long driveway and stopped in front of the door. Everything was slick with ice, and he walked over the frozen grass, which crunched beneath his shoes, rather than trust his smooth-soled shoes to the glazed sidewalk.

Milton Caine opened the door before Draper could knock. "Those police officers got here right fast," Caine said. "Seems they were in the neighborhood. Ms. Phelps thanked them and sent them on their way. Come on in. It's cold out."

Caine extended a hand as though to welcome Draper, and there was something in that hand. Draper's body convulsed as a bolt of pain crackled through his arm, shook his shoulder, splintered his brain.

The first words he heard, when he came to, were, "Sorry about zapping you, Doc. But there are worse ways I could have put you down." Slowly, Milton Caine came into focus, his face red, a wool cap pulled down over his ears.

"We are here for an exorcism," he said. "I gave it some thought, and it ain't your client's fault how she is. It's a demon that has got inside of her. There is plenty in the Bible about this condition, and you and I are gonna bear witness to the truth of it. Right here and now."

Draper lay prone on a sofa, on his right side, his arms bound behind him, his feet tied. Rachel was tied to a straight-backed dining room chair across from him. He assumed it was Rachel. This was the way she dressed. A gray skirt, black leotards, a blue-and-white striped blouse.

"Rachel? Are you all right?"

"Dr. Draper? I am not so good?" Her voice was muffled. Her head was wrapped in a portion of a black plastic bag, and duct tape was wrapped around her throat to seal the bag. A garden hose entered the bag and was also sealed in duct tape. The hose trailed away, beyond Draper's field of vision.

"I'll be right back, Doc. Don't go anywhere." Caine left the room. Draper heard some sounds, not immediately identifiable, and then the sound of a car's ignition. Draper knew then. Caine entered Draper's field of vision again.

"Let her go!" Draper said.

Caine shook his head. "Can't do that. We are gonna chase that demon out with carbon monoxide. I think that will get it."

At first only a terrible stillness filled the room, and then Rachel began to vibrate and then Draper experienced a strange dislocation, as though he'd been injected with some powerful hallucinogen, because, as her body trembled, a second figure emerged, oscillating on a different ghostly axis around Rachel and then *standing up.* This second Rachel, naked and wild-eyed, screamed and fell back against the wall and took on weight and substance and the opacity of flesh as she slid down the wall. She tried to rise again but couldn't, and she hugged her knees and looked away from Caine and spoke, a single word, only a whisper but sharp and distinct: "Father."

"Gotcha!" Caine howled.

The front door blew off its hinges, spinning into the room and smashing into a bookcase, which toppled, vomiting books. A giant entered the room, a human form but partly beast with a great horned helmet and a white beard of twisted braids, a face half-human, half-gargoyle and missing an eye, its absence a black pit. Milton Caine backed away, holding the forked stun gun in front of him. The giant reached out and clutched the high-voltage weapon, and his huge fist held, for a moment, a nest of blue lightning. He tossed the stun gun away and drew a broad silver sword from its sheath and swung it, and Milton Caine's head leapt up, like a startled rabbit, thumped against the fireplace mantle, and rolled under a table as though seeking shelter.

The giant walked to Rachel and gently removed the tape and the plastic from her head. He knelt and cradled her in his arms. She had passed out, but she was still breathing. The giant stood up and walked back to Draper and crouched before him and leaned down until his face was inches away from Draper's. "I believe you are a doctor of the soul, a doctor for curing pain and the sadness of life. I want you to go from here with my daughter. I want you to help her."

With a great effort, Draper said, "Who are you?"

"I think you do not know me. Of your profession, there are none who knows me now. Do you know of Carl Jung? He would know me. He would call me Odin or some such name. It is Christmas. You might call me Santa Claus."

❋ ❋ ❋

AS IN a dream, Draper drove Rachel Phelps back to his house. She was awake and she seemed alert. She kept turning her head to regard her twin in the back of the car. Her twin was dressed now in sweats and bundled in flannel blankets, and she slept, quiet and pale as one dead.

Draper parked in the garage and gave Rachel the keys to open the door that lead into the kitchen. He carried Rachel's twin into the house and into the guest room. There were two beds in the guest room, and he lay Rachel's twin on one and turned to Rachel.

"Both of you can sleep here tonight," he said, "and tomorrow—" He realized he had no thoughts on the morrow. "Well, it will be another day, won't it?"

Draper walked out into the hall and heard a faint squeaking sound. It came from the hall closet. He peered inside—of course, Mr. Trip!—and saw his cat being *eaten by mice!* He'd never heard of this phenomenon. Did mice occasionally rally en masse and attack their oppressors? He scooped up one of the mice and hauled it into the light. It was a kitten. This was still extraordinary. Where had Mr. Trip acquired these tiny miniatures of himself?

A light went on: Mr. Trip was *not*, in fact, a guy. It was just like Angie to play this last joke. But... *I'm an idiot*, Draper thought. *How could I be so oblivious?* He tried to think if he'd said or done anything inappropriate when he and Mr. Trip were just a couple of guys batching it. Well, too late to worry about it now.

And there, sitting on the rug in the hallway holding a tiny kitten in his hand, he had an authentic revelation. It was as though he had shaken a box with a thousand puzzle pieces and when he poured them onto the table they settled perfectly into that picture of windswept dunes and sea waves and a sky of clouds and seagulls. Voila! He knew, for instance, that DID (Dissociative Identity Disorder) had once been called MPD (Multiple Personality Disorder) a condition created by childhood sexual abuse in which a person fragments into a number of separate personalities. These personalities, or "alters" as they are often called, are created by the process of dissociation, as a way of escaping or distancing trauma.

Rachel Phelps was suffering from Dissociative Identity Disorder. In her case, the additional personalities were flesh and blood entities, which was a little unusual, but then Rachel Phelps was the daughter of an ancient God so you might expect some divergence from the norm. What had Odin said when he had bid his daughter farewell? "We seek out pain for the wisdom in it. But then we must leave the pain behind and guard the wisdom."

As Dr. Gertz noted, the disease was controversial. Some therapists discounted it entirely. The treatment was suspect. A therapist would try to address all the alters and help them merge into the single complex self from which they had fragmented. Was this something Draper could do just by reading the literature?

Why not? *Bring it on.*

* * *

THE NEXT morning, at breakfast, Dr. Draper learned that not-Rachel called herself Eve. She said she was an actress and used to live in Hollywood.

"Rachel," Dr. Draper said, "I'd like you to meet Eve. I think you two are going to be good friends. And when you are comfortable with each other, we'll be looking for some of your sisters. I think we'll find quite a few of your family just outside of Clovis, New Mexico. They might be frightened, but we'll be very kind and patient."

They sat at a small, round table in the kitchen. They were all eating cornflakes and bananas, because that's what Draper had. He reached out his hands and clasped Eve's left hand and Rachel's right.

"Can we do this?" he asked.

"Yes," they answered.

It was weeks before Draper's methodical mediation began to show results and weeks more before that day when he watched Rachel and Eve embrace and merge into Rachel alone, and the process was exhausting. He tended to her while she lay under the covers, bringing her food and water and trying to keep the kittens off her bed.

"I like them," she said, and so they stayed.

Draper closed his office, referring his patients to colleagues and vowing to return in a month or two. He engaged the teenage daughter of a neighbor to look out for Mr. Trip and the kittens. He paid her very well to stay in the house.

"You are maybe worried too much," Rachel said.

"Maybe," he said, but he didn't really think so.

* * *

CLOVIS WAS the true test if tests are measured by how close they court despair. They stayed in a motel called MOTHERS.

Draper maintained that the absence of an apostrophe suggested that the motel's name was a truncated obscenity.

When they first visited the burned-out shacks where Rachel had been tortured, where a host of alters had been born, where love had been brutalized and humanity demeaned, Rachel could not get out of the car. For three days in a row they drove to the site, and each day, Rachel could not walk among those ruins.

On the fourth day, when they awoke, the snow was falling thickly. They drove through it in their rented Jeep, and the white blanket blessed the land, and Rachel got out of the car and breathed deeply of the cold air.

On the third day after this, the first child came out of the woods. It seemed she might flee. But Rachel reached out her arms and called her name. And the girl had not heard her name in so long that it had a kind of magic in it, and she could not turn away.

And Angela was the first of the rest.

The Love Song of
A. Alhazred Azathoth

Let us go then, you and I,
When the star-spawn wake and writhe
Like nightgaunts drunk on blood;
Let us go, beyond the nameless city,
Streets drained of pity,
Following Yog-Sothoth's ancient journey.
Oh, do not say, "No, never!"
Else all your tentacles I'll sever.

In the void the Azathi come and go
Gibbering and all aglow.

The black miasma that enfolds your carapace,
The eldritch light that hisses in your carapace,
Made darkness glitter like a feast of dreams
And brought exalted madness to our schemes
Until we lay enraptured, sated on dead things.

Time there will be beyond Time,
Time to read the *Necronomicon* at leisure,
Time to devastate a race of heretics
Or fashion some grand galactic seizure
As a sign of our displeasure.

In the void the Azathi come and go
Gibbering and all aglow.

And indeed there will be time
To don my mottled coats of slime.
And some will say, "His cilia have lost their shine."
["His spines," they'll say, "are thin and oscillate."]
They'll think me old, but not an Elder, not a Great.
Still there is time; it's not too late.

For I have heard the worlds go dying,
Heard Time itself unwinding, crying,
And I have measured out my years
In a bar in Sarnath, drinking beers.

And I have known the eyes that skitter
And I have watched the black hordes winter.
Long before the Yith had bodies,
I scavenged Chaos for my dinner.

I should have been cold mandibles
Scuttling across dead R'Lyeh's corpse
Under the heavy, somnambulant sea.

And would it have been worth it?
Not to smite them with a blow but say,
Instead, "You are mistaken. Love is all, yes, all."

No, smiting is my heritage.
I smite, therefore I am.
Between the stars there is always
Thunder without a mouth
And wizen Death full of rage.

I grow old...I grow old...
I shall sheathe my ganglia in mold.

Shall I wear my enemies on strings?
I shall torture them and feed them fetid dreams.
I have heard the hounds of Tindalos, howling as they run.

I do not think they will howl for me.

I have seen them rending the black moon,
Shaking Chaos with their sharp teeth
In Kara-Shehr amid the blighted ruins.

We have drowsed in the blood-red desert
Bound by implacable dreams,
Caressed by Cythonian tongues,
Till Cthulhu's cries wake us and we scream.

I am, I suppose, inordinately fond of this poem. I have read it a couple of times at science fiction/fantasy/horror conventions, and it has been politely received, but some member of my audience has always noted that the poem refers to those bogus beasts that are not part of the Lovecraft canon, beasts and gods that sully the power of Lovecraft's work by trying to codify it and contain it. Chaos cannot, after all, be contained.

They are right, of course, but what I was really shooting for was a T. S. Eliot homage or parody. I should have known better. In the circles I move in, T. S. Eliot cannot hold a candle to H. P. What was I thinking?

Copyright Information